In Memory of Us

Also by Jacqueline Roy

The Fat Lady Sings
The Gosling Girl

JACQUELINE ROY

In Memory of Us

**SIMON &
SCHUSTER**

London · New York · Sydney · Toronto · New Delhi

First published in Great Britain by
Simon & Schuster UK Ltd, 2024

Copyright © Jacqueline Roy, 2024

The right of Jacqueline Roy to be identified as author
of this work has been asserted in accordance with the
Copyright, Designs and Patents Act, 1988.

1 3 5 7 9 10 8 6 4 2

Simon & Schuster UK Ltd
1st Floor
222 Gray's Inn Road
London WC1X 8HB

Simon & Schuster: Celebrating 100 Years of Publishing in 2024

Simon & Schuster Australia, Sydney
Simon & Schuster India, New Delhi

www.simonandschuster.co.uk
www.simonandschuster.com.au
www.simonandschuster.co.in

A CIP catalogue record for this book
is available from the British Library

Hardback ISBN: 978-1-3985-0425-7
Trade Paperback ISBN: 978-1-3985-0426-4
eBook ISBN: 978-1-3985-0427-1
Audio ISBN: 978-1-3985-2881-9

Typeset in Palatino by M Rules
Printed and Bound in the UK using 100% Renewable
Electricity at CPI Group (UK) Ltd

MIX
Paper | Supporting
responsible forestry
FSC
www.fsc.org
FSC® C171272

For my dear friends, the three Anns:
Ann Sarge
Ann Germanacos
A.K.
With love

PART ONE

ONE

ZORA

We were joined at the hip – that's not a metaphor. We walked
with disjointed, ambling steps in perfect symbiosis, swaying
from side to side, but never falling. We were dressed in two
pink-and-white smocks that billowed into one from the waist
down. There were no photographs, but I would picture us as
babies, joined together, smiles wide.

I remembered every detail of the separation. Tubed and
monitored, we shared a hospital bed side by side, the only possible position. You were a kicker; your left leg swung into my right
at regular intervals all through the night. From our window
we saw the Houses of Parliament and boats drifting down the
Thames. The chimes of Big Ben resonated hourly, vibrating
through our diaphragm (always referred to in the singular).

Our separation was the talk of the hospital. Piercing whispers circulated round us.

'Aren't they sweet?'

'Such pretty little things.'

'How does anyone tell them apart?'

'Look at that black curly hair . . .'

'... And those lovely dark eyes.'

'Coo-ee. Come on, darlings, give us a smile.'

'It must be strange for them.'

'They don't know they're different. To them, all this is normal.'

'They're joined here, and here, you see? They're very fortunate. No vital organs are involved.'

Doctors and nurses stood above us, proclaiming the phenomenon we were. They examined us minutely, measuring each response and finding new ways to emphasise our difference, a source of sorrow for you – you couldn't bear the thought of us divided. Eventually they split us in two. I've always thought that two were better than one, but of course you begged to differ.

Our scars were long, fibrous lumps that ended mid-thigh. You would run your finger over yours, claiming it was testimony to the whole that we once were.

There was a wall in our bedroom filled with collages you'd made, each piece overlapping, faces doubled, carefully cut from magazines. Twin girls. They were there for years, even when we had outgrown them, because you were compelled to keep them visible. When I asked you about it you said that if you had been a doctor of medicine, or a psychologist, your need to study twins wouldn't have been seen as strange, it would have been rewarded with research grants and sabbaticals. You always wanted to grasp why the pair of us existed. There was a documentary you watched that said identical twins were a kind of cosmic joke, God's little prank on an unsuspecting world. You relished the description.

Our mother, Viv, found us exhausting. She'd only wanted one baby, but she'd got two. When our father Rudy came home from work, she looked at him tearfully and said, 'They only want to be with each other, they're hardly aware of anyone else. How can I look after them? They don't even seem to notice me. I don't feel like their mother. I don't know what to do with them.' Viv believed that we were everything to one another and had no need of her.

'You're exhausted, Viv, that's all,' Rudy replied. 'Two babies at the same time when you already have a toddler would exhaust anyone. They're doing fine, everybody says so. Just give it a bit more time. We'll manage.'

'Of course we will, Rudy,' our mother said, though it was clear from the anxious look that was still on her face that she didn't really believe it.

Our mother had pale, slightly freckled skin, and long, thick hair, parted in the middle. Each morning, she would brush it with impatient strokes. She disliked its auburn colour, but we knew it was beautiful – our mum was beautiful. Her smile was warm (though she didn't allow herself to smile often enough) and she had long, slim legs; her hips swung elegantly when she walked. Our father was tall and muscular with tight black curls, brown skin and glasses that gave him the look of a Caribbean Clark Kent. I often hoped he'd turn into Superman. And then there was our brother: kind, generous Cal, the only other person we wanted to play with. Eighteen months older than us, he knew the best games. He had racing cars, planes and Meccano. He taught us to make cranes, complete with string, that would lift tiny objects when we turned the handle. We loved the story of Little Red Riding Hood, so our mother made you and me red cloaks from old velvet curtains, and a wolf suit for Cal, cut from an old fake fur coat, with pointy ears and a tail. At first he chased us all over the house, his growls loud and rumbling, but we soon tamed him, and he went to live in a den at the bottom of our tiny garden, where the Riding Hoods fed him biscuits and cake – much tastier than grandmothers or small children. Do you remember Cal? Do you remember how it was when there were five of us in our south London house?

Perhaps you don't remember living there. Perhaps, in time, you won't remember much at all. I will keep reminding you. But whatever happens next, I know you will remember Harriet. I know you will remember her.

Two

SELINA

Lydia is late. The café is full. The only available table is squeezed into a corner by the door. Whenever anyone enters or leaves, I feel a blast of cold air around my neck. A small boy is running up and down the narrow space between the chairs. He jabs me in the calf with his action figure, laughing at the joke. He is impervious to my hard stare. The local mother and toddler group has commandeered most of the space. Women struggle to make themselves heard over the shrill sounds of free-range children. I feel out of place. The mothers are dressed competitively in designer casuals. Short jersey dresses with chunky lace-up ankle boots are the order of the day. My trousers are khaki-dull. My shoes are scuffed. My baggy shirt is frayed at the sleeves. I could have dressed up for this meeting but I'm tired of making an effort.

I peer out of the window onto the street, hoping to see Lydia. There is no sign. Perhaps she's changed her mind about coming. I'll give it another ten minutes, then go. I decide to get a choux bun from the counter. Anxiety fuels a need for cake. As I walk back to my table, I see that the small boy with the pointy toy has nabbed my seat. He is poking his finger into the dregs of my coffee cup. This time, he does respond to the stare I give him and scuttles off. The victory boosts my confidence, although the ability to suppress a three-year-old really shouldn't count for much.

The smell of bacon fills the air as the mothers' breakfast subs are carried to their table. They squeal about self-indulgence and the need to return to the diet tomorrow. They are all as thin as celery sticks, pretty and pale. At school, if we'd been contemporaries, they would have been a clique. They would have despised my awkwardness and the golden glow of my skin. They would have preferred Zora by a small margin, despite us being the same. They would have been fascinated by our twinship however much they would have wanted to ignore us. Lydia would have scorned them without mercy. Zora would have turned her back on them (literally). I would have stayed silent in the face of their contempt.

Just as I decide Lydia definitely isn't coming, I see her pushing open the glass door. She is still recognisable after all these years. I doubt if the same can be said of me so I wave to get her attention. She peers at me as if she thinks that I'm an imposter. Then she smiles coolly. She embraces me before taking a seat at the table.

We were close once, Lydia and I. But I haven't seen her for decades. I don't know if I want to be here. I don't know why I asked her to come.

'It's so good to see you,' she says, but I'm not sure she means it.

'You too,' I reply, and yet I feel uneasy. Perhaps there's a reason we haven't kept in touch.

She orders coffee, speaking dismissively to the waitress, who responds with extra nods to 'madam', as if condescension is all she deserves.

Lydia has continued to be beautiful. Her hair is still dark, dyed expensively. There are subtle colour tones and small streaks of grey. Retained for ... author something? What's the word I'm looking for? I'll have to concentrate. I can't afford to use the wrong words. Lydia might see there is something wrong with me.

She is wearing a brown dress. Her jacket is the same shade of green as her eyes. Her make-up has been cleverly applied to emphasise her perfect mouth. I know my chin has sagged. My face has filled and coarsened with age. But Lydia's has retained the fragility of youth. I am envious of her poise and her ability to put me in my place with barely a word. I feel fourteen again, wanting to impress, wishing I'd made an effort with my clothes.

'So how have things been?' I ask as the waitress brings the coffee to the table.

She smiles to convey the impossibility of summarising almost four decades in a sentence or two, surrounded by the young in a coffee shop. She doesn't reply.

My fingers grip the corner of the tablecloth. I don't want Lydia to see I'm anxious about this meeting.

She leans forward and her expression changes to one of concern. 'I heard about Zora's—'

I cut her off, panic rising. 'We're not here to discuss Zora, I'm not talking about her now.' I don't want to talk about Zora. I can't.

Lydia leans back in her seat again. 'What are we here to talk about, then?' she says. 'I was surprised when you got in touch. I wasn't expecting to hear from you. But I am wondering why you asked me to come because it's obvious that you still haven't forgiven me, not even after all these years. I saw it in the fixedness of your smile as I came through the door. No one can hold a grudge the way you can, Selina.' She drains her coffee cup.

'Forgive you?' I ask, hoping she'll say more. I need to fill the gaps.

'It was all a very long time ago,' Lydia replies, gazing towards a point beyond my head.

She examines her empty coffee cup. She's left dark red lipstick on the rim. Then she says, in a softer tone, still not meeting my gaze, 'I do regret it, you know, but we were very young, all of us. And I am pleased to see you, Selina, though I know you find that hard to believe. It's been too long and I've missed you. Rupert and Amy and my youngest daughter, Laura, visit every now and then, and the entire family comes down at Christmas. But it's not the same.' She waits, as if she is hoping I'll say my life hasn't been the same without her either. I remain silent. She changes the subject. 'I'm to be a great-grandmother, did anybody tell you? Emily – my oldest grandchild – is expecting a baby any day now. Isn't that extraordinary? You never expect to reach an age where such a thing is possible.'

I've also reached old age with some surprise, though the alternative would have surprised me even more.

'There's no point in denying it: we are old now, Selina.

I'm feeling it far more than I used to. Perhaps I should have exercised more or drunk a little less alcohol – who knows? But most of all, of course, it was the cigarettes. Do you remember how we all smoked like chimneys when we were young? No one told us it was bad for you. It was a sign of sophistication. They even said it was good for you once upon a time – cleared the lungs. Well, I'm paying for it now.'

Does she mean she's ill? Is that why she's agreed to meet with me? I ask her if an illness has been diagnosed. She waves the question aside. 'You don't expect to be in the peak of health at our age, do you? What I mean to say is, life's too short for holding on to grievances. Why can't we put the past behind us? When I was younger, I could afford to be patient, but I'm too old now to waste time with someone who sees me as the source of all their ills. The past is the past, Selina. It's time to stop wallowing in things that can't be changed.'

'What do you mean?'

'Did that sound cruel? Insensitive? I'm sorry, I'm just tired of all the blaming. I've fallen out with a lot of people over the years – you know me, I've never suffered fools gladly. But I don't have the energy for it anymore and that's the truth of it.' She looks put out.

I start to ask Lydia what she means once more. Before I can get through the phrase, I've forgotten how to reach the end of it. I'm stuck, without words, somewhere in the middle, not quite knowing what I wanted to say. Lately I've had to adapt the way I think and speak. I can't seem to do long sentences anymore. Only short ones. My sentence was too long. I change the subject as quickly as I can.

Lydia is looking at me in a funny way, though she says nothing. She rummages in her Mulberry bag and pulls out a pair of glasses. She glances at the menu. 'I think I might have some lunch. Adrian is away at the moment, so it will save me bothering to cook later on.'

'Adrian?'

'My husband.'

'Which number is he?'

Lydia frowns slightly and says, 'Michael and I divorced in the early eighties, you may remember. I married Julian in 1986, but he died in 2008. I met Adrian a couple of years later.'

Husband number three, then. Or have I missed one? I can't seem to hold on to details anymore.

'He's taken his grandsons – by his first marriage – on a boating trip. There's no incentive to cook when it's just me, it's too tedious. I'm sure you know about that even better than I do. Or perhaps you're with someone now?'

I decide not to answer her question. I don't want Lydia to know I'm on my own. She'll never see it as a choice. To her, it will seem like failure. I'll be someone that she pities. 'What happened between us?' I ask softly.

Lydia stares at me. 'What do you mean?'

'Why did we stop being friends?'

'I'm not sure we did stop being friends as such, we simply drifted apart. People grow up, nothing stays the same. And I went back to America, of course. When it's no longer possible to meet up with people it's just too difficult to keep in touch. Do you fancy something to eat?'

I shake my head. I'm still full from cake.

Lydia places her order. She snaps the menu shut and hands it to the waitress.

There was something that altered our friendship, I know there was. Maybe I blocked it out years ago because it was too painful to remember. Or perhaps my illness has recently sucked it away. It's there, in the back of my mind. It was my reason for getting in touch with Lydia again. I need to find out what happened. There are too many gaps. 'Was it to do with Harriet?'

Lydia doesn't reply. She takes a cigarette from her bag. I expect her to light it. But then she seems to remember that smoking in indoor, public spaces is no longer allowed. She puts it back again.

I'm afraid of Lydia. No, not afraid – what's the word? Weary? Not weary, something else. I don't quite trust her. She gives me a sense of unease. And yet, at the same time, she is familiar. Since the diagnosis, retaining a sense of the familiar has become so much more important.

As the waitress brings her lunch to the table, Lydia says, 'I can see I should have made more of an effort to keep in touch, phoned you perhaps, but these days most conversations only take place in my head, which at least saves the disappointment of dealing with replies; the usual responses are trite and simply prove that the person you're supposed to be conversing with hasn't been listening at all.'

Yes, this makes total sense. If anyone disagreed with Lydia, she always assumed they hadn't been listening. Otherwise, they would have seen her point of view.

Lydia pushes her glasses to the top of her head. She says, 'I've often thought of writing to you. Not a letter as such – nobody writes those anymore, which is a pity I think – but perhaps an email. Only I don't have your email address, and I couldn't find any trace of you on social media. I've become quite good with technology. I thought if a six-year-old can master it, how hard can it possibly be?' Lydia picks at a lettuce leaf and adds, 'You think any difficulties we had were rooted in some kind of game I played with you. They weren't, you know. Amy will bore you to death on the subject of where I went wrong with her if you give her half a chance. She says I don't care for anyone because I have no feelings. It's unkind, obviously, but it's also wholly untrue. I'm just good at conceal-ing what I feel. It was expected of you when we were growing up. I don't understand why everybody wears their heart on their sleeve so much these days. Who was that awful man? Jerry Springer? And that British version – Kyle somebody? – always getting everyone to air every little grievance. It's time to let go of the past.'

I start to laugh loudly and I can't seem to stop. I am letting go of the past. It's all slipping away from me. And I've asked Lydia here because I am desperate to hold on to every bit of it. She is one of the very few people who can help me to do it.

Lydia glances at me. 'Are you all right?' she says.

'Something did happen between us, didn't it? Something to do with Harriet? Is she the reason we haven't kept in touch?'

She looks at me quizzically once more, as if I've said some-thing stupid. Perhaps I have. I am starting to feel unnerved. My hands are sweaty. I try to breathe in through my nose and out through my mouth. Or should it be the other way round? But I can't control my fear. I have to leave. I run towards the door. But just as I try to open it, I feel myself fall.

I awaken in a strange bed. Shafts of light flicker through the half-closed blinds. My mouth is dry. My throat is sore. I can taste the salty, metallic tang of blood. There is something covering my face. I pull it off. My head aches.

There is an elderly woman sitting in a chair beside me. She leans over. 'You'd better keep the oxygen mask on for now, at least until the nurse comes back.'

She looks familiar but I can't quite place her. 'Who are you?' I say, aware that my voice sounds rumpled and strange.

The woman gives a tight-lipped smile. 'It's Lydia,' she replies.

This isn't Lydia. This woman is old.

And yet there is a resemblance to Lydia in the woman in front of me. The cut of the hair, sleek and bobbed – expensively dyed. Narrow shoulders, graceful in her movements, even though she must be at least seventy. I don't understand. I try to sit up but I can't. My head aches too much.

'Just stay still,' the woman says.

'Is Zora here?'

She just stares at me, this version of Lydia, who seems to have come from my dreams. Perhaps she'll tell me where Cal has gone. He argued with Zora and ran from the house. 'Where's Cal?' I ask.

'I think you're confused.' The woman gets up. 'I'll fetch a nurse.'

I look around and realise I'm in hospital. There are five other beds in this room. Each has a curtain and a bedside cabinet. Women in dressing gowns are sitting in armchairs. One is reading. Another is knitting. A girl in her late teens or early twenties is listening to music. Her oversized headphones look too heavy for her. She sways to a beat. At the far end of the stark, white space there are open double doors. They probably lead on to a corridor. My head hurts.

The woman called Lydia (who isn't really Lydia) returns. She is with someone in a navy-blue top. Matching trousers. She says she is a nurse.

I want to ask why she isn't wearing a uniform. She should be wearing a stripy dress and a white apron. A starched hat with a frill. I try to say this to her. I can't form the words. Why won't they come? Why is everything so strange? I am choked with fear.

A man comes over. He has a stethoscope around his neck, so I know he is a doctor. But there is no white coat. With rules so lax here it's hard to believe they actually know what they are doing. I sit up. I need to know what's going on.

'Do you know where you are?' the doctor asks. He has pale, freckled skin and light brown hair.

'Hospital,' I reply.

'And can you tell me what day it is?'

'Tuesday?' I have a one in seven chance of getting it right.

He doesn't respond, so I know I've got it wrong.

'You fell over in the café and you hurt your head,' says the stand-in for Lydia. 'Don't you remember? You asked me to come and see you. We met in the café by the bridge.'

I don't recall a café. I just remember being in an armchair watching television. It's happened before, being somewhere one minute and somewhere else the next. I'm like a time traveller moving through different dimensions at the flick of a switch. I'm in the future now. Maybe this Lydia is the real one after all. An old, more mellow version. Perhaps tomorrow I'll travel to the past. I must be careful not to go back too far. I could end up being mistaken for a slave, like Dana in *Kindred*.

'Mistaken for a slave,' says Millie-Christine. She is standing by the nurse. I reach out to touch the bustle of her dress but she has gone.

Some words leave my mouth. 'What happened?' I ask. 'Why am I here?'

'You had a fall and hit your head,' the doctor says, returning to my bed. He is wearing a turban and there is a stethoscope around his neck. 'You're concussed. You'll need to stay in overnight and we'll see how you are in the morning.'

'Where's Zora?'

She should be lying here beside me. We've had our tonsils out. At teatime we'll be getting jelly and ice cream, the nurse promised. But not even the thought of ice cream is enough to stop me crying. Zora puts her arms around me. She says we'll feel better soon. Our throat hurts.

'When can I go home?'

'Soon,' the nurse replies.

*

Our home has cracked and broken windows and a roof that leaks. Down the street, our neighbours have put a cardboard sign in the window. We see it each morning as we walk to school. The writing is in thick black ink. There is a blot at the bottom of the page. Mum looks at it and makes tutting noises. She shakes her head. We know she is cross and it's not about the blot. Zora and I read it out loud, both at the same time: *Room to Let. No Coloureds.* Are we coloured? we ask. I look at my hand, the one that is identical to Zora's. We can't be coloured. If we were coloured, our skin would be green or blue. There would be red stripes or polka dots. 'Shush,' says Mum, and she holds Zora's light brown hand on one side of her and mine on the other. She pulls us away. As we hurry past the windows, Mum whispers the words *ignorance* and *prejudice*. We don't know what they mean but we guess that they mean stupid.

Our dad always goes past without saying a single word. When we walk to school with him on his days off, we pretend not to see the window. We know the words make Dad sad.

Dad has a big red bus. We are six years old and we want to be bus conductors like our dad when we grow up. Cal says he wants to be a driver. Cal is nearly eight, so he will be grown up before us. He will be a good bus driver but he'll have to be careful not to drive too fast. He likes to go fast on everything. When he puts on his roller skates, he goes very, very fast.

The bus jolts to a halt. I look out of the window. We've stopped at traffic lights but nothing is familiar. I don't know where I am. Have I missed my stop? Did I get on the right bus? I can't remember if I checked the number on the front. Perhaps I just got on without thinking. I stand up in panic. 'Is this the number 35?' I ask the woman sitting next to me.

'Yes, dear,' she says, pointing to an amalgamated sign above our heads. *Clapham Common next stop.* I start to feel better. I know where Clapham Common is. Where is the conductor? There doesn't seem to be a conductor on this bus.

Dad hurries up and down the aisles of the bus calling, 'Fares, please.' His voice sounds like sunshine and the sea. We scoop up the tickets the passengers throw away as they get off the bus and keep them in our pocket. 'They are souvenirs,' I say to Zora.

'What's a souvenir?' I ask, as we stick little red, white and blue flags called Union Jacks on the tops of the sandcastles we have built.

'A souvenir is something that helps you to remember your holiday,' Mum replies.

We don't go on holiday. We just go for day trips sometimes to the seaside. The buses at Southend are different to our father's London bus. The buses in London are red. We like red buses best.

We are sitting on Dad's bus, Zora and me. A woman gets on. I grab hold of Zora, and get her to look. The colour of her face is just like ours. We stare and stare, joining hands. Zora's thoughts and mine are exactly the same: this is what we will

look like when we're grown up. We've never seen a grown-
up before who has one parent who is black and one who is
white. We smile at her. We try to get her to look at us but she
gets off the bus without noticing.

The bus is going too fast. It shudders to a halt, brakes screeching. We almost hit a ... pedicure. I'm relieved there hasn't
been an accident. Clapham Junction. I'm so glad to recognise
it, but Woolworths has gone. Everything looks shiny where
it used to look grey. An orange car goes past. I once had an
orange car but it was small ... a Dinky car. No, not Dinky –
Mini. The orange car is going too fast. The world is going too
fast, I'm having trouble keeping up, everywhere is strange.
I fumble in my bag and pull out that portable thing I can
use to speak to people. I need to get away from here. I lean
against a wall, trying to compose myself. I'll speak to Zora.
She will tell me where I am. I start to punch the numbers
in. I must have done it wrong because there is nothing, her
name doesn't light up the ... The ringing doesn't sound. And
then I remember; I can't ring Zora anymore. The weight of it
causes me to slide down the wall and I fall on my knees on
the pavement.

'You are in hospital,' the doctor in the turban says. 'You had
a fall. Remember?'
    I take the tablets the doctor gives me but the headache
doesn't stop. There is a cut, I think. They stapled it together
as if I am a cardboard box. I'm prone to falls, they tell me.
Perhaps I keep forgetting to look where I am going.

'When can I go home?'

'Soon,' says the nurse.

The house is still where I thought it was. I feel a rush of joy as I recognise my home.

I'm relieved I've remembered my keys. It's easy to forget to pick them up. I push open the door, kicking aside a small pile of ... papers with advertising on. I fumble for the light switch in the dark.

At the hospital, they said I was concussed. I'd been afraid I'd slipped into my future – one of hallucinations, confusion – forgetting the people I know. But it was the bump on the head. Perhaps it was a taste of things to come, but I can't afford to think like that.

It's the thought of losing the familiar that scares me most. Not so long ago I took a bus to see my old home. Everything familiar had gone, even the house where we all used to live. It was as if it had only ever existed in my imagination – a bewildering feeling. I am often bewildered these days. Too many things to process and my processing tools are becoming less sharp.

There are notices all over the place, reminders of what needs doing. Trouble is, if I don't remember to check them, they aren't a lot of use. Rubbish and recycling every Wednesday. Grocery delivery on Thursday afternoons. Walk with Fran on Sundays. It's more manageable if everything happens at the same time each week, as long as I remember what bloody day it is. A notice on the mantelpiece says: *Date and Time: check your phone,* as if I am an idiot. Sometimes I feel like one. Still, I'm managing – more or less. What day is it? Perhaps a souvenir would help me to remember. *Check the phone.* It isn't in my pocket. It must be in my bag. Did I leave it in the hall? What time am I meant to be meeting Lydia? I'll have written it down; I have to write everything down these days. The trouble is, half the time, I can't remember where. But I've already seen her, of course I have. She was at the hospital. She was wearing a dark pink dress.

THREE

ZORA

We were playing ball when a girl in a deep pink dress peered over the top of the wall at the end of our small back garden.

We'd been talking to each other in our own language, the one we never shared, which made me go bright red; she must have heard. Her skin was pale, and her two long plaits had green ribbons on the ends of them. She flicked one across her shoulder and said, 'We've just moved here. Our house cost a bomb, Daddy says, even though he got it cheap on account of the neighbourhood being so run-down.' She pointed behind her. The house loomed; it was huge, like a castle. The branches of the tallest tree in her garden hung over onto our side of the wall; its leaves were turning brown and apples were starting to fall.

'My name's Lydia. What are your names?'

'I'm Zora and she's Selina.'

'I heard you talking funny just now. Are you savages?'

'No, we're not, we're as English as you are.' I knew all about savages; I'd seen them on television. Tarzan lived in the jungle. He wasn't savage; he was white. Mostly the savages left him alone, but every now and then they would appear, waving their spears and speaking gibberish.

She looked us up and down. 'Well, you're not really English, are you? Where do your mummy and daddy come from?'

'Our mum is English and our dad is from Jamaica,' I said. 'And we were born here,' I added, just to make sure she knew we definitely were English because it was sounding as if she didn't believe us.

'What language were you speaking just then? Was that African?'

'Twinola,' I replied. 'It's a very rare language, like gold is rare. Not many people speak it.'

'My daddy is a very clever businessman. He has big piles of gold, in a bank.'

'Prove it,' I said crossly, aware that our mum and dad were definitely lacking in the gold department, though I could say, with total truthfulness, that our dad was very clever too.

'You two are twins, aren't you?' said Lydia.

'What gave it away?' I replied sarcastically.

Lydia ignored this and said, 'How old are you, then?'

'We are nine. Our birthday was in June.'

'I was nine in May,' she said, looking pleased with herself. 'You can come to my house if you like. There's a swing we can play on.'

You went to go over the wall but I pulled you back. She

was a show-off and she thought an awful lot of herself. 'Not today, thank you,' I said in the voice our mother used when she was cancelling the milk.

Lydia didn't seem to care. She just said, 'Which school do you go to?'

'St Joseph's,' I answered.

'Are you Catholics, then?'

'Yes,' I said to her.

'I'm just a heathen. You should be heathens too, seeing as how you're savages.'

'We're not savages!' I answered angrily.

'What are your teachers like? Are they nuns? My teachers are so tedious.'

Tedious. It was a good word, I had to give Lydia that much, even though I wasn't sure what it meant.

'I bet you can't climb this,' said Lydia, pointing to the apple tree.

'I bet I can,' I answered.

'Go on, I dare you,' Lydia replied.

I didn't hesitate. I hauled myself onto the wall and looked up at the branches. They were sturdy enough and well within reach.

'Don't, Zora,' you said.

'She's dared us,' I replied.

'You'll never be able to do it,' said Lydia.

I began to make my way up, you watching anxiously. We'd only just met, but I was determined to impress Lydia, especially when she was so certain I would fail. I climbed higher and higher, reaching up to grab the thickest branch that hung over our side of the wall. And then my foot slipped and I crashed to the ground, a burning pain coursing through my arm.

You ran towards me. 'That hurt,' you said, your face twisted with pain, as if you'd been the one who'd fallen.

I said nothing. I wasn't a baby and I wasn't going to cry; I didn't want Lydia to see how badly I'd hurt myself.

'Are you all right?' Lydia asked, peering down at me from the other side of the wall.

'Yes,' I said, though the pain was so great I could scarcely squeeze the word past my lips.

A woman started calling Lydia's name.

'I have to go in now. Bye.' She turned and ran off.

You put your arm around me and helped me indoors.

'I've hurt my arm,' I said to Mum.

'We've hurt our arm,' you echoed.

Mum took us to the hospital in a taxi, just you and me; Dad was still doing a shift on the bus and Cal had to finish his homework. We'd never been in a taxi before. If my arm hadn't been hurting so much I would have savoured the journey.

'How did you do this?' the doctor asked as he looked at the X-rays that had been taken. You were mesmerised as he showed us the X-rays: photographs of the inside of the body. You couldn't stop staring at them.

'I tripped,' I said, silently telling you not to contradict me. I didn't want Mum to know I'd tried to climb the apple tree – she'd warned me about doing it too many times.

'Well, it's broken, I'm afraid. We'll need to put it in a plaster cast.'

A cast. I was elated. For at least six weeks, I would look different to you, and everyone would see that I was Zora.

FOUR

SELINA

There are so many books in this library. I don't know where to start. I used to know how to find things. There were index cards in cabinets, stacked alphabetically. Now there are computers. I used to be good with computers. But this library has a different system and trying new things is a lot harder than it used to be. I daren't ask the librarian – a stern-looking woman in her forties dressed from head to toe in black. She might notice this forgetting thing. It's embarrassing, my inability to remember.

Ironically, I want to find books on forgetfulness. I don't want to use the proper name for my condition, it makes me too afraid.

Too many books. Once, Zora and I believed that too many books was an impossibility. We longed for too many. We wanted to read them all. We believed, when we were small, that we would find a book about the two of us. Two brown-skinned identical people joined together. Impossible, we thought, yet maybe one day ...

*

I find the book in the college library. I open it and I can hardly believe that it exists, this book from America about Millie-Christine. Twins, born conjoined on a plantation. I turn the pages, expecting to wake up, but I am awake, it's real. There is a picture of Millie-Christine on the cover. Their skin is darker than ours but the resemblance is clear. I slip it under my coat and take it back to halls. It's mine, it's meant for me, I haven't stolen it. I read it from cover to cover. Then I read it again. Two identical people joined as if they were one. Zora's absence hurts less and more at the same time as I study their picture on the front of the book. It's comforting, but I wish with all my heart that Zora and I could share it. If only we'd found this when we were young and hungry for a book about us. Or, if not *us*, anyone who wasn't white. There was next to nothing about children of colour back then, unless *Little Black Sambo* counts.

In the corner of our class, there are lots of books on shelves and in wooden boxes. Every week we are allowed to choose one. We look for books about us but we can't find anything with coloured children in it. Only white children are in story books. Except one day I find one with a coloured boy whose name is Little Black Sambo. He has an umbrella and very bright clothes. He looks a bit funny. He has big red lips and curly hair that sticks right up and dark brown skin. I think he's meant to look like us. Zora is cross. She says he doesn't look like us, he is a mistake. He is horrible. She doesn't like him. He comes in her dreams at night and makes her so scared, she is shaking all over. I have to cuddle her and say it will be all right like I always do when Zora is sad and scared. He makes her cry. I hate it when Zora cries, I feel like crying too.

'Go back home!' a man is shouting at me. He is following me down the street. His mouth is twisted with rage. 'Leave means leave,' he cries. The familiar slogan is becoming a personal attack. I hurry away from him. Where will I go if I have to leave the country of my birth? Will I become an asylum seeker, fleeing persecution, travelling to an unknown place in a boat? Will I be told to go back home again when I arrive?

After school, I tell Zora we have to go to our secret place – the falling-down house. Cal told us a whole street got bombed when the war was on. Nothing has been fixed up yet. We slip in through a small gap in the fence. The sun is out. We are too hot. Zora brushes the sweat away from her face with her hanky. Then she reaches across and wipes my face too. It feels nice. I take *Little Black Sambo* out of my satchel.

'What are you doing with that?' asks Zora, backing away from me. 'Why did you have to bring that here? Did you steal it from our class?'

'I took it when Miss Allison wasn't looking.'

'What are you going to do with it?'

'You'll see,' I tell her.

'I don't want to see, I want to go home,' Zora replies. 'We have to go home now.'

'Go home. Go back to where you came from.'

*

It's not time to go home yet. We go into the tangled-up garden of the falling-down house. I've got a spoon – I nicked it from the hall at dinner time. I use it as a spade. I start to dig a great big hole. At last, the hole is big enough. I drop *Little Black Sambo* inside and cover it with earth. 'Gone,' I say, brushing the dirt from my hands. Now Zora won't have nightmares anymore. Now she will feel much better.

When we get home, we are giggling and we can't stop. Sad Zora has gone away now and happy Zora has come back. She whispers our special words, the ones that mean I love you, and I feel so glad. I have made Zora better again. I have made everything all right. At tea time, she holds my hand so I have to eat my spaghetti hoops on toast with my left hand and she has to eat them with her right. It takes ages and ages. Mum gets cross. 'For goodness' sake let go of one another and finish your food, it's getting cold,' she says. We just carry on giggling, which makes Mum even crosser. The things that hurt Zora hurt me too. When Zora is happy, I am happy. When she is sad, I am sad.

We are sad. Our throat hurts. I am sad because we are hurting. We lie in bed together and Mum takes our temperature. The doctor says we'll have to go to hospital. We hold one another tight in case they try to separate us like they did when we were joined. When they try to take me away from Zora for the operation, I scream. When they try to take Zora away from me, she screams too. We are both screaming. In the end, they take us both away together to have the operation at the same time, lying side by side.

*

We are cut apart. It hurts. We start to scream.

Millie-Christine are joined. Two who are one – they look like us. We read about Millie-Christine side by side on the hospital bed. We look at the picture of them. We are the same as Millie-Christine, twins who have brown skin, even though our skin is a little bit lighter. No one could ever make them come apart. We are twins who are joined as well. No one will ever make us come apart either.

The phone rings. I must have fallen asleep. It's Lydia. When did I give her my number? Her voice is different – deeper – and the vowels are less pronounced. Sometimes she hesitates. She never used to hesitate. She sounds old.

'How are you?' she says. 'I was worried about you at the hospital.'

'I'm fine,' I reply.

'I could come and get you in the car if you want to change your mind about staying with me.'

'No, I'm fine. It's a sunny day, I think I'll sit in my garden.'

'It's going to be very hot. You might be better off lying down indoors where it's cooler.'

'No, the garden's fine. It's peaceful. There's a . . . a . . . something to sit on by the tree. I can get some shade if I need it.'

In the garden we are eating the apples that have fallen on our side of the wall. Lydia hears us speaking in our special way and she jumps over to our side and lands next to us. She says we've stolen her apples and we must be savages. Zora is angry. She hits Lydia. 'Don't ever call us that!' she shouts. Lydia is angry too. She hits Zora back and Zora falls into the wall. Our arm hurts so much. Our arm is broken, the doctor in the turban says.

I can hear Lydia lighting a cigarette. She inhales deeply.

'There was an apple tree in the garden,' I say to her.

'An apple tree?'

'In the garden of your house, the one that backed onto ours.'

'Yes, there was an apple tree, wasn't there? My father and his brother sold stuff on the black market during the war and when it was over, they bought houses that had been bombed with the proceeds, renovating them and selling them again. You said it was like a castle – or maybe that was Zora? The very first time we spoke, wasn't it over the garden wall? When I asked your names, you said you were called Selzora.'

Selzora, the name we used to call ourselves to save everyone the bother of trying to distinguish between us.

'Zora hated the Selzora thing, didn't she? She used to get really cross when I called her that,' Lydia continues.

'I don't remember Zora being cross. She was the one who thought of it first.'

'Oh, she always said it was you. Well, look, enjoy your afternoon in the sunshine. It really is a glorious day; you should make the most of it. I might follow your example.' She asks once more if I'm sure I am all right. It's annoying, the way people check up on me. They assume I don't know what I'm doing.

My fingers start to tingle. I'm gripping the phone too tight.

'When we first met, did you and Zora fight? Was that how Zora broke her arm?'

'Goodness, it was all such a very long time ago, I really don't remember now,' Lydia replies.

FIVE

ZORA

We were late and I was cross; you'd forgotten your camera. If you hadn't gone back home again to fetch it, we would have been on time. I wasn't sure Lydia would still be waiting for us. She was the kind of girl who would get bored and go off with other friends if we took too long.

You stopped dead. I almost tripped over you. I knew what was wrong; there were dogs in the park. One was bounding up to us, small and skinny, but still a dog. We held each other tight, unable to move. As the woman put the dog on the lead, we managed to start walking again. I looked around, praying that Lydia hadn't seen us. She would never let us live it down. 'It was tiny,' she would say, and she would laugh and laugh.

Luckily, Lydia hadn't seen anything. She was lying in the grass by the water, with a book spread out in front of her. A boy, taller and wider, whose posture mirrored hers, was lying beside her. They were each wearing khaki shorts and sunglasses. Lydia looked up as we approached. 'You took your time,' she said. She pointed to the boy beside her. 'This is my cousin, Adam.'

He barely glanced at us. We murmured some sort of greeting that wasn't reciprocated. Now that we were closer I could see there was a family resemblance. Both he and Lydia had thick, dark hair. Their mouths turned down very slightly at the corners, giving the impression they were always rather bored.

'Say hello, Adam,' said Lydia, giving him a nudge.

'Hello Adam,' he muttered, without looking up from his book.

Lydia laughed. 'He's so rude,' she said, but she sounded proud of him.

'Who are they?' he asked.

'They're the twins. They're called Selina and Zora Bunting, but they like to be called Selzora.'

'That's stupid,' said Adam.

I turned red.

Lydia gave the kind of shrug that said he might have a point but she didn't really care. 'They live round the back of my house. Look at them, I told you they were very nearly the same.'

Adam raised his head and studied each of us, seeming to take in every twin-ish detail. 'It's the baby Buntings. Bye, baby Buntings,' he said, and he waved his hand at us dismissively.

You looked unsure about what we should do but we still remained where we were. Lydia and Adam laughed so hard that Lydia got hiccups.

'They're interesting, aren't they?' said Lydia, as if we were exhibits in a glass case.

'They are interesting,' Adam replied. He gave us one final, penetrating stare and then returned to his book, continuing to read while we played catch with the big red ball Lydia had brought. 'Keep the noise down, can't you?' he said intermittently.

I threw the ball at his head when he wasn't looking. He sat up sharply and stared at the three of us. 'Who did that?' he demanded.

You looked worried and said nothing, but Lydia replied, 'It was Zora, and she did it on purpose,' as if there was nothing wrong with telling tales.

Adam jumped to his feet. He loomed over me. 'Do that again and I'll knock you into the middle of next week.' His voice was disconcertingly quiet but I could see that he meant it. I wandered over to a patch of grass, a safe distance from him, acting like I wasn't bothered in the least, and I picked some flowers for a daisy chain, threading them with dignified concentration.

'It's far too hot to keep on running about,' said Lydia, flopping down and pushing the ball back and forth along the bumpy ground with the flat of her hand. She smiled as you took a picture with the camera you'd brought. You took one of Adam too.

He looked up. 'Did I say you could take a picture of me?' he said to you crossly.

'She didn't think you'd mind,' I answered. I could see his hostility was making you anxious.

'Well I do mind. She should have asked.'

'Leave her alone, Adam, you love having your picture taken really. He's so vain, you know,' said Lydia.

Adam glared at her.

'We go back to school the day after tomorrow,' I said gloom-ily, tossing my daisy chain into the flower bed behind us.

'I don't start back for another ten days,' said Lydia, sound-ing pleased with herself. 'I'm being sent away to boarding school. Daddy says it's to rub the corners off me.'

Adam looked across at us. 'Best of British luck with that,' he said, and Lydia put her tongue out at him.

I looked down at the grass; I was so bitterly disappointed that Lydia was being sent away that I could have cried. Lydia was the first real friend I'd ever had and I knew how desper-ately I was going to miss her.

We were thirsty. Lydia got bottles of ginger beer for her and Adam from the pink Tonibell ice cream van but you and I didn't have any money. She gave us a sip each but it wasn't enough. Our throats were so dry we were starting to cough. 'We'd better go home now,' I said reluctantly.

'No, don't go,' replied Lydia. 'Come back to my house instead. Joyce won't mind, as long as we're quiet, and it is nearly tea time. We've got proper lemonade, with real lemons, and we'll put some ice in.'

'Who's Joyce?'

'My stepmother. She's very wicked you know. It's why she made Daddy buy a house with an apple tree in the garden. It will come in very handy when she decides to bump me off.'

'Never eat her apple pie, you'll die,' said Adam.

You and I looked at them, unable to tell if they were joking. Then they burst out laughing again.

Lydia said, 'Come on, let's go home. I'm dying for some iced lemonade.'

We didn't even have a fridge, so we stood up eagerly.

'They'd better not come back with us,' said Adam, 'not without your dad or Joyce saying it's all right. We hardly even know them.'

'*I* know them,' said Lydia.

'Well I don't. We've only just met. They could be anyone.'

'Well, we're not anyone,' you said, quite bravely for you. 'We're friends of Lydia.'

Lydia stared at you, surprised to hear your voice. You hardly ever spoke to anyone outside the family.

Adam looked us up and down again. Then he said, 'My father doesn't like coloured people. He says they've got no manners and they're ruining everything, taking over the whole country. They eat funny food as well and the stink gets everywhere.'

You and I began to walk away, our angry footsteps in perfect sync.

'Don't go,' said Lydia. 'Adam didn't mean anything, he was just being stupid.'

'I'm not stupid,' Adam answered coldly.

'You are,' said Lydia, glaring at him.

To our surprise, he backed down. 'Oh, all right, I suppose they can come back to the house, but don't blame me if Joyce has a hissy fit.'

I wasn't sure I wanted to go back with Lydia and her cousin anymore, but the lure of lemonade was strong and Lydia said there would be biscuits too.

Lydia's street backed onto ours, but it was called an Avenue. A long drive led up to each front door and fuchsia bushes hung over the walls shedding pink and purple petals over newly mowed lawns. I could tell you wanted to take a picture of Lydia's house as we approached, but you remembered Adam's anger and kept your camera in its case.

'Don't just stand there, come in,' instructed Lydia as we hovered on the doorstep.

We followed her into a hall that had stained-glass windows that cast orange and blue light onto a tiled floor.

'We're home,' called Lydia, but nobody answered. 'Joyce has probably gone out and Daddy's busy I expect. Let's go into the kitchen.'

We went down a flight of stairs into a room that was almost the same size as the whole of the upstairs part of the house we lived in. A thin, sharp-faced woman was standing at a table. Her knuckles were pounding dough.

'Is that your stepmother?' I asked in a low voice.

Adam and Lydia laughed until they couldn't laugh anymore. Then Lydia said, 'Of course it isn't. That's the woman who does for us.'

'What are you doing down here?' the pastry-pounding person asked, suddenly paying attention. She was looking at you and me, waving her rolling pin with menace.

'It's all right, Billy, they're with us,' said Lydia.

'Billy's a funny name for a lady,' I whispered to Lydia.

'It's Mrs Billington really,' she replied, without lowering her voice, 'but we always call her Billy.'

'Does Mrs Russell know you've brought them here?' Billy asked, still staring at us.

'See? I told you not to bring them back,' said Adam.

'Don't mind Billy, her bark's worse than her bite,' Lydia told us. 'She's a billy goat gruff.'

'She can't cook though,' said Adam. He was chewing a home-made biscuit he had taken from a large glass jar and pulling a face.

They were talking as if Billy wasn't in the room. We went red again. We'd never heard children speaking to a grown-up like that before.

'Go on, be off with you,' said Billy, 'and take both of them with you. Who are they anyway?'

'Selina and Zora. They like to be called Selzora.'

'Do they indeed? Does your mother know you're here?' she said, looking at us both once more.

I said nothing. You shook your head.

'You'd better be off home, then, hadn't you?'

'I want them to stay,' replied Lydia imperiously.

Billy sniffed as she considered this. Eventually she said, 'If they're going to stay, don't let them get up to anything. I know their sort.'

We didn't know what she meant, but she'd obviously taken a dislike to us. Her lips were pursed and there was a frown across her forehead.

'They never get up to anything. They're pretty boring really,' laughed Lydia, getting out some glasses and pouring lemonade from a jug in the fridge. She took a few more biscuits from the jar and handed them round. 'Come on, we'll go up to the playroom.'

We drank the lemonade in a room that had stuffed dogs and teddy bears piled up against a wall. An electric train set covered a large part of the floor. We knelt beside it, examining the metal station and the track with its signals and points.

'Adam is staying here for a few days,' said Lydia. 'He didn't think I'd have any decent toys so he brought that with him.'

'And I was right, wasn't I?' replied Adam, gesturing towards the stuffed animals. 'Do you want to see it working?' He picked up a controller and put a train on the track. We watched as it circled a little model village.

'Can I work it?' I asked.

'Girls can't do train sets,' said Adam scornfully.

This statement infuriated Lydia. She kicked the station master onto his side and threw a metal tree across the room. Adam launched himself at her and they fought wildly. Adam was much bigger but Lydia was speedy and her blows landed with greater precision; their shouts and screams filled the house. Billy burst into the room and pulled them apart. 'What are you, a couple of savages?' she said, with a pointed look at you and me, as if our very presence had caused the fight. 'There'll be no pudding for either of you this evening.'

Adam stood up, brushed his knees and said, 'Leave us alone. You can't tell me off. You can't do anything to us, you're not allowed. You're supposed to be in the kitchen.'

'Your uncle asked me to keep an eye on you today and that's what I'm doing. I'll be telling him all about this when he comes home.'

'He won't care,' said Lydia defiantly.

'No, he won't,' agreed Adam.

The two of them were united again in the face of Billy's threats. We stood there awkwardly, not understanding why Billy didn't tell Adam and Lydia off for being so rude. 'We'd better be going home now,' I said.

'No, stay,' replied Lydia.

We wanted to stay. There were so many things to explore; in addition to the stuffed toys there were shelves full of children's books, all with colourful covers. It was like a library, only better – the books all looked brand new. But Billy was glaring at us again, as if the disruption was all our fault, so we made our way downstairs.

'Come round again tomorrow,' said Lydia, standing by the front door.

'It's Sunday tomorrow,' I replied. 'We'll be at church.'

'Monday, then.'

'We're back at school on Monday, I told you that already,' I answered crossly.

'Don't be angry,' Lydia said. 'I'll write to you when I go to boarding school and we'll be together in the holidays. We'll still be friends.'

I nodded; I so much wanted it to be true. Lydia was naughty and funny and she didn't worry about things the way you did; when I was with Lydia, I didn't feel I had to take care of her, I could just be myself. She never mixed us up; even Mum, Dad and Cal sometimes confused us with one another, if only for a moment. Lydia never did; she knew the difference between us, and I loved her for that.

In the weeks that followed, I ran to the front door each morning, hoping to find a letter from Lydia – not addressed to both of us; a letter just for me – but no letter ever came. You and I went round to the house in the Christmas holidays, then again at Easter, but no one was home. The house looked empty. There was a sign up outside: FOR SALE, it said. Lydia had gone and she hadn't even bothered to say goodbye.

I remember crying while you slept, determined to keep my tears hidden because you wouldn't have understood. You thought our bond was all we ever needed, but I wanted more; I wanted to be in the world as me, not one of a pair or two of a kind. Why hadn't Lydia told me she was going? Why had she never even written? Had she cared about me at all? I felt the loss as an ache that lasted far longer than the broken arm I'd got when we'd first met, but when you asked how I felt about her departure, I only said, 'I couldn't care less about Lydia.'

Six

Selina

I am awoken by the shrill sound of the doorbell. Who can be calling round at this time of night? I heave myself out of the armchair and a book slides to the floor. Whoever is there has started knocking as well; they'll break the door down if I don't open it. I am quivering with fear; has something happened to Cal?

'What's the date, Miss Bunting? What year is it? Do you know where you are?'

The sun is shining through the open curtains, so it can't be night. The clock on the mouthpiece says just after three o'clock – it must be afternoon. As I reach the hall, the knocking and the ringing stop.

The letterbox pops up and someone says, 'It's Gemma, Miss Bunting.'

Gemma? Who is Gemma? If I'm being called Miss Bunting, she will be somebody official. I open the door cautiously. I think I recognise the pale-looking woman in her forties or fifties standing on the step but I can't quite place her. 'You missed another appointment. I did phone earlier. You are expecting me.'

I sigh. Why does everybody have to interfere so much?

'Can I come in?' she says, but she doesn't wait for a reply. She just barges her way into the hall and then into my living room, where she sits, uninvited.

The house is tidy – I'm relieved. Sometimes I can't be bothered to do the vacuuming or the tidying up. Sometimes it seems as if it needs doing again even though I only did it yesterday or the day before – one long round of cleaning that doesn't have any real effect.

I tune in and out as the woman speaks, catching snatches of one-way conversation. 'I should be able to arrange for you to have some assistance with day-to-day living when you come to need it,' she says, in a tone that suggests I should be grateful. 'And you have a daughter, is that right?'

I nod.

'I expect she's a help to you.'

When did I last see Harriet? When was she last here? Did she bring the dog? What's its name again?

'I think you said you had a twin sister as well last time we spoke. Will she be able to help out if you need her to, with shopping and appointments, that kind of thing?'

It's impossible for me to speak. I miss Zora so much that for a moment, I can't move. She will be here in a minute, I keep saying to myself. She will be here with all her assumptions that she remembers everything better than I do.

I am hoping that what's-her-name will see that her

questions are intrusive and stop, but she continues to inter-
rogate me. I sit as still as I can, half-turned away from her,
expecting her to get the message and leave, but she doesn't.
Who is she anyway? Some kind of social worker? Today, I'm
having trouble keeping up. My mouth is dry. Perhaps it's
anxiety. I'm anxious whenever someone comes to the house.
What if things don't look right? What if I seem strange to
them? Will they put me in a home? I wish my mouth wasn't
so dry; it makes it hard to speak. Did I get her a cup of tea?
Did I even think to ask? I should have made her tea. Now
she'll think that I'm not managing and she'll try to put me in
a home. I interrupt her mid-flow.

'Would you like a cup of tea?'

She says she's got one and points to the cup in front of her
on the coffee table.

'Do I seem all right to you?' Should I have asked that? Is it
a silly question?

'Why do you ask?' she says, failing to give me an answer.

I don't reply, I'm too afraid.

She gets up and wanders over to the far wall. She looks at
the framed photographs. 'Did you take these?'

I don't answer her.

'They're very good. There's a group at the community
centre I told you about, a photography group. They share
their old photographs and they take new pictures too. You
should come, I think you'd enjoy it.'

I shake my head. It's hard, dealing with strangers. 'I might
forget something.'

'That won't matter. It's a group for people in the same boat as you, people who are living with dementia. Why don't you give it a go? I'm sure you'd like it – your photos are really good. The group meets once a fortnight. If I message you the details will you be able to access them?'

I nod. I have no intention of accessing anything, but maybe she'll leave me alone if I say yes.

At last she gets up to go. I breathe a sigh of relief as soon as she's through the door. It's exhausting, trying to keep things in my head – pretending to remember. To wind down, I turn on the television. There's a football match, a women's team. I can't quite tell who is winning or losing but I enjoy the skill of the game. Cal liked football, the skill of the game, and cricket too; he played for his school teams. He got into the grammar school; he passed the eleven plus exam. Mum and Dad were so proud. Zora and I were determined to get into the girls' grammar school and make them proud of us too.

'Do you like your new school?' we ask Cal as we are doing our homework.

'School's all right,' Cal replies. Then, after a while, he adds, 'They make fun of me sometimes. They're all white except for me and my friend Joe – his dad owns the record shop. They call us Sambo and chocolate drop.'

'What do you do then?' asks Zora.

'We fought them once, but we got into trouble for it – not the boys who started it, just us. If it happens again we'll probably be expelled.'

'That's not fair,' I say to him.

'No, it isn't, but it's how it is. Joe and I are targeted for being different. Does that happen to you?'

'Nobody likes us very much,' Zora replies.

'At least you've got each other,' answers Cal.

'At least we've got each other,' Zora and I agree, saying the same words at the exact same time.

Cal is the cleverest person we know. When we have our tonsils out, Cal sits on the bed and recites a very long, funny poem. It's called *The Hunting of the Snark* and it's pages and pages long. He knows it all by heart. He pulls funny faces as he says the words and makes us laugh a lot, even though it hurts. Cal knows everything. He knows the name of every single cricketer who has ever played for the West Indies. Cal can throw a ball faster and harder than anyone else. We go to watch him play cricket for his school, all of us: Zora, me, Mum – Dad comes too; he takes half a day off work. We shout and cheer for Cal. He gives us all a thumbs-up and he goes red but he also looks proud.

Norman Tebbit asks who we cheer for during a cricket match. The answer is the West Indies, of course. Garry Sobers is Cal's hero.

Mum and Dad buy Cal a cricket bat for Christmas. He loves cricket. And football.

There is a photograph of Cal at Christmas somewhere, I know there is. What's-her-name said to bring some photographs to the photography group at the community centre so I try to take the red album from the top shelf but I can't stretch high enough. I used to be able to reach it. Have I got smaller? They do say you shrink with age – everything shrinks with age, come to think of it. I drag a chair across the floor and climb onto it. As I reach for the album it slips from my fingers and crashes to the floor. I scramble down in panic – if I've damaged the photographs, how will I ever remember once things really start to deteriorate? Sometimes I fear I'm nothing more than the sum of my misremembered parts. If that's true, who will I be as memory fades? I flick through the pages, but no harm done, the photographs are all intact. Most of my life, I've taken the pictures that hold the family memories. What was it I wanted to see?

'It's only second-hand,' Dad says as I open the present. I pull a camera from the box. It's in a leather case that looks a bit battered. Even though it isn't new, I can tell from its weight that it's a proper camera that cost a lot of money. I take a big breath. 'Wow,' I say as I breathe out. 'I've always wanted a camera.' Mum and Dad look pleased. Zora is peering at it over my shoulder. She wishes she had a camera too. Her gift is a wooden box with paints and brushes in it. Usually I mind when Zora and I are given different presents. I like it best when we have exactly the same thing even if we have to share, but not this time. This is mine. I am proud to be the only person in the family with a camera. I take a picture of Zora. I take a picture of Cal.

*

Here it is, the picture of Cal, the Christmas one I took. Seeing photos of him hurts even now. The next photo also marks a celebration: it was incredible to think that Cal was going to university.

'How many black boys get into university to study law? You'll have a career, a decent wage, you'll be somebody one day. Lawyers are respected by everybody,' Dad says to Cal. He shakes Cal's hand as if he is a big man now. I take a photograph. We celebrate with Mum's home-made angel cake and McVitie's chocolate biscuits. Mum pours us each a glass of wine. Zora and I feel grown up as we sip our first alcoholic drink. We are all so excited, it's just like Christmas. I take another photograph.

These photographs, they're all in black and white, yet I see them in colour. Mum is wearing her green woollen dress. It's her favourite and she wears it on special occasions like Christmas and birthdays.

Zora and I are ten today but Zora looks different; her arm is in a sling. I am cross with her for looking different on our birthday. We have a cake. Mum wrote HAPPY BIRTHDAY SELZORA in pink icing right across the middle. It should say SELINA AND ZORA because today we don't look the same, we look like two people not one, and I feel sad. We blow out ten candles. I take a picture of Mum and Dad and Cal but I flat out refuse to take a photo of Zora because today we don't look the same.

*

Endless photographs these days, an obsession with capturing the moment; an obsession with being visible. Endless selfies on ... Scrapbook?

'People never notice you unless you make them look,' says Lydia, who is very good at making people look. 'You two get noticed all the time without even trying. It isn't fair.'

We are always visible. Our brown skin makes us stand out, plus there are two of us the same.

'It isn't fair,' says Lydia.

I pick up a picture of the three of us; Lydia is smiling, pale-skinned and beautiful. I am smiling too, because you have to smile when someone takes a photograph. But I'm not looking at the camera. Zora isn't looking at the camera either. It's 1968 – I scribbled the date on the back of the picture. Teenage girls of Jamaican and British parentage were rare back then.

We are self-conscious. We stand out. We don't look like other people. We don't want to have our picture taken but Cal has asked to borrow my camera. He says he wants a photo of the three of us: Zora, Lydia and me. The camera clicks. Cal winds on the film.

I must have taken a photo of Zora with her arm in a sling because it's here, in front of me. She's eating a slice of birth-day cake with her good arm. How strange, I could have sworn I didn't take a picture of her then. And it's June; our birthday is June. But wasn't it autumn when Zora fell in the garden? Weren't we eating apples picked straight from a tree?

I need to capture moments, hold on to them, freeze time. I have to find my camera, take pictures again. Once I was obsessed with taking photographs. These pictures are not the thing itself but its likeness, preserved, yet also distorted. Fragments. A part of the whole. But these fragments are all I have of the past, apart from my memories, and my memory is full of holes.

You're obsessed, Dad says as I snap him again and he laughs his deep, warm laugh.

Zora hates having her picture taken. 'What's the point?' she says. 'Everyone will think I'm you in any case.'

I hold a grainy image to the light. Zora is in the kitchen, gazing towards me. She isn't smiling; she never seems to smile when she has her picture taken. Perhaps it's me in the picture, not Zora after all. But that can't be the case. She wouldn't have taken the photograph and I would have smiled.

PART TWO

Seven

Zora

A new girl arrived in our form halfway through the autumn term. I knew who she was straight away: Lydia Russell. She had been small and skinny when we'd last seen her but now she was nearly as tall as us, with the kind of curves that meant she would never be short of boyfriends.

I looked for signs that she recognised you and me but there were none. She unscrewed the cap of an emerald-green fountain pen and took a bottle of matching green ink out of her leather briefcase.

Most new girls would have spent the day keeping under the radar, but not Lydia. In French she demonstrated her cleverness, conversing with a much stronger command of idioms than Sister Mary Anthony had ever managed. At break time, she ignored everyone, standing by the netball court, watching with disdain as girls from our form practised shooting. When the ball came her way, instead of tossing it back as she was asked to do, she let it roll into a corner and walked away. It was obvious she had no intention of courting popularity by exerting herself. We watched with grudging admiration but

I was determined not to speak to her. She had left us without a word – it wasn't up to us to make the first move. Eventually, she sauntered over to our corner of the playground. 'Hi,' she said. 'Fancy seeing you here.'

'Just fancy,' I replied. Of course she had recognised us – we were unmistakable.

'What's this dump like?' she asked, slipping into the small space between us and leaning against the wall.

'Terrible,' I replied; it was the standard answer.

'How are the nuns?'

'Terrible,' I repeated.

Lydia tucked one hand under my arm and the other under yours and we had no choice but to walk with her towards the school building.

'We're not allowed indoors until the bell rings,' I said.

She snorted derisively and steered us inside. 'At least it's warmer in here, though they could do with turning up the heating.'

'Are you here for good?' I asked.

Lydia nodded and perched on the top of the radiator to warm herself.

'What about boarding school? Did you leave?'

'Got chucked out. Me and the other girls in my dorm got drunk on some whisky, and we smoked a bit of pot, though I was the only one who was asked to leave. They said I was a bad influence.' Lydia seemed more proud than chastened.

'How come you're here?' I asked. 'You're not even Catholic.'

'My father lied. He was desperate to get me into a decent grammar school. He told Sister-So-Bloody-Superior we were among the faithful. And he offered a sizeable donation towards the new school library.'

'You mean they took a bribe?' you asked incredulously. *'Nuns actually took a bribe?'*

Lydia laughed. 'Don't be so naïve, Selina,' she said, recognising, without hesitation, that you were the one who was speaking, not me.

The bell rang for the end of break. The other girls filed into the classroom. They barely looked at us but they stared at Lydia admiringly. On her first day, without even making an effort, she had become a person of importance.

I hadn't intended to forgive Lydia for forgetting all about us and not keeping in touch, but I did, of course. Before long we were even closer than we'd been before she left. After all, we'd only been about ten when she'd disappeared; too much time had passed to let that get in the way of friendship. Besides, she was good company and we went up in the estimation of our classmates by association. If Lydia Russell thought we were all right, we must have had hidden attributes – everybody wanted to be her friend, but she had chosen us.

EIGHT

SELINA

I can tell that the doctor has no real interest in me. He barely even looks at me and he keeps repeating himself, like someone with dementia. I feel patternised. 'Why don't you just get to the point?' I say to him crossly. He frowns but then he starts explaining that irritability is one of the symptoms I can expect to experience. I just sigh. What I can expect to experience is endless conversations like these, where everything I say will be seen as a symptom of worsening illness.

'And you live alone?' he says.

'Yes, I live alone.' I told him this ages ago. Don't they make notes anymore?

'You're still in the early stages of dementia and from what you have said, you're managing well. We'll focus on medication . . .'

As I walk past the reception desk, a woman calls out to me. 'Miss Bunting!'

I don't want to stop; I just want to get out of there, so I keep walking.

She catches up with me. 'Remember me, Miss Bunting? It's

Gemma. I was hoping to see you at the photography class for the Dementia Group? Do try to come next time. I think you would enjoy it.'

I just nod, wanting to end the conversation. Sometimes, it's hard to hold on to the thread. I don't remember her. The thought that we might have met before unsettles me but I try to keep a calm look on my face. She writes on a card and pushes it into my hand.

'This is where the group meets, and I've written down the time and day. I know it's hard, but put this card in a prominent place, on your fridge door, somewhere like that. I really think you'll enjoy it if you come.' She pats me on the shoulder as if to water down the irritation that she feels.

I don't irritate people on purpose, but everyone I speak to seems to be holding in crossness these days. I'm too slow and I'm often forgetful; people think I should be quicker on the uptake but I just have trouble keeping up. It's a youth ... a youth ... what's that word that means using a nice word for something instead of the real one? I'd rather use nice words; the real ones are too scary. Sometimes I just have trouble keeping up. I nod at what's-her-name, shove the card in my pocket and hurry through the double doors.

It's a relief to be outside in the fresh air again. The street is littered with beer cans and empty bottles of cider. There are wrappers, crisp packets, cigarette butts and a single woollen glove, riddled with holes. My feet brush against an old newspaper, sodden from a recent downpour. I pick up everything, even though I can't think what to do with it. I worry that I'll end up like my father. He once took to hoarding as if his life depended on it. But there are too many useless things cluttering up the pavements. And there is so much sound. It seems so loud, so insistent; voices, traffic, a clamour of sound. A feeling of frustration overwhelms me. I want to shout about the too-muchness of everything. Perhaps I do shout, because two women turn around to stare at me. 'What are you looking at?' I shriek at them, like someone spoiling for a fight at closing time outside the local pub. The women turn away again. I should find a bin, but there doesn't seem to be one. I place the rubbish in a neat pile by a lamp post. I just want to tidy everything up. I'm sick of mess, of loudness, of chaos. How can I think when the whole world is so disordered? But perhaps it's evidence that I am not myself.

Then I remember my camera. I squat on the ground and dig through my bag until I find it. It's almost dusk. Silver paper from a pack of half-eaten sandwiches glistens in the gloaming. Water rests in the holes of the glove, shimmering and shifting as it shines. I take a photograph. Rubbish is ugly. Rubbish is chaos. Yet it gleams. I hurry out of sight of the doctor's surgery. If he sees me doing anything that isn't normal, I'll be shoved into a home. I half expected not to be allowed to leave the surgery at the end of my appointment. I could see an ambulance being called. What would it be like never to go home again? I shut out the thought. I put my camera on the ground, wanting to lose the evidence that I am not myself. But the camera is me. Photographs are me – I *am* myself. I pick up my camera again. The rubbish shines. I take another picture of the ugliness that shifts to beauty as the water shimmers on the cellophane.

NINE

ZORA

I sat behind Lydia in class, observing her cockiness, and envying it. She got away with things that were impossible for us. She was always visible, just as we were, but her visibility strengthened her, whereas our visibility was perceived as a problem, a sign of something not quite right; a mark of difference doubled by our sameness.

She turned to me as we listened to a nun droning on about Michelangelo in Art Appreciation and passed me a note. It had a drawing on it, meant to resemble the statue of David. The area around his groin was ringed: *I appreciate this*, was scribbled beside it. I grinned at her. The nuns would be outraged if they saw it, always a plus for Lydia. Another note followed. She wanted to see *Bonnie and Clyde*. Did I fancy it?

'Yes, but it's an X certificate,' I scribbled on the bit of paper, passing it back.

Lydia wrote: 'We'll still get in. I'll do your make-up.' 'DON'T TELL SELINA, IT WILL BE MORE FUN IF IT'S JUST THE TWO OF US' had been scrawled hastily at the bottom of the torn page and underlined.

*

'I didn't think you'd come,' Lydia said, as she applied blusher and eyeliner to my face. 'I didn't think you'd do anything without Selina.'

'We're not joined at the hip anymore,' I replied crossly, glad to have proved her wrong.

At the Odeon, in full make-up and our most adult clothes (miniskirts and blouses so tight the buttons almost popped), we sat as far from the screen as we could for the Saturday afternoon screening of the film. Lydia had wanted to go in the evening but Mum would never have allowed that.

We leaned back, our feet resting on the tops of the thread-bare seats in front of us. We shared the salty popcorn Lydia had bought. Its texture seemed the same as the polystyrene tiles on our kitchen ceiling. As pieces melted on my tongue, I wished she'd chosen sweet. She'd also got some Coke with two straws in it. She held it between us and we sucked alter-nately from the same cup, slurping noisily, the way I might have done if I'd been with you.

'Warren Beatty,' said Lydia loudly, as he came on screen.

She got a chorus of shushes from the rest of the audience.

'He's just to die for,' she added, without lowering her voice.

We watched the rest of the film in silence. I kept turning to see your reaction before remembering that you weren't there.

We stood for the National Anthem, our seats clattering noisily as they folded upwards. In the light, I was aware that the only brown face was mine. I felt self-conscious. If you had been there too, I would barely have registered being out of place.

'That was fantastic,' said Lydia, gripping my arm excitedly.

'Oh my God, that hail of bullets at the end! Come on, let's go and get a burger.'

'I should be getting home. I said I was going to the library and it closes early on Saturdays. Selina will be worried.'

'I'm paying,' replied Lydia, as if this would make you worry less.

In the Wimpy Bar, over cheeseburgers and chips, Lydia and I savoured the best moments of the film. Lydia ordered two more coffees. We sipped them between bites, falling silent once Lydia had exhausted the topic of Warren Beatty. We had a window table. I looked out at the street, wondering what to say. You and I communicated seamlessly, without thinking, but talking to outsiders – even Lydia – was hard. 'How's your cousin . . . ? What's he called?' I said eventually.

'Adam. How do you know him?' asked Lydia, seeming surprised.

'We met up with you both at Battersea Park when we were young. We went back to your house. There was some woman there who shouted at you and him for fighting.'

Lydia frowned, prodding a stale piece of bun with her fork. 'That can't be right. Adam and I have never fought. We've always got on pretty well.'

She would have been annoyed if I'd contradicted her, so I said, 'Do you still see him?'

'Of course. He's at boarding school, in the sixth form, but I see him in the holidays. His parents are often away so Adam comes to stay at ours. He'll be here again at Christmas, I expect. He's nearly eighteen now. He thinks he should be allowed to live on his own in vacation time but his mother put her foot down completely on that score. Shame really. Think of the parties he could have had.'

'I expect his mother did think of them,' I replied.

'I expect she did,' said Lydia, laughing. She picked the onions from her bun and put them to one side in case a snog from a stranger was suddenly in the offing.

'Don't look now,' I said, 'but the boys at the corner table are eyeing you up.'

Lydia did look, of course: two boys, roughly our age, were glancing in our direction. They were skinny and prone to spots. Lydia looked back at me and shook her head. 'Why can't I meet someone different, someone exciting?' she said. 'I'd like someone a bit older – not by much, just a year or two. Younger boys are so gauche, don't you think?'

I nodded, wiping ketchup from the corner of my mouth.

Lydia looked at me with a sly smile that I didn't understand until she added, 'But you don't really like boys, do you?'

I could feel a flush extending from my neck to my forehead. 'What do you mean?'

Lydia lit a cigarette. Smoke curled towards me. 'You'd rather spend time with girls,' she replied.

'You're completely wrong. I do like boys,' I said unsteadily.

Lydia shrugged in that take-it-or-leave-it way she had.

'What makes you think I like girls better?' I asked after a few moments, determined to get to the bottom of it. I looked through the window towards the betting shop. Three young men appeared on cue. I studied them. Was I interested or not? They were wearing tight trousers and fitted shirts, Mick

Jagger-style. If Lydia hadn't had her back to them, she would have been eyeing them up with a smile. ·

'Well, you do prefer girls, don't you?' said Lydia.

'But what is it that makes you think that?' I asked, desperate to find out what it was so I could change it.

'I can't explain, it's just a vibe you give off. Don't worry, the rest of the girls at school are far too slow on the uptake to have noticed. Selina hasn't, has she?'

I didn't reply but I knew Lydia was right – on all counts. It felt odd to realise that she had recognised something about me before I had – before you had – though perhaps I did know. Perhaps I'd been pushing it to the back of my mind, hoping it would go away.

'Nobody cares about that sort of thing anymore,' said Lydia, kindly but inaccurately. 'Homosexuality is even legal now.'

I remembered the things I heard last year as the legislation was being debated – all the slurs – Harold Wilson allowing poofters to shag whoever they fancied from now on, expressed with anger and revulsion: *it isn't natural, a change in the law will lead to total moral degeneration*. I knew it had never been illegal for women to be with other women but that didn't mean it wasn't feared almost as much.

I sat back in my seat. I'd only been pretending to fancy Warren Beatty and Lydia had seen through it. But then I hadn't fancied Faye Dunaway either. What did that mean? I realised I was shaking. I wasn't sure why. Perhaps it was to do with the exposure I was feeling. 'Can I have one?' I said to Lydia, looking at her cigarette.

'Help yourself,' she replied, pushing the packet towards me.

I needed to change the subject and there was a question I'd been meaning to ask. 'You don't have to tell me if you don't want to, but what happened to your real mother?'

Lydia looked at her hands. 'I never actually knew my mother. She died not long after I was born.'

'You must miss her.'

'You can't miss what you've never had, can you? My father married Joyce when I was three or four. I remember being a bridesmaid.'

Lydia gazed past me towards the counter where a waitress was putting money in the till. When she looked at me again, she was crying silently; a large tear plopped on top of the onions on the side of her plate. I'd never seen her upset before. I took her hand. It felt good to hold her – warm and inviting – too good. I let it go again.

'Is she really a wicked stepmother?' I asked, remembering what Lydia had told me when we were young.

'Joyce? Good God no, she's too feeble. She's Catholic, quite devout. There are rules against being wicked if you're Catholic, you know. That's what got me into St Mary's. She's always in church, being holy, and that was enough to seal the deal. No, not wicked, just deadly dull and vacuous. We tolerate one another, I suppose – just about. Anyway,' she said, dabbing her eyes with a pale pink handkerchief, 'we'd better get going, Selina will be wondering where you are.' She took out a compact and checked her mascara in the mirror, relieved to see the tears hadn't caused it to smudge.

'Where have you been?' you asked accusingly on my return.

'Just the library,' I said.

'What's the matter?'

'What do you mean?'

'You're sad about something.'

'Why would I be sad?' I replied, though I knew I had every reason to be. I wondered if you had come across the word 'lesbian'. I had, but only recently. I'd heard it used on television in a documentary and I'd looked it up in the dictionary. I'd been shocked by the definition. *Really?* Women loving other women? How complicated the world had seemed. And then a question had popped into my head, just for a moment. Could I be one? How would I know?

I hadn't known, or not completely. But as soon as Lydia had said it I'd realised she was right. Lydia had seen it, so it showed somehow. It was visible, this secret thing.

I hadn't really thought about who I might love one day until then. I'd assumed there would be a boy I felt attracted to sometime in the very distant future. I believed I was just a little slower in this respect than the other girls I knew, who talked about boys constantly. Even you would nudge me when boys from Cal's school were about, giggling self-consciously if one of them looked in our direction, admiring his hair or his eyes, hoping Cal knew him and would introduce us. I'd behaved as if such silliness was beneath me, all the while thinking I'd start to have feelings for boys myself very soon, I was just a slow developer. But the conversation with Lydia had made me aware that feelings for boys had never actually been on my horizon and probably never would be.

I played back some of the scenes from *Bonnie and Clyde* in

my head, begging God to make me fancy Warren Beatty, but no bolt of lightning struck and turned me heterosexual. I knew that once you were asleep, I would sob quietly into my pillow, wishing you and I could change places and you were the lesbian and I was straight.

You were starting to get ready for bed. 'Are you really all right?' you said. 'You still seem down.' You were looking wounded, trying to understand my withdrawal from you, knowing I was concealing something. I looked back at you, and said once again that I was fine. I put on the radio. Desmond Dekker was singing 'Israelites', your favourite song. I turned it up, hoping it would distract you enough to bring an end to your prying. As you swayed to the rhythm, I wondered what would you think of me if you knew that one day I would probably touch a girl, that I would spend the night running my fingers up and down her naked body, kissing her, in the certainty that this was the only way that I could be? You would be shocked. The Catholic in you would see it as a sin. You would see me as sinful, someone to be ashamed of. And perhaps you would be right.

I turned over. I could see us being divided, and separation from you, the thing I wanted more than anything else, was starting to become the thing I most feared.

TEN

SELINA

'Did I tell you there's an art group I'm thinking of joining? They have photography classes. I'd love to do some of those.' I'm not prepared to confess that it's actually a group for people with dementia. Lydia will only pity me.

'You take more than enough photos as it is,' says Lydia. 'Why would you want to learn to do something you already do all the time? Wouldn't you be better off learning something new?'

Learning new things is hard. I'm more comfortable with the familiar. But to cover this up, I start to explain that I want to take more polished photographs, more professional ones. Lydia cuts bread to go with the soup she's made us for lunch with an absent look on her face. I've probably told her about the photography group before. It's why I start lots of sentences with 'Did I tell you?' I don't want to keep repeating myself. Conversation isn't as smooth as it used to be. I know I say the same thing more than once, and sometimes I start a sentence and I just can't think how to bring it to an end.

*

There is a card attached to my fridge with a magnet. Harriet unfastens it and reads it aloud. Something about a photography group. 'You should give this a go,' she says. 'Come on, Mum, you need to get out and about, meet new people, get your confidence back.'

I shake my head. But Harriet is like her birth mother, she doesn't take no for an answer. Before I know it, she is driving me to a community centre, insisting I'll like it once I get there.

There are eight people including me in the photography group. Seven, counting Harriet. She is hanging on to my hand as if I'll run away unless she keeps hold of me. But it's still good to feel her there, to feel her touch. A woman – in her fifties, I would guess – says her name is Gemma and introduces us to one another. I think she's just conducting the group, or maybe she's a relative, like Harriet. There is an elderly man in a grey jumper that's been darned in places, and navy tracksuit bottoms. He is asking to look at my photographs. I open the album. The first pictures are of me and Zora when we were small. I didn't take these, of course. Mum or Dad must have taken them. But wasn't I the only member of the family who ever had a camera?

Me and Zora are standing together. It is our first communion. We are wearing the same long white dresses, like brides. We are trying to look holy even though Cal is doing his best to make us laugh by pulling silly faces. I ask Zora if trying to stop people being holy is a sin. She is cross. She says of course it isn't, Cal's just having fun and God doesn't mind.

*

God seems to mind a lot of things, like kissing boys and not going to church on Sundays. I go to church quite a lot and Zora thinks it's because I'm a true believer, but the thing I want to believe most is that the world is safe and not utterly cruel. I worry that Lydia is right when she says God doesn't exist. Starving children in Africa and India pray to God to give them food to eat but nothing happens. They're on television all the time with swollen bellies and large, hopeless eyes. God only seems to listen to white children. I say some of this to Father John in the confessional. He says God works in mysterious ways. He's certainly right about that. I keep going back to confession in the hope that Father John's answers will be better and I'll feel safer about everything but they never are. He says that God isn't responsible for all the cruelty, man is responsible, and man has free will. 'You have to have faith,' he says. 'It's arrogant to question your faith like this and think you know better than the Pope and all the holy nuns and priests. Pray to God to give you some humility.'

I do my best to pray for this, but it's hard.

When I made my first communion I prayed to God to give me a camera. When it didn't fall from the sky and onto my bed one morning, I waited a while. Then I wrote a letter to Father Christmas with the same request, and this got me the result I'd been hoping for. I took a lot of pictures.

'Show us the next photograph,' says Harriet.

The next picture is of Lydia. She is in shorts and there are leaves on the trees so it must be summer. She is drinking from a bottle of pop and wearing sunglasses. There is a boy beside her, also wearing shorts and sunglasses. They are stretched out on the grass side by side. Zora is just visible on the very edge of the photograph but it isn't possible to see her face.

'Who's she?' asks darned-jumper man.

'That's Lydia,' I reply.

'Who is the boy?' asks ... Emma?

I stare at the photograph and try to remember. He looks a bit like Lydia. Did she have a brother? 'I don't know who he is,' I tell her, and then I add, to cover the gap in my memory, 'I used to go to school with Lydia.'

'That must be Adam,' says Harriet. 'How old are you all here?'

I try to work it out. 'Eight? Nine?' I remember Adam. He was probably ten or eleven. He was older than us.

'Is that the Common?' darned-jumper man asks.

'It's Wandsworth Common, isn't it?' says Emma. 'There's a railway track.'

I can't see a railway track. Did Zora and I go to Wandsworth Common with Lydia once? I can't remember now.

Lydia is standing by a long window. Her husband ... Michael? ... has been for a run on the Common and he is taking a shower, I can hear the water running. Everything is open-plan in this apartment. There are big, coloured statue things that glisten in the sunlight; I like to run my fingers along their smooth edges. All the rooms are on the ground floor, including the two big bathrooms, and there are no doors, just sort of cubicles. Even the bedrooms are like very big cubicles. I prefer old houses with proper doors you can shut. But perhaps I'm just not keeping up. The world has changed and everything is almost bare of homely things. Lydia obviously likes the modern look. She is old now but she is still recognisable as the girl I used to know. Her face has a few lines but mostly her skin is smooth. I don't think I'm recognisable as the girl I once was. I look at Lydia again. Her face is almost perfect even though she is old. There is something I want to ask her. I open my mouth to speak, but I can't remember what it is I want to say.

'What were you going to say?' asks Harriet as I close the book of photographs.

'I'm not sure,' I answer. I think it was something about Lydia, but the words have slipped away from me.

Eleven

Zora

Lydia had a new record – *Absolutely Free*. She put it on the turntable; although her record player was compact, it was stereo and it sounded much better than our radio. Frank Zappa shrieked and moaned, very much out of tune. Lydia assured me he was doing this on purpose. 'It's a musical fuck you,' she said, glancing at me to see if I looked shocked. She seemed disappointed when I just nodded.

I sat on the bed with its deep pink cover while Lydia danced. Her fingers clutched the air as if she were playing an invisible harp above her head. Her nails were long. Mine were bitten, like yours. She closed her eyes as she absorbed the music and continued to sway. She opened them again and held out her hand for me to dance too. I shook my head and remained where I was. I felt self-conscious with Lydia, and besides, I'd never find the beat, buried as it was beneath discordant wailing.

As 'Call Any Vegetable' started to play, someone came into the room. I sprang up from Lydia's bed in case I wasn't meant to be there.

'What the hell is this racket?' a man asked. He had to stoop to avoid the butterfly mobile in psychedelic shades of yellow and green that spun slowly while Lydia continued to dance. He was trying to loosen his tie with abrupt, tugging movements.

Lydia gave the rhetorical question an answer. 'It's the Mothers of Invention, Pa.'

'Turn it down now! Who's this?' he asked, looking at me.

'This is Zora Bunting. She's one of the twins I told you about. She used to live at the back of us when we were at the old house.'

He nodded almost imperceptibly but he didn't look pleased to see me. 'Joyce said you were rude to her this morning.'

'Sorry, what? I couldn't hear,' said Lydia.

'That's because the music's still too bloody loud.' He went over to the record player and turned the record down with an angry flick of his wrist. He repeated his statement about Lydia's rudeness.

'I wasn't rude, I was just truthful.'

'Try to be a little less truthful in future or you'll find your-self without an allowance.' As he went towards the door, he added, 'Dinner will be on the table in five minutes. We need to eat promptly. Joyce and I are going out for the evening.'

'Okay, I'll be down in a minute. Can Zora eat with us?'

I thought he was going to say no, but he nodded curtly and left.

'I shouldn't really stay,' I said. I didn't want to spend the evening being polite to Lydia's 'pa' and the not-so-wicked Joyce. I wouldn't know what to say to them.

'Please, Zora, stay for a bit longer,' Lydia wheedled. 'Pretty please.'

'What was the rude but truthful thing you said to Joyce?'

'I told her God didn't exist, that it's one big lie to keep us all in line. I said it was no wonder they called Jesus the shepherd. If she's an example of the faithful, they are indeed just a load of sheep.'

I laughed.

'You will stay to dinner, won't you? I can't promise it will be particularly nice – Billy's cooking is very mediocre – but at least we could spend a bit more time together.'

It was always hard to say no to Lydia. 'I'll need to phone Mum or she'll wonder where I am.'

'The phone's down there.' She pointed to a space on the floor beside her bed.

I looked at it enviously. 'You've got your own phone?' There was just one phone in our house and it had only been put in last year. 'It must be nice to be rich, never having to worry about money.'

Lydia looked surprised. 'We're not rich,' she replied.

'You can buy anything you want.'

Lydia laughed. 'Not anything. I suppose you could say we're reasonably well off but rich would be stretching it.'

I thought of her big old house, the one that backed onto ours and had turrets. It had been turned into luxury flats. I picked up the phone.

'Be careful what you say – it's not exactly private. Joyce keeps listening in via the extension in the sitting room, nosey cow. It's one of the things we were arguing about. Tell your mother you're staying here tonight. Then you won't need to worry about getting the bus. It'll be fun; with Pa and Joyce out for the evening we'll have the place to ourselves.'

I picked up the receiver, feeling anxious as I pictured Joyce listening to every word, even though it was hard to imagine anything more innocuous than 'I'm with Lydia, she's invited me to stay over, so I won't be back tonight, if that's okay.' I thought of you hovering next to Mum, asking where I was and when I would be home. I knew you would be envious. It was bad enough that Lydia had asked me round, and not you, without a stopover being included.

The LP came to a halt. It made a hiccupping sound as the needle reached the final grooves and got stuck. Lydia strode over to it and lifted the arm off the vinyl impatiently. 'Come on, we'd better go down to eat.'

The dining room had a large oak table, already set with heavy silver cutlery. There was no tablecloth, just placemats. The red wallpaper darkened the room, which was in shadow, lit by ornate table lamps, one at each end of a sideboard. Joyce was standing by her chair when we arrived, looking slightly perplexed. She nodded to me just as Lydia's father had done but said nothing. 'Is Harry coming?' she asked Lydia, who didn't reply. 'We're going out shortly. We'll be late if he doesn't get a move on.' Joyce was slender, with backcombed hair in a beehive that was too young for her, yet three or four years out of date. Her wine-coloured dress clung to thin, shapeless legs that showed pale beneath it. Lydia's father finally arrived and we all took our seats, me opposite Lydia, and Joyce and Harry at either end of the table.

Joyce clasped her hands together and bowed her head and I realised she was about to say grace. I glanced at Lydia, who rolled her eyes but still looked down with a suitably demure expression as Joyce muttered the prayer. I thought of you – you wouldn't have been embarrassed by this sign of devoutness; you would have lapped it up.

There were three courses: homemade tomato soup, thin and rather bitter, followed by cod in a thick parsley sauce, and finally, fresh fruit salad with single cream, which was the most edible part of the meal. When we had fruit salad at home, it came out of a tin and was topped with evaporated milk.

I'd been expecting animated conversation that I would struggle to keep up with, but instead there was silence, broken only by the sound of cutlery clattering on plates. There was no discernible tension; it was as if the Russells simply had no inter-est in each other. When our family had a meal together, there was barely a pause in the conversation. Mum would ask how school had been or what we'd eaten at dinner time. She would tell us which flowers were in season at the florist and describe the wedding bouquets she'd made up. Cal would repeat a bad joke he'd heard and we'd all be helpless with laughter. We would chat about things we'd watched on TV or listened to on the radio. Then the conversation would become more serious. We would be angry, collectively, about calls for immigration to come to an end. We would talk proudly of Arthur Ashe and Muhammad Ali, and Dad would tell us about Althea Gibson. We would repeat the gist of speeches by Marcus Garvey, Martin Luther King and Malcolm X. Then we would shift back to lighter topics and Dad would share stories about awkward passengers on his bus, like the man who sang opera very loudly all the way from Clapham Common to Liverpool Street station, and the woman who stripped naked to dance on the top deck of Dad's bus because, she said, she couldn't do the splits in tight trousers. Sometimes Dad reminisced about the way things used to be back home, and we'd realise how much he missed Jamaica; he'd come here after being in the merchant navy during the war, but he'd always meant to go back – he would have done, if he hadn't met our mother.

Lydia rested her spoon on top of the slices of orange she hadn't been able to finish. 'May I leave the table?' she asked. I assumed the request was a throwback to her childhood.

'You may,' her father replied.

Lydia got up, beckoning me to follow.

'What about the washing-up?' I whispered.

'Billy will do that. She's here till eight. It's a pity she's such a lousy cook. I've asked Pa to get rid of her and get someone else instead but he says she's cheap and she's willing to do split shifts, so we're stuck with her, worst luck.'

'You just can't get the help nowadays,' I replied as we ran up the stairs.

'I know,' said Lydia, failing to detect any irony.

'Your dad doesn't speak very much, does he?'

'He's a man of few words. Joyce used to chatter but she's given up now too. I suppose I should be thankful for small mercies.' She went over to the record player. 'Shall we listen to the other side of this?' she said, turning over *Absolutely Free*.

It wasn't the kind of music I was into. 'Can't we listen to something else?'

'You're such a philistine. There's a stack of albums over there. You can pick something out if you want.'

I knelt on the floor and looked through the pile of records: the Doors; the Rolling Stones; the Grateful Dead; Buffalo Springfield. 'You've got Jimi Hendrix,' I said, pouncing on *Are You Experienced*.

I sat on the bed again. Lydia joined me. I listened to the rapid, intricate chords of Hendrix's guitar and pictured him plucking the strings with his teeth. Lydia's leg was touching mine. I could feel myself turning red. There wasn't much space on Lydia's bed; two tops, a pair of jeans and three dresses were piled up on the other side of me. Perhaps it was just that there wasn't room to move. But Lydia edged closer, and I knew she was doing it on purpose. I felt strange, wanting to be touched yet fearing what this might mean. Lydia definitely liked boys. Why would she want to do this with me? Her body curled into mine and then moved away again, almost as quickly; a little tease perhaps, a show of what could take place if only I would let it happen. But Lydia liked boys, I thought again to myself. And then she was kissing me. I kissed her back, confused by the ease of it.

I pulled away. 'Your father might come in again,' I said.

'He's out for the evening, remember?'

'They might come back.'

'Relax, they'll be gone until dawn, I expect.'

'They might come back early.' I was thinking of you. I knew that Lydia would swear me to secrecy and this would be something else I'd be required to keep from you. And it would be such a secret that it would threaten to break us apart. Yet it was impossible not to welcome Lydia's touch as she caressed the space between my thighs. I responded in kind, breathing in the flowery scent of Diorissimo as Hendrix sang 'The Wind Cries Mary'.

I woke up while it was still dark, and everything felt wrong. I shook Lydia's shoulder until she was awake too and I told her I had to go home.

I got dressed silently, ducking to avoid the green and yellow butterfly mobile that spun slowly in the night breeze. Lydia covered her naked body with a pale blue dressing gown and walked me to the front door. Her father had locked it so she had to get the key from his study. She didn't hug or kiss me as I left, she only said, 'It was a one-off, you do understand that, don't you? It can't go anywhere. I'm straight, we both know that. And you mustn't breathe a word to anyone, especially not Selina, not ever.'

I don't know why I nodded. I was desperate to ask why she'd wanted it to happen in the first place if she was so dismissive about it now, so certain that it couldn't work between us, but I couldn't find the words. In the dark of the night, it all seemed grubby, and I was full of loneliness.

I walked the three miles home, remembering when we'd first met Lydia. I'd climbed the apple tree that hung over the garden wall because I'd wanted to impress her. She'd thought I couldn't do it and I'd wanted to prove her wrong. I seemed to spend a lot of time trying to prove Lydia wrong. What had I wanted to prove by sharing a bed with her? And, more importantly, what had she wanted to prove by sharing a bed with me?

I let myself into the house as quietly as I could. As I slipped into our room, you stirred and muttered something, but you were asleep again almost at once. I don't know what I'd been expecting. I think I'd assumed you'd be fully awake as soon as I walked through the door, anxious about my absence, worried that in asking me to stay, Lydia had preferred me to you.

I stepped out of my clothes, acutely conscious of my body; my skin, the areas that Lydia had touched. I'd touched her back willingly; her body and mine had been intertwined and I had been full of a delirious kind of joy that had now turned to a sharp sense of unease. What did it all mean? I'd had the feeling, even as we had held one another, that Lydia had been playing some sort of game. Why? I knew that I could love her; perhaps I already did. She liked me, yes – some of the time, when it suited her – but she didn't love me, and I knew beyond a doubt that she never would. Perhaps tomorrow, Lydia would say that we were no longer friends – let alone lovers – if that's what we had been. In my bunk above yours, I was full of fear.

Twelve

Zora

You knew I had a secret. You kept asking what was wrong, your face contorted with ... what? Anxiety? Dread? These were the things I was feeling. I tried to behave as if everything was normal, even though I knew nothing would ever be normal again.

Being around you gave me a sense of shame and foreboding. You enjoyed going to Mass. You were always at confession and it never seemed to occur to you to question anything the church said or did. You believed everything you were told, so you would have no trouble thinking I had sinned if you ever found out about me and Lydia. The Pope was infallible, according to you and Father John. Mary was a virgin when she gave birth to her son. You even believed there was an actual ark that Noah had built and populated with two of every single animal.

'It's not even possible,' I said as we walked home with the grocery shopping one Saturday afternoon. The bags were so heavy that I set mine down for a moment and sat on a low wall to rest my aching arms. You perched beside me.

'Do you know how many species of animal there are in the world? There would have been tens of thousands of animals, all milling about in the hold. Imagine the stink of all that manure. They would probably have suffocated, buried under steaming great heaps of it.'

You looked towards the sky as if the answer was in the heavens above, and then you said, 'The ark was probably like Doctor Who's TARDIS.'

As I was opening my mouth to say what a ridiculous idea this was, you laughed and I realised you were joking.

You believed we each knew what the other was thinking, but lately, I'd sometimes thought you were being serious when you weren't. It felt strange to realise we were no longer quite understanding each other. I knew it felt even stranger to you.

That evening as we were all watching some variety show, you whispered to me, 'Come into the garden.'

I knew you wanted to speak in private so I shook my head – a secret conversation with you was the last thing I needed.

'Please,' you said.

I gave in eventually, the way I always did.

We squatted on the damp grass in the shadow of the apple tree that hung over the wall. The air was cold; our breath smoked.

'Tell me exactly what happened when you stayed over with Lydia. Did you argue? Why are you being so odd about it?' You were barely pausing for breath, let alone answers to your questions. 'Why won't you tell me anything? Did Lydia say you mustn't? She always says don't tell. Why do you keep listening to her when she says that? Why does everything with Lydia have to be such a secret?' Your tone shifted from hectoring to beseeching. 'I wish things could be the way they used to be between us, before Lydia came.'

I wished that too. The world had seemed so safe when we had been everything to one another, and had only needed secret words to tell each other how we felt. But all I said was, 'Nothing happened when I stayed with Lydia,' and I went back inside the house, determined not to cry.

SELINA

Zora wants to speak to me, so she asks me to go outside with her. We always go into the garden when we want to be most secret. Perhaps she's going to tell me what happened when she stayed over with Lydia. She's been so unhappy since then. I think Lydia must have said something spiteful. Zora is easily hurt even though she pretends she isn't. But when we open the back door, the garden is full of puddles from all the rain we've been having – there's nowhere for us to sit. Zora steps back.

'We can talk in our bedroom,' I say to her.

She just shakes her head and I see that she is using the rain to back away from telling me what's wrong with her.

I take her arm but I don't say anything more. I can tell that Zora no longer wants me to speak.

Once, Zora and I wouldn't have hesitated to share whatever we were thinking – it would just have come out of our mouths before we even knew it. I feel so cold as I stand beside

Zora, willing her to talk to me again. But she stays silent and I feel more afraid than ever – the space between us is getting bigger all the time.

The space between us contracts and expands as I sit by my bed, trying to hold on to all the memories of us. I miss Zora. I miss her so much.

Thirteen

Zora

Lydia wanted to get a birthday present for Adam. 'Do you fancy coming?' she said to me over the phone. 'Just you,' she added, the way she so often did. I leapt at the chance. Perhaps, afterwards, we would go back to Lydia's house and repeat the night we'd spent together. She'd said it could never happen again, but I didn't want to believe her.

You were continuing to ask what had gone on that night. I was determined not to tell you. Perhaps I felt ashamed. I definitely felt embarrassed. Every time I looked at Lydia, my embarrassment intensified. My body, so different to hers, in its brownness, its adolescent fullness, had been exposed; I had been exposed and I had been humiliated too, not during the intimacy we'd shared, when there had been an equal sense of pleasure, but in the days afterwards when Lydia had been distant, tacitly making the point that whatever had happened between us was completely inconsequential to her, even though she knew exactly how much it had meant to me. I saw that I should have it out with her, but I also knew that Lydia wouldn't think twice about ending the friendship altogether if it became any sort of difficulty. It was better, I thought, to collude with the idea that nothing out of the ordinary had ever occurred.

I followed Lydia along the high street, wishing she cared for me the way I cared for her.

'Let's try in here,' said Lydia, opening the door of an antique shop.

I watched, standing to one side, as Lydia browsed through rows of worn, old-fashioned things, thinking how pretty she looked in her white, wet-look coat and matching boots.

'It's hard buying stuff for boys,' she said. 'I never know what to choose.' She settled for a wooden ink stand with cut-glass bottles that cost a fortune even though it was second-hand, and we decided to go for a coffee. I thought it would be the Wimpy Bar as usual but Lydia wrinkled her nose and said, 'The Wimpy's so passé. I've found this little Italian coffee bar; it even has a jukebox. Let's go there instead.'

The café was obviously new, with wipe-down tables and benches upholstered in psychedelic fabric. Lydia put some money in the jukebox and 'Hole in My Shoe' began to play. She wanted to pay for my drink but you and I had just started holiday jobs at the local supermarket, so I told her I'd buy my own. It was a statement of independence; I needed to conceal my longing to be closer to her than she would allow. I offered to treat her too, but Lydia looked irritated and I realised she was disappointed that I was failing to allow her to patronise me. I got a knickerbocker glory. Lydia only wanted black coffee; she said she had to watch her figure. She looked at me critically as I wolfed down ice cream and said I needed to mind I didn't get any fatter.

The words stung, as they were meant to do. 'I'm not fat,' I muttered, wondering what touching me had felt like to Lydia. Had she been repulsed by rolls of flesh? Was that why she'd said the night could never be repeated? Did this mean she wouldn't be asking me back to her house that evening? The ice cream suddenly tasted too sweet and I pushed it to one side.

'There's an album I want to get,' said Lydia as we left the café. 'Everywhere in town has sold out, so I thought I'd try that little record shop round the corner.'

'Cal works there sometimes in the holidays, with his friend Joe. He might be there now. He might give you a discount as you're with me.' Now that I had something to offer Lydia, through being Cal's sister, I felt a little more significant.

As I pushed open the door of the record shop, I saw Joe, leaning over the counter, talking to one of the customers, a young black man with dreadlocks that reached his waist.

'He looks weird,' said Lydia.

'Be quiet,' I said quickly. 'He's a Rasta.'

'He's a what?'

'A Rastafarian. It's a religion.'

'What kind of religion?'

'I'll tell you later.' I didn't want to give Lydia the chance to be scornful about Haile Selassie and Ethiopia. She would say how silly it was, loudly and insistently, though she would probably relish the idea of the ganja. I distracted her by pulling her over to the aisle that was labelled Psychedelic Rock.

Lydia flipped through the album sleeves and found the one she was looking for: *Surrealistic Pillow* by Jefferson Airplane. At that moment, Cal entered the shop from the stockroom.

'Hi, Zora, what are you doing here?'

'This is Lydia. She's getting a record,' I told him.

Lydia looked up. 'Hi,' she said to Cal.

'Hi,' he replied. 'I've heard a lot about you.'

'Same here,' said Lydia.

The words seemed loaded and I realised, with a stab of pain so sharp that it almost made me gasp out loud, that they were flirting with one another. There were lingering looks. Lydia flicked her hair across her shoulders and I looked on, feeling apprehensive – and humiliated – but trying not to show it. Yet perhaps I was imagining it all. Perhaps my longing to be with Lydia was making me see things that weren't actually there.

Cal took the empty cover of *Surrealistic Pillow* and dug out the vinyl from the shelf behind him. He inserted it into the sleeve and put it in a carrier bag, pausing to gaze at Lydia before giving it to her with a large discount.

'Do you like Jefferson Airplane, then, Lydia?' he asked.

'No, I hate them, that's why I've just bought their album,' Lydia replied.

Cal looked awkward. Perhaps his chat-up lines would have been better if he hadn't been so aware of me, standing by the Soul section. 'What I mean is, what other groups do you like?'

'The Stones, of course. Big Brother and the Holding Company. The Beatles, I suppose, but everybody likes them, don't they? Are you into Jefferson Airplane as well?'

Cal glanced at me, aware that I would know, if he said yes, that it was a lie. 'I'm really into music with a bit more bass,' he replied.

'What kind of thing?'

'Stevie Wonder. James Brown.

'James Brown? A bit short. A bit full of himself.'

'What about Mick Jagger? If anyone's full of himself it's him.'

'Part of his charm. Who else do you like, then, apart from Little Stevie Wonder and the diminutive Mr Brown?'

Cal smiled, realising Lydia was teasing. 'Charlie Parker, Miles Davis, Dizzy Gillespie, Duke Ellington.'

'*Who?* I don't know any of them.'

'They're four of the greatest jazz musicians there's ever been. We could listen to some jazz if you like.'

'What, now?' Lydia paused. Then she said, 'Oh, all right then,' as if Cal had twisted her arm.

Joe slipped *Kind of Blue* out of its cover and placed it on the turntable with reverence. The mellow notes filled the shop.

I could tell Lydia didn't get it. She looked bored as she leaned against the counter. But Cal said, 'Miles Davis is unbelievable, isn't he?'

Lydia nodded. Cal didn't seem to notice her lack of enthusiasm. They listened without speaking further. Joe served a couple of customers with bad grace – they were disrupting his enjoyment of the album. When side one finished, Lydia said, 'I wouldn't mind a dance now. Do you have anything with more of a beat?'

Cal looked at Joe, who pulled out *Cold Sweat*. Lydia, remembering their earlier disagreement over James Brown, smiled at Cal; he smiled back. She held out her hand, beckoning him to join her in the dance.

Fourteen

Zora

There was plenty of booze, and the woody smell of marijuana filled the air. Joe's living room was too small for all the
bodies gyrating to the rhythm of James Brown. We danced
well enough on our own, but with other people you and I
were awkward and self-conscious – uncoordinated. A single
strobe light flashed on us intermittently, illuminating our
failure to look grown up. We were wearing make-up we had
each applied to the other's face. Our eyes were large, ampli-
fied by kohl and khaki-coloured eyeshadow. Our mascara
shed particles that pricked the surface of our eyes, causing
them to redden and water unflatteringly. Determined to look
partyfied, we'd put on tops designed to show our cleavage.
Our necklines were edged with sequins we'd stitched on that
morning. I'd been determined to make myself look irresist-
ible; I knew Lydia would be there and I wanted her to know
what she was missing – then perhaps seeing her with my
brother would hurt a little less. At the last minute, you had
decided that even more embellishments were needed, so you
had covered our white plimsolls with glitter, glued on with

Gloy. It hadn't had time to stick, so most of it was now on the floor, sparkling in the light.

We were confident we would fit in at first but, as the other guests arrived, we knew different. Their clothing was casual and understated. The gaucheness of our home-made adornments was all too obvious.

'Lydia isn't here yet,' you said.

As Cal's girlfriend, Lydia had a proper invite. She wouldn't need to stand at the front door begging Joe to let her in. She wouldn't be there on sufferance, allowed in solely because she was related to Cal. She wouldn't be seen as an embarrassment, and Cal wouldn't wish she'd clear off home.

'I don't care about Lydia,' I told you.

'I never thought she'd start going out with our brother.'

'Me neither,' I replied, trying to keep the edge from my voice.

'Lydia said something to me, but I'm not supposed to tell you.'

'What?' I asked, pushing back the anxiety that was causing my whole body to quiver.

'She said she isn't a virgin. It happened before she met Cal.'

'Did she mean she'd been with a boy?' I wasn't sure I wanted to know the answer, yet at the same time, I was desperate to find out.

'What else could she mean? She said he was called Raoul, and it was when she was on holiday in France last year. She said, and I quote, "It was just a holiday fling." But she told me she was hoping to see him again in spring. Do you think Cal knows? Do you think we should tell him? I mean it's probably none of our business and it probably doesn't matter, she might not even want to see Raoul again now she's met Cal, but—'

I started to walk away but I couldn't go far; the house was too small so you soon caught up with me.

'What's the matter? You've been weird for weeks now. I do wish you'd tell me.'

Then Lydia arrived. She was wearing a purple minidress with full sleeves. Brown leather boots showed off her perfect legs. Three boys approached as she entered the room, offering her paper cups of wine, and cigarettes. It was as if their actions were choreographed. Soon they would burst into song and it would form a scene in a musical. Cal rushed to Lydia's side, staking his claim. The other boys backed off. I watched, feeling hopeless. Coming in just behind, I saw her cousin Adam. He was grown up now, and barely recognisable. He was wearing brown trousers and a cream shirt. His thick hair fell into sideburns that brushed his ears. You whispered to me that he was even better-looking than you remembered, assuming that I would appreciate him too. He took in the dancing and the drinking. Then he caught your eye and came over. 'Hello, Selzora,' he said to both of us.

He chose you, despite remembering us as Selzora – two moulded into one. You were too surprised to resist. I felt your panic as he drew you away from me but your fear faded in seconds and then you followed willingly.

I watched in disbelief. Even though I had no interest in Adam, it hadn't occurred to me that he would choose you when – as far as he knew – he could be with me. I was the lively one. You barely even spoke. I heard him telling you how nice you looked (clearly a lie in the light of the glitter-covered plimsolls) and offering to get you a drink.

Across the room, Lydia danced with Cal, her chin resting on his shoulder. His hands were round her waist. I tried not to look but I couldn't stop torturing myself as they shuffled across the floor to the distorted sound of 'See Emily Play'. I stood beside the buffet table eating sausage rolls and slices of leftover Christmas cake, feeling invisible, yet utterly conspicuous. I wanted to go home, just run away and never look back. But it was New Year's Eve. Who went home at quarter to eleven? I shoved chunks of marzipan into my mouth.

Joe took the Pink Floyd single off the turntable and replaced it with 'Soul Man'. I stood up defiantly and moved to the beat, a paper cup of wine in one hand and a cheese straw in the other, but I couldn't dance for long, I felt too miserable. You were continuing to chat to Adam. You looked animated and more than a little pleased with yourself.

Lydia was sitting opposite me now, still beside Cal, smoking something pungent. She glanced across at me and then, with slow, deliberate movements, she leaned into my brother, putting her arm around his neck. She tried to pass him the joint but he shook his head, aware that the music that was rocking the house could soon attract the attention of the police. He knew he couldn't risk getting a record and being barred from university. He and Joe would be the first in the van if there was a raid. He'd probably be accused of supplying the party guests with all the illegal substances that were doing the rounds. But Lydia was oblivious to this. She had no real conception of the difference between her cosseted life and ours.

You had disappeared from sight. I dragged myself away from Lydia and Cal and went upstairs to find you. As I reached the top of the stairs, I saw you and Adam. You had your tongue down his throat. As I got closer I thought I could smell marijuana on you, but you were far too strait-laced to smoke anything more than a cigarette, and you didn't even like those very much, so the woody smell must have come from Adam.

'For God's sake, Selina, have some self-respect,' I said.

You laughed – Adam too.

We never laughed at one another, we just didn't, but you and Adam were laughing like I was nothing.

It was as if you had kicked me.

I turned away from you.

You'd never hurt me like that before and I couldn't understand it, not from you, the only person in the world I completely trusted. How could you have done that? I felt dizzy with bewilderment – and anger. I didn't know what to do; how could I stay and see in the New Year with you after that? It was half past eleven but I couldn't wait until midnight. I had to get out of there and leave you behind.

SELINA

When I look at Zora, I see myself reflected back and I feel more confident than I have ever felt. We look fabulous in our tight tops and brand-new black shoes – not school shoes either; they are strappy and gorgeous. We bought them with the money we got from working part-time at the supermarket.

Tonight I'm shining bright, even though Zora is on one side of the room and I'm on the other. She looks cross that Adam has chosen me, not her. I try not to feel triumphant because it's not a nice characteristic and, besides, Zora's feeling awkward on her own, and sad too. It radiates from her.

I'm enjoying talking to Adam. The music is so loud I'm having to shout to be heard, but Adam is interested in me, and I'm feeling so good about myself . . . maybe it's the wine, or the joint we've been sharing. Conversation is coming easily to me. I've never been chatty before; it's a good feeling. Adam is so sophisticated. I keep staring at him, even though I'm trying not to make the attraction too obvious. He's really good-looking, with dark brown hair and big green eyes.

Zora is standing by the buffet table, drinking from a bottle of rum that somebody has brought. She is filling her mouth with Potato Puffs, which ruins the adult persona she is trying to project. Maybe I should go over to her but if I do, Adam might go off with someone else. He starts talking about his studies. He's doing classics at Cambridge. I tell him he must be very clever to be doing Latin and Ancient Greek at the best university in the country and he seems pleased. When I remember to look over at Zora to check that she's okay, I realise I can't see her. Has she gone upstairs? I should try to find her but I want to stay here with Adam, though I'm worried he's thinking I'm too young for him. He must be nineteen, something like that. He's in his first year at university and I'm just a schoolgirl. At least I'm wearing make-up. Soon we are laughing uncontrollably at the memory of a sketch from *At Last the 1948 Show* and we sing the song from last week's episode at the tops of our voices. People turn to look but I don't care.

Two women turn to look as I scoop up rubbish from outside the doctor's surgery. I have to clean things up. I'm tired of all the useless things cluttering up the place. I have to make everything clean again; it's impossible to hold things in my head when everything around me is so chaotic. I just want to make everything less disorganised. The women turn to look. Let them look, then. What does it matter?

'Let's go upstairs,' Adam says.

I follow him, not sure what I will do if he wants anything more than just a kiss. Beside the bathroom door, he whispers something: 'Dusky girls are so sexy.' His lips find my mouth. He pokes at me with his tongue but I pull back; he tastes of wine and marijuana and I'm not sure I like it. What did he just say to me? I'm not certain; the music is so loud it's hard to hear. He can't have said what I think he said. I stare up at him, flushed with the realisation that I've actually been kissed by a boy. At last, I've done something before Zora, and I can't wait to tell her. Where is she? The bendy opening bars of 'See Emily Play' drift up the staircase. It's Lydia's favourite song.

Martin turns up the music on his car stereo. 'I've always liked this track,' he says.

'See Emily Play'. Who sang this? Lydia used to love this song.

*

'See Emily Play' is coming to an end. I want Adam to dance with me before the music stops. He whispers to me but the music is so loud I can't hear what he's saying.

Martin parks the car but he keeps the engine running so 'See Emily Play' doesn't stop. 'This was the first single I ever bought,' he says. Then he starts kissing me, but his kisses are wet; he tastes of wine and cigarettes so I pull away from him. He says he is turned on by me. Turned on, as if he is the radio that's playing. He places a hand on my thigh. I pretend it's not happening but perhaps it's time to sleep with him. I'm at college now, too old to still be a virgin. I'm not sure I'm turned on by Martin but I still agree to go back to his flat. I can't remain a virgin for the rest of my life.

Emily plays as Adam kisses me. He whispers in my ear. He tries to kiss me again. This time, I let him, but only for a moment. I don't recognise the next song. It's something loud, and the repetitive beat is annoying. It incites a load of boozed-up people to grab one another and form a conga. They coil unsteadily down the stairs. Zora still isn't anywhere to be seen. Just as I am starting to panic about her absence, Adam looks over my shoulder and says, 'It's the other baby Bunting.' I turn and see her behind me.

Adam called us that when we first met, years ago now. It seemed funny then but we aren't babies anymore. I still laugh but Zora continues to look cross.

'What are you doing?' she asks.

'I'm with Adam,' I reply, stating the obvious.

The mood is broken. I can't kiss Adam anymore, so the three of us go back downstairs and sit on the sofa in the living room. Cal and Lydia are still dancing, though they have also avoided the conga. They look good together. I can't help wondering if Adam and I look good together too.

Zora says, 'I'm going home,' her speech slurred.

Perhaps I'm slurring too, I've had such a lot to drink. 'Don't go home,' I say to her.

'I'm really bored now,' she answers with a pained expression on her face.

I want to stay with Adam, so I say to Zora, 'It's too early to go home, we've got to wait till after midnight.'

'I'm not waiting, I'm going home now. Are you coming with me or not?'

Zora gets to her feet, but before I'm even aware that I've made the decision, I say to her, 'I'm staying here.'

We stare at one another, each unsettled by my resistance. It can only have happened because of the wine I've been drinking – it wouldn't have occurred to me to be apart from Zora on New Year's Eve if not for that. We always see in the New Year together, holding hands, each making a silent resolution, each knowing our resolutions are the same.

Zora turns to leave. I can't believe she's going. I think I expected her to decide to stay with me after all. As she reaches the door, she gives me a look that says she feels betrayed. I should go with her; I can't leave her feeling like that. I get up to follow, but Adam pulls me back down on the sofa. I watch her go, scared to be without her, but also relieved, in a way. It will be easier to spend time with Adam now she's gone.

Adam puts his arm round my waist but we don't dance. 'A Whiter Shade of Pale' blasts through the speakers.

I can hear 'A Whiter Shade of Pale' on the radio as I search for Potato Puffs in the corner shop, not the flavoured ones, just plain. I can't find them. I ask the assistant, a spotty boy who can't be more than seventeen. He shakes his head without looking up from the car magazine he's reading.

The man behind me in the queue says, 'Potato Puffs? You're going back a bit, aren't you? I don't think they make them anymore.'

'I just thought they might have them.' I'm sure I ate some the other day. Turning to look at the man behind me, I realise he is old – old enough to be forgetful or to get things wrong.

'Used to love those,' he says with a smile. 'Bought them after school when I was a boy. They used to disintegrate, though. You'd get them and sometimes it would be just a load of crumbs at the bottom of the packet. Used to love them, though. They should bring them back.'

I pick up some crisps instead but I can't seem to find the right money. I can't think how much each coin is worth and how to make them all add up. The boy behind the counter is impatient. He sighs loudly and then he rolls his eyes, clearly wanting to return to the car magazine. I think about leaving without the bag of ... so it doesn't become obvious that I don't know what I'm doing. But instead I tip all the coins in my purse onto the counter. I wait as the boy helps himself to the right change.

On the radio that's playing in the shop, a DJ says, 'A blast from the past, a number-one hit from way back in 1967. They don't make them like that anymore: Procol Harum and "A Whiter Shade of Pale".'

'I remember this song as well. I used to chat up girls to this, back in the day,' the old man behind me says with a chuckle.

'I remember it too,' I answer.

'A Whiter Shade of Pale' is blasting through the speakers. I want to dance with Adam. Soon it will be midnight on New Year's Eve, but Zora is no longer here.

Fifteen

Zora

I'd woken up a couple of hours before sunrise, my head still
full of the misery the party had caused, making it impossible
to sleep. I was angry with you, angry with Lydia and angry
with Cal. I didn't know what to do with myself. In the end,
I'd gone downstairs to make myself a drink, and as I'd sat in
the kitchen, I'd heard a key in the lock.

I thought it was Dad at first. He was doing a shift on the
night bus. But then I realised from the lightness of the footsteps
that it was Cal. Before I'd even thought about it, I ran into the
hall. 'Where have you been?' I said, trying to control my fury,
because I knew, of course; Cal must have been with Lydia. They
must have been in bed together and now he was sneaking back,
hoping not to get caught, just as I had done a few months earlier.

Cal didn't answer.

'Where have you been?' I repeated.

'Just out,' he said.

'Are you sleeping with Lydia?'

'Mind your own business, Zora,' he replied, and he went
upstairs to his room.

Cal was hardly ever abrupt. I could see he was embarrassed to have been seen. I hated him, even though he wasn't to know he'd taken Lydia away from me – he hadn't done it on purpose – and besides, this was Cal, our big brother, who had shared his sweets and games with us when we were little, and had tried to comfort us when we had fallen over or got a telling-off from Dad. I wanted to follow him to his room, make him see that Lydia was just playing games with him, the way she'd done with me, but I remained where I was, unable to move. I'd been harbouring the thought that soon Lydia would tire of Cal and want me back in her bed again but that was impossible now. I saw that it was Cal she wanted, not me – and it always would be.

Now, standing beside Lydia at the bus stop, lost in the wave of humiliation that came with the memory of Cal entering our house at 5am, I thought I would never be happy again. I was only here because Cal was away on a school field trip and Lydia was at a loose end. Otherwise, she would have been with him. I leaned against the panel of the shelter, wishing I'd told her where to get off. I was allowing myself to be used, but I couldn't seem to do anything about it.

'Why are you going out with Cal?' I asked shakily. I really wanted to ask why she was sleeping with him and not me, but I knew I wouldn't like the answer.

Lydia blew a smoke ring towards me. It hovered in the air. She smiled enigmatically and said, 'He's a good-looking boy, your brother.'

'So you just fancy him, then?' Had she fancied me, or hadn't she been interested at all – just pretending for a reason only she knew?

'I don't *just* fancy him. I really like him. He's easy to talk to. And he's so passionate.'

I became still. 'Passionate?' I said, very softly. Lydia wasn't meant to hear, but she did.

'I don't mean in bed, though of course he is. I mean he's passionate about life. Things matter to him.'

Cal was passionate, as Lydia described it, about a lot of things: nuclear disarmament; apartheid; the Vietnam War. Cal was passionate about these things to the point where he often couldn't sleep. The possibility that he wouldn't get the grades he needed to go to LSE also kept him awake at night; Mum and Dad were counting on him going, they'd told all their friends about their brilliantly clever son, and how he'd been offered a place at the best law school in the country. Two or three weeks on from this conversation, he would be in despair about the assassination of Martin Luther King. He would cry bitter tears. 'When will things ever change? Why do they hate us so much?' he would say. I wondered if Lydia knew this aspect of Cal but I couldn't imagine them having deep conversations about racial violence in the dead of night. I thought once more of the time Lydia and I had shared a bed with a dull ache. It seemed so long ago now and it was obvious that she wanted to hurt me by letting me know she was sleeping with Cal, and that he was passionate, and then pretending she hadn't meant that at all.

'What do your dad and Joyce think about Cal staying over with you?' I asked.

'They're hardly ever home,' Lydia replied.

'They leave you on your own?'

'I'm nearly seventeen now, Zora. I don't need a babysitter.'

I wanted to ask Lydia more questions about her and Cal but I knew it might entertain her to tell me in full and it was unthinkable for me to hear about the physical side of her relationship with my brother. It would also hurt too much. I wished I could end the friendship, but being Lydia's friend seemed better than not seeing her at all.

We huddled in the bus shelter as it began to rain. I felt water from a leak in the roof trickle down my neck.

'Adam hasn't been in touch with Selina since the party,' I said, desperate to move off the subject of Lydia and Cal, even though I'd been the one who'd brought it up. 'I think she was expecting to go on a date with him. Do you know why he hasn't phoned her?'

Lydia took a final drag of her cigarette and tossed it into the gutter, where it smouldered red before turning grey and going out. Then she said, 'Adam's in his first year at Cambridge. He's still a bit of a fish out of water – too clever by half, and rather cocky with it, in that shy-yet-full-of-himself way boys often have when they think they might be geniuses but are afraid they're actually not. He's still feeling his way round things. Selina isn't really his type. He's more into blondes.'

Did Lydia mean what I thought she meant, that Adam only wanted to be with white girls? I was full of indignation at the possibility that, ultimately, you had been rejected by Adam because of our Jamaican heritage. 'Are you saying that Selina wasn't good enough for him?'

'Don't be silly, of course I'm not. I just meant that Adam's quite awkward around people. He thinks everyone should fall over themselves with eagerness to spend time with him and when they don't, he can't work out what to do. He would have been talking to Selina to cover that up. He would have found her easy to be with – unthreatening. Not like you.'

'What do you mean? Why do you think I'm threatening?'

I was still in my school uniform, but Lydia kept a light, black coat in a tote bag to conceal her school skirt and blazer whenever the need arose. She was putting it on now. Beside her, I looked like a child, even though I was taller.

'Why do you think I'm threatening?' I persisted.

Lydia hitched up her skirt and turned up the collar of her coat to make herself look even older. 'I don't think you're threatening. Of course I don't. Why would I think you're threatening?' she said, the repetition making this sound insincere. 'The point is, Adam would.'

I put this aside, aware that Lydia wasn't going to enlighten me further. In any case, there was something else I needed to ask. It had taken me all afternoon to build up to saying it, but finally the words came out. 'Why did we sleep together that night?'

Before Lydia could reply, you came up behind us. 'Sorry I'm late,' you said breathlessly, 'I smashed four eggs at the end of the cookery lesson. I had to clear it all up. Sister Mary Anthony went nuts.'

So it wasn't just me that Lydia had invited to the shops. She'd invited you as well. I should have realised.

I'd been furious since the party about the way you'd laughed at me with Adam, and bitterly disappointed that we hadn't seen in the New Year together. That night, I'd watched you both drinking vodka and devouring cubes of cheese and chunks of pineapple on sticks, feeling too miserable and angry to eat or drink anything myself. I was losing weight; our similarity to one another was waning, which gave me a spiteful kind of pleasure. Now, seeing you here, I felt angrier than ever; I'd been desperate to spend time alone with Lydia and that possibility had gone. I could have cried with frustration, but I wasn't going to show Lydia how much I minded. Instead, I looked at you warily and you returned the same gaze. We had been avoiding each other for weeks. At night, we each pretended to fall asleep as soon as we got into bed to ward off any possibility of conversation.

But then I glanced towards Lydia and I saw a fleeting smile – she was enjoying the tension between us. I didn't want to let go of the anger I felt towards you. I didn't want you to think you were forgiven, but I needed you and you needed me, and besides, I couldn't let Lydia win – she'd won far too much already. I forced my face to wear an expression of warmth – or if not warmth, neutrality – and I took your arm. You looked surprised, and then, understanding the gesture as I knew you would, you leaned into me, full of relief that we were almost back to normal.

The next bus arrived. We ran up to the top deck. Lydia passed round her cigarettes and we all lit up. I wanted to think, so I sat behind the two of you and let you chat together. I returned to the time Lydia had said I preferred girls to boys. I wished she could have said exactly how she knew this. It must have been something more than just 'a vibe' or she wouldn't have guessed. I still didn't know what this would mean for me. I wouldn't be normal, I supposed. I wanted to add, *So what?*, convince myself it didn't matter. I wanted to believe I would be fine standing outside of things while you – and Lydia too – had nice, tidy lives, doing what everyone expected of you: wives, mothers – good women. So would I be a bad woman, then, by that reckoning?

It wasn't fair. You and I were meant to be the same. We had the same genes. So why were you straight and not me? There would be a book about twins somewhere that studied deviations between identical pairs with regard to sexual preferences. I thought about the word deviation – deviant must have its root in this: I would be considered the deviant, the one who wasn't normal. Nature versus nurture, that would be the question, as if being an identical twin, and of dual heritage, didn't throw up enough deviation from the norm already. I remembered Cal talking once about being bullied at school: I'm targeted, he'd said, not realising how targeted I would be if anyone found out the way I was.

At home that night, I almost told you about me and Lydia, but we were speaking again – laughing together – and our New Year animosity had almost faded. I couldn't bring myself to risk another rift between us; I had missed you too much for that.

Sixteen

Selina

I am watching the news. Nothing seems to stay the same and all the changes are bewildering. A Cabinet reshuffle. A new Budget.

Adam Russell stands by the dispatch box, the youngest ever Cabinet minister. Isn't he related to Lydia? 'I am not and I have never been a racist. I have always been committed to stamping out racism in all its forms.'

Who is the prime minister?

I know the answer to this, but in case of forgetfulness, I wrote the initials on my wrist.

What is today's date?

It is April 20th 1968.

We are watching the news. Enoch Powell is standing at a table, talking to grey-haired men and a handful of women. He reminds me of a cartoon villain. In a minute, he will narrow his eyes even further and twirl his moustache. He reads from a sheet of paper: 'In fifteen or twenty years' time, the black man will have the whip hand over the white man.'

Cal sits up and puts aside the book he is reading. Zora and I look at one another. Our dad gets up to turn off the small television in the corner of the room. 'No, please, Dad,' says Zora, 'we have to see what he's got to say.' Dad nods and sits down again. Mum is frowning with anxiety. She is scared for all of us. The whip hand: I think of slaves. He is saying that one day white men will be slaves, even though 'Rule, Britannia!', sung every year at Last Night of the Proms, insists that this will never, ever, ever be the case.

'This man is dangerous,' says Dad, looking away from the screen. 'He's going to stir up all kinds of hatred.'

He's going to stir up all kinds of hatred, I think, as I stare at Nigel Farage. His face is enlarged by the fifty-inch TV that hangs on my living room wall. 'Since 2000, we have gone mad, we opened the doors to much of the world but in particular we opened up the doors to ten former communist countries, and as a result of our EU membership we have absolutely zero control over the numbers who come.'

Control. He wants control. I take a biscuit from the plate on the coffee table. I don't know why I bought Bourbons; I wanted custard creams. I almost forgot to pay. I was walking out of the supermarket with them in my hand. Luckily I remembered before I got to the door. I turned round and scanned them through the machine. No one would believe that a person of colour just forgot. Immigrants and their descendants are scroungers who take and give nothing back. Nigel Farage doesn't say it outright, but this is what he believes. There is zero control over the numbers who come. There are too many of us, that's what he is saying.

There are too many, Enoch Powell states, and I know he is talking about us – there are too many of *us*. White people no longer have a place in their own country. He says there is an old woman. She is very upset. She doesn't want to let her rooms to coloured people, but if the Race Relations Bill goes ahead, she won't have any choice. I pick up the pair of tights I've been trying hard not to darn and thread a needle. I wonder if the old woman has a room-to-let notice in the window of her front room like the ones we used to pass on our way to school with Dad. *No coloureds*, it will say. Zora looks at me. She thinks that starting to sew during something like this shows I'm not really paying attention. But I am listening. I just need something to distract me, to make this seem more bearable. The old woman doesn't want to see coloured people in her street. But we've turned up anyway, with our loud music and our fighting spirit, ready to beat up white people. We need to be stopped, sent back home before it is too late. The old white woman is afraid, Enoch Powell says to us.

Breaking point. We are at breaking point. They are flooding into our country. Nigel Farage points to the poster behind him. Lines and lines of migrants are crammed together, trying to get in.

*

Mum is afraid. I can tell that our dad is also afraid, our dad who is never afraid of anything.

I am afraid. I can see by the look on Zora's face that she is afraid too. Cal is scratching his book absent-mindedly with his fingertips, so I know he is afraid as well. We are at breaking point. We are not wanted here. Where will we go if we are sent back? We thought our home was here in London; it's all we've ever known. We've never been able to afford to visit Jamaica; we've never even been there. We won't know anyone. We won't have a place to call home.

All the hatred is taking us to breaking point. Vote Leave. Get them out. Send them back. Take back control or the old white woman won't have a place in her own country. If you want a nigger for a neighbour vote Labour. Breaking point. Broken Britain. Migration broke Britain but we can take back control. It's a victory for common sense. Leave means leave.

None of us are speaking, we are listening to Enoch Powell's speech. Dad takes off his glasses and wipes them slowly. He is still not looking at the TV screen. Soon, Enoch Powell says, there will be a war. Black people will be fighting white people. The River Tiber, or maybe the River Thames, will be running with blood.

Seventeen

Zora

We were sitting at the table, all of us together, you and me side by side as always; Sunday dinner was a family ritual that was only missed if Dad couldn't swap a Sunday shift on the bus.

You and I were full – we'd eaten too many roast potatoes – but we were still looking forward to Mum's homemade apple crumble. Then, as if he had to say it quickly or not say it at all, Cal blurted out, 'I've asked Lydia to marry me.'

You and I looked at one another. This was impossible; Lydia was the same age as us.

Mum was bringing the crumble to the table. She almost dropped it as she said, 'You've *what*?'

Cal's body stiffened but he repeated his statement in a firm voice and awaited the inevitable objections.

'How can you even think of getting married? You're only eighteen. You're about to go to university. Do you know how hard your father's worked so you could stay at school and study?'

Cal stared at his empty pudding bowl. 'I want to marry Lydia,' he said.

'Well, you can't,' answered Mum briskly. 'You're going to university. I've never cared for that girl. She's a bad influence. Look at the effect she's had on the twins. They would never have started smoking if it wasn't for her. And what about that New Year's Eve party they both sneaked off to?'

'It isn't fair to blame Lydia for whatever those two get up to,' said Cal. 'They've got minds of their own.'

'It wasn't anything to do with Lydia,' I chipped in. 'We needed to be more . . . more sophisticated. Everybody smokes nowadays. You can't tell us off. It's really hypocritical when you smoke all the time.'

'That's just what I'm talking about. Before Lydia came along, you would never have spoken to me like that.'

'We were children before Lydia came along. We're grown up now,' I persisted. 'Lydia doesn't influence us; we make our own decisions.'

Ignoring me, Mum turned to Cal and said, 'You're too young, you don't know what you want at your age. Lydia doesn't know what she wants either. Just give it time, please. Don't throw away your whole future out of impatience to be more adult than you are. Marry her, if you really must, but wait until after university.'

'We want to get married now, Mum. We don't want to wait.'

'How many handbags does Lydia Russell have? How many pairs of shoes? Do you really think she's going to want to settle for a bedsit somewhere and a few second-hand sticks of furniture?'

'We love each other. Nothing else matters.'

'If you love each other, she'll wait until after you've got your qualifications before expecting you to settle down.'

'We have to get married now.'

'Oh my God! Don't tell me you've got her pregnant,' said Dad, throwing down his unused spoon. It pinged against his empty bowl, making you and me jump.

Cal was silent. I was silent too as I thought about the implications of this for my own relationship with Lydia.

'How could you have been so stupid?' Dad picked up his spoon again and waved it angrily.

'Has Lydia said yes?' you asked, your tone suggesting that if she had, it would be a good thing, bringing her into the family and making us related.

'She hasn't decided yet,' Cal replied.

'What do you mean, she hasn't decided?' asked Mum, as if she couldn't conceive of anyone having the audacity to turn down her son.

'She could get rid of it,' I said, more in hope than anything else. A baby would seal Lydia's relationship with Cal for ever.

'Get rid of it? She's a Catholic. She'd never do something like that.' Mum had conveniently forgotten that Catholics didn't have sex before marriage either.

'Lydia isn't a Catholic. She doesn't even believe in God,' I replied.

'But she goes to St Mary's.'

'Her dad gave the nuns a donation to get Lydia in,' you said.

Mum looked sceptical, as if you'd made it up.

'You're not marrying anyone,' Dad said to Cal. 'You're going to university.' His face was full of tension; he had told everyone at the bus depot about his clever son who was going to university in the autumn. He'd been so proud, prouder than we'd ever seen him before. And now Cal was talking about getting married and ruining his future.

'I could still go to university. It doesn't mean I can't.'

'You really think a student grant will run to nappies and baby clothes?' said Dad.

'I'll get a part-time job. We'll manage somehow.'

Mum put a hand on Dad's arm. 'This changes things, Rudy. If Lydia's pregnant, Cal has to stand by her, of course he does. It's as much his responsibility as hers. He's doing the right thing.'

'I'm not having this. I don't care if she's pregnant or not. Cal is going to university and that's the end of it,' said Dad.

I took a sip of water. Turning to Cal, I said, 'Have you actually seen proof that she's pregnant? She could be making it up.'

He looked at me in disbelief. 'How can you say something like that? Lydia would never lie to me.'

He doesn't know Lydia at all, I thought.

Dad was still speaking. 'You're putting your whole future at risk. You'll end up in some dead-end job, moving boxes round a warehouse, or being ... or being a bus conductor.' Dad spat out those last two words. For a moment, I feared he would cry – our dad was so crushed that he was almost in tears.

'I'll only be working part-time. I'll get an evening job. The rest of the time I'll be at university. I've thought it all through, Dad. I wouldn't be telling you if I hadn't. Lydia and I are in love. It will be all right. You're going to be a granddad. That's something to celebrate.'

'*If* Lydia goes through with the pregnancy,' I said.

'Why wouldn't she go through with it?' you asked.

'Can you really imagine Lydia settling down with a baby? Has she definitely said she's keeping it?'

'She's still thinking about it,' Cal replied.

'You can't let her have an abortion. That would be wrong,' said Mum.

Dad flung back his chair so hard that it crashed to the floor. He fled from the room. Mum hurried after him. The apple crumble remained untouched on the table. You put a spoon in the jug of custard and pushed back the skin that was now resting on the top. We could hear our parents shouting at one another. Words like 'ruined' and 'sacrifice' echoed through the house. Cal's face was taut, as if he hadn't been expecting this. What had he been expecting? I thought.

'It's all going to work out,' you said, squeezing his hand. You and Cal were equally naïve.

'What did Lydia's father say?' I asked.

'She hasn't told him yet.'

The words, *But would you want your daughter to marry one?*, bandied about so often after Enoch Powell's speech, circled round my head.

I went to our bedroom and sat on the top bunk, leaving you with Cal. I needed to think. Lydia was pregnant. Cal intended to marry her. Our parents were still arguing, their raised voices impossible to shut out. And I was numb with confusion. A pregnancy was absolute proof that Lydia and my brother had an intimacy that was no longer open to me and never would be again, and she was the only person I could ever see myself being with. I felt the sting of humiliation once more. I doubted that Lydia had ever wanted me in any real sense. I'd been her little experiment, her way of proving to herself that no one, male or female, was immune to her charms.

One day it would probably please her to tell Cal what we'd done. She would be tired of him. She would want to hurt him. She would want him to know that she'd never really been his. She would want to set us against each other. I lay on the bed, my body still. I had to tell Cal before she did. At least then, he might not marry her, and something would be salvaged. Cal would go to university. He wouldn't break Dad's heart.

It grew dark. Our parents' angry voices were still audible, but they were quieter now. You came into the room. 'Are you all right?' you asked.

'Yes.'

I felt your hesitation, your awareness that I wasn't all right at all. 'It will work out with Cal and Lydia,' you said. 'They'll sort it somehow. Cal will find a way of going to university. Mum and Dad will calm down about the baby.'

'Yes,' I repeated, in the hope that this would shut you up.

'We're going to be aunties. That's pretty amazing.'

I didn't reply.

'What's the matter?'

'What do you think is the matter?'

'It will work out,' you said again.

'Where's Cal?' I asked.

'He's gone to his room.'

'I need to talk to him.'

'He's upset. I think he wants to be left alone.'

'You've spent most of the afternoon with him. It's my turn now.' I slid off my bunk and went to find him.

Cal was sitting on his bed when I entered his room. 'I don't want to talk about this anymore, Zora, I'm all talked out.' His eyes were ringed black and there was a frown on his face.

'I need to tell you something,' I said.

'Can't it wait? I'm really not in the mood for anymore talking.'

I sat beside him. 'No, it can't wait. I need to tell you something about Lydia, something important that you really need to know.'

He listened in silence as I told him about the night we'd spent together, the frown on his face deepening.

'She plays with people, Cal, you must have seen it. She doesn't care who she sleeps with or who she hurts. I had to tell you, to warn you.'

'Get out, Zora,' he said.

'You have to listen to me.'

'You're a liar.'

'I'm not lying. Why would I lie?'

'You would never do something like that with another girl, nor would Lydia.'

'Cal—'

'You're feeling left out because Lydia can't spend as much time with you as she used to. You're the same with Selina;

you always want her all to yourself. You're just jealous and you want to split me and Lydia up. Get out now.'

'You have to listen to me. Lydia told me about the pregnancy. She told me that she didn't want the baby, she's going to get rid of it. She doesn't love you, Cal, that's what she said.'

'I don't believe you.'

'It's true,' I said, but my voice was unsteady and I couldn't look at him.

Cal was trembling. 'All right then, I'm going to go and ask her. I'll prove what a liar you are.'

I followed Cal from the bedroom, anxious now as I watched him go into the hall and put on his jacket. What would he say to Lydia? What would happen once he told her what I'd said? She would deny it of course, and then she'd stop being friends with me. Cal would hate me too.

He yanked open the front door and dashed out of the house.

Eighteen

Zora

Someone was trying to break in. The sound of the front door being rammed reverberated, and each of the windows smashed one by one, leaving jagged shards of glass sticking up out of the floorboards. You tried to crawl to the other side of the room, but you began to bleed; rivers of blood sprang from your hands and knees.

You were shaking me awake. 'Something's happened,' you said, your face pale in the glow of the bedside lamp.

We could hear frantic knocking on the front door. Our mother's voice, tight with fear, was calling out repeatedly, 'Who is it?', and then came the sound of our father running down the stairs. We followed, reaching the hall just behind him. Our mother was peering down from the upstairs landing. Dad's friend, David, stood on the doorstep, breathless. 'You have to come,' he said, tugging on our father's sleeve. 'Your boy is hurt, he's in the alley.'

Our father ran. We followed, the soles of our bare feet slashed by the broken glass that was strewn along the pavement. You were wearing pyjamas that were too small for you – was I wearing the same? – but you didn't seem to notice you were only half-clothed. You didn't seem to notice the chill of the night or the trail of blood we were leaving.

We overtook our father and reached Cal first. He was lying on the ground, blood on his face, his eyes closed. Lydia was beside him, begging him to wake up; she was holding his hand but there was no movement, no sign that he was still alive. 'Cal!' you screamed, but your voice was drowned by the sirens that filled the night air.

PART THREE

Nineteen

Selina

We drift through the house in a daze, unable to take in the news. Sometimes I think I know how Cal must have felt in the moment before he died; his fear, his hurt, and I am so cold inside and nothing will ever make me warm again. God is cruel. God is callous. Not even Father John could disagree. I am invisible now, fading into the furniture, my face buried in the print of the big armchair.

I am invisible now. I am old. I am invisible except to the people who don't want to see me. 'Go back home,' a man shouts. I turn in surprise. I don't know when I last heard that phrase. Back in the eighties, I think. Brexit has altered everything. It's all right to tell us to our faces now that we're not wanted here. I am old. I am no longer visible, except to the people who don't want to see me.

I am invisible. I sit in the armchair, fading into the fabric. Cal used to sit here. Sometimes he would squeeze up to make room for me and we would share. Zora would get cross then.

She didn't like it when me and Cal shared instead of me and her. Everything is empty now. I can't look at Cal's room; its emptiness feels too strange. Our mother barely speaks. She is broken into tiny pieces. Dad cries but he pretends he is coping. He is fine, he says.

I say Cal's name over and over as if this will make him come alive. Or perhaps I want to burn him on my memory in case I forget what he looked like. Or the way he used to sound.

Cal. Cal. Cal. Cal. Cal.

I am forgetting things, getting confused. The familiar is becoming strange. So I go to the doctor. He asks me lots of questions and then he refers me to a clinic at the hospital. I don't want to go. I miss two appointments before I find the courage. Questions. Tests. And then the results: not the best news, the doctor says. I keep telling myself they must have made a mistake but the evidence continues to grow. The other day I left the kettle on the hob and it boiled dry. There's a hole in it now. I'll have to get a new one – when I can remember. I can't help smiling at the feeble joke. Yesterday, or the day before perhaps, I left my house keys in a vase full of flowers (*why on earth?*). I only found them when I went to change the water. So the evidence is there. I'm trying not to panic, trying to take it one day at a time like they say you should. Good days and bad days. I am forgetting things. I'm having trouble keeping up. But I am not forgetting Zora or Harriet. And never Cal.

I have to keep the memory of Cal alive so I say his name over and over. Zora shakes me, hard. I didn't know I was screaming. Zora is very angry. Zora is angry because she doesn't know how to be sad.

The police come. They pound on the door. We let them in. 'We have a warrant to search the house.'

They rifle through everything, all our things – nothing is private now. A policeman picks up one of my school notebooks. Its pages flap as he shakes it in the hope that something will fall out. They are searching for evidence. 'Evidence of what?' shouts Zora. She is angry, raging. Our brother is dead – punched to death by a stranger, Lydia said. We saw his broken body, the stuff of nightmares that will haunt us through our days and nights. We are the victims but we are being treated as if we've done something wrong. Perhaps they think we are the ones who killed Cal. Maybe they think it was us. They don't understand about loving people. They don't understand about us.

People don't understand when you have problems with your memory. They think you could remember things if you just tried hard enough. I do try hard, all the time. It's exhausting. The news is on. I focus very hard on the things the newscaster says so I will remember them.

It's everywhere, in the news. Cal dealt drugs, they say, he was killed in a gang war over drugs. But we know it isn't true. Cal hated drugs. He feared them. He knew that if he ever took them he wouldn't have a future. Zora's anger leaps from her to me and back again. She is angry, so angry that she doesn't know how to stop it bursting out. She lashes out and catches one of the policemen in the mouth. A policewoman holds her back. 'If it wasn't for your brother being dead, we would be arresting you now. That was the assault of a police officer,' she says. She turns to our mother. 'You need to keep your daughter under control,' she tells her, as if Zora is a four-year-old having a tantrum.

'Do try to remember your next hospital appointment,' the blonde woman says. She is speaking loudly to me, as if that will help my memory. She is speaking down to me as if I am four years old. I'd like to smack her but I know I must control myself.

The police think if Mum had kept Cal under control, he wouldn't have died. Mum doesn't speak. She can't stand up for us. She is too deep in shock. We saw Cal lying on the ground but our mother wasn't quick enough; she was held back as the police arrived at the scene. I am so glad our mother didn't see him like that, though she says she wishes that she had – she wishes she had held Cal in his final moments.

'I will do my best to remember the next appointment,' I say to the woman, like a child who is promising to be good.

Once Zora's promised to be good, the policewoman lets her go again. I hold her hand. Rage passes between us, zapping back and forth.

*

I try not to be angry but I can't help it. Beneath the surface, I feel rage – panic and rage. This illness is so big, so terrifying. I want to scream about it, rage about it all night long. Instead, I push the fear deep inside of me and tell people that I'm fine. But inside I am raging. *Why me?* I say to myself. *Why not me?* is the answer that springs back.

We feel rage. Rage and fear. We are desperate to clear Cal's name. How dare they accuse him? His life was ended before it had really begun and now they are saying he brought it on himself. A black boy, top of his year, all set to go to university – who is going to believe that? Another version has to be told, even though they can't find any evidence to support it.

'We'll sue them!' our father shouts when he reads the stories. He scours the streets. He gathers up the offending tabloids from Tube trains, buses and park benches. He deposits them in our living room. They form a leaning tower, like the one in Pisa.

A policeman comes round. He is very tall, not quite real, almost like a cartoon character. He sits in the big armchair, his feet planted between the piles of papers. Zora and I can't concentrate on what he is saying. We are too embarrassed by the state of the house. All the newspapers our dad has gathered are building up around us.

It's hard to concentrate. I can't focus anymore. In my mind, everything feels blurry all around the edges. I am starting to lose words. Words are slipping away from me. I am forgetting what they mean. When I write, I can't remember how to spell

the words I've always known. Easy words, not even long ones.
I have to concentrate so hard on everything.

It's hard to concentrate
A black man's been arrested, the tall policeman says
We tell ourselves to concentrate
We start to listen, slowly tuning in
We hold our breath until we almost burst
He killed Cal, the tall policeman says
A photo in the paper and on television
A man blank-faced, eyes extra wide, wild hair
Rivers of blood are running now
The black man murdered Cal
But still, white people are afraid
Wading through the rivers of blood
The black man is done with Cal
And now he is coming for them

Twenty

Zora

It was October before we were allowed to bury Cal. The details of his funeral have always been hazy; the memory was too painful to be stored. I remember it in fragments, but large parts of it aren't there, however hard I try to recall them. Perhaps, over the years, I made up things to close gaps in my recollection, but I can't be sure.

I do remember being cold. Someone had forgotten to pin back the porch door. It banged in the breeze, punctuating Father John's words, and sweeping debris into the space beneath the holy water font. As we entered the church, we trudged through heaps of confetti mixed with leaves from the horse chestnut tree that shaded the path. They resembled the stacks of useless things our father had started to collect, that were piled up in heaps all over the house.

You and I stood side by side, holding hands, as Father John's loud, flat voice portrayed the altar boy, pious and quiet, not the Cal we knew, but the Cal who had been on his best behaviour for Father John – an aspect of Cal, I suppose, but not really him. Perhaps no one could have described him as he'd been when he was alive. In the time since his death, we had each misremembered him, elevating him to the level of the angels with true Catholic sentiment that did Cal no favours. He'd committed all the usual childhood sins. He'd smoked, as we all did, hiding it from our parents. He'd nicked sweets from shops. He'd sneaked into the pictures via the back exit to watch films without paying. He'd stolen a car when he was fourteen because the local boys had called him stuck up and no longer one of them now he was at grammar school; he'd had to prove them wrong. Dad had been raging when one of the neighbours had told him. 'You're lucky you didn't get caught by the police. Do you know what happens when black boys get caught even bending the law, let alone breaking it? There's no leeway for us, you get a record and that's it, in and out of prison, the end of everything.' Cal had managed not to do anything wrong since then. Dad's fear and disappointment had been too much of a warning. I looked across at Dad as he sat at the end of the pew next to Mum. His last words to Cal had been spoken in anger, and regret was written in the blankness of his face. I thought of Lydia and wished, once more, that she and Cal had never met.

Lydia hadn't been in the church but she was at the grave-side. I didn't want to see her, and yet I did, both at the same time. I still didn't know if Cal had been attacked after he'd told her what I'd said or if it had happened before he'd had the chance. I hoped she didn't know; she certainly gave no sign of knowing. You grabbed hold of her and gave her a tearful hug. There was a tremor in her shoulders as she hugged you back. 'How are you?' you asked. And then before she could answer, you asked the question that was uppermost for you: 'How are you doing with the baby?'

'I'm starting to show now,' she said, though I couldn't see it; I thought she'd actually lost a little weight. She was wearing a dark blue cotton coat that flared out above the waist, tailored to hide indiscretions.

'You're still pregnant,' you said, squeezing her arm. 'I was scared that after ... that night ... and having to be on your own, you wouldn't be able to go through with it.'

Lydia looked at you with empty eyes. 'I'm sorry I haven't been round to see you. My father wouldn't allow me to come. He's been confining me indoors like a prisoner. I'm a disgrace to the family, getting knocked up by somebody like Cal.' She gave a hollow laugh, failing to see that although she'd used the words ironically, they were hurtful to us. Somebody like Cal? I couldn't bring myself to ask exactly what she meant; she was carrying Cal's child – a living piece of him – and I couldn't afford to alienate her. She took a pack of cigarettes from her handbag and lit one with a slightly shaky hand, inhaling deeply before saying, 'Dad said he'd never forgive me. Joyce was even worse. She was almost hysterical, said I'd burn in hell. How dare she? Adam told me his dad had said that she and Pa were shagging while Mum was still alive, fucking hypocrites. I thought they'd understand how terrible it was for me to be there that night, to see Cal attacked, to hold his hand as he slipped away from me, but all they can think about is themselves and how much I've embarrassed them.' She paused – waiting for sympathy perhaps?

You were ablaze with it. You raised your voice, attracting

the attention of some of the other mourners who turned to look at us. 'It must have been so terrible for you, being there with Cal when it happened. I expect your father is just in shock about the baby. He'll come round in the end.'

Lydia's eyes filled with tears. 'He won't come round. He's made that very clear. Cal and I were going to be married. How can I give up this baby when it's all that's left of Cal?'

'Of course you can't,' you said. As you squeezed Lydia's arm again, I saw that the people around us were staring. Cal's death was the source of endless gossip from the neighbours. Had he dealt drugs? Perhaps he'd pulled a knife that night, or a gun. Perhaps someone had killed him in self-defence. He looked the part of a bad boy, in spite of his stuck-up ways and his grammar school education. Did you know that Vivian Bunting had been quite well off before she'd married beneath her? I'm sure she regrets it now. The son turned out just like his father. They can't control themselves, they always wind up in trouble in the end.

Lydia held her hand to her belly and said, 'You know, I'm not at all sorry about this, however much everybody wants me to be.' Her eyes now sparkled with defiance. 'They're sending me away, can you believe that? I've been in such a state. I've lost Cal, but that doesn't matter to them. All they care about is hiding me away somewhere.'

I tried to absorb Lydia's words, feeling sick inside. 'You're going away?' I said.

'Pa says I can't stay here, there will be too much gossip.'

'Don't go, Lydia,' you said desperately, 'we don't want you to go.'

'It's no use. Pa won't budge. I'll have to come back for the trial so at least I'll see you then. I'm a witness, I expect you've heard.' Her voice dropped; there was a tremor in it. 'They arrested a man – well, a boy I suppose, no older than us. Did they tell you?'

You and I nodded.

'I don't know if I can face it, going over everything again.'

'You'll manage somehow, Lydia, I know you will,' you said, squeezing her hand. 'I'm so pleased you came today. Cal would have wanted you to be here so much.'

'What will you two do now?' asked Lydia.

'We're going to university,' I told her.

'I didn't think you wanted to go.'

'We have to go,' you said. 'Mum and Dad were so proud to think that Cal was going.'

We were desperate to return hope for the future to our parents, the hope that had died when Cal had been killed. For their sake, we had to succeed, we thought.

We could see our mother up ahead, struggling to speak to the friends who had gathered to support us. Across the road, a newspaper photographer was taking pictures. Mum was wearing a red, hand-knitted jumper under a pinafore dress. She'd said she wanted to be nice and bright in memory of Cal – he liked to see her looking cheerful, she told us – but her clothes were incongruous, wholly unsuitable for the occasion; they made her look childlike and in need of care. Her lipstick was smudged and there was a circle of deep red blusher on each cheek that made me think of clowns. We should have stopped her showing herself up like that but neither of us had the heart, or the energy, to coax her to get changed, and I'm not sure Dad even saw that anything was wrong. The following day, Cal's death would be headline news again, and pictures of the funeral would fill the front pages. Mum would look deranged. I wanted to warn her that we were being photographed, but I decided it would be kinder to keep her in ignorance. She would only worry about how she was behaving and whether anyone was seeing the cracks, and that would engender a self-consciousness that would make her seem more odd, not less. Dad was beside her. He had been almost silent since Cal's death, as if words had been sucked out of him. Words couldn't describe the way he felt, so he was losing his ability to use them, retreating to a place we couldn't reach. We were afraid for him, even as he stood beside our mother, shielding her with arms outstretched, his posture seeming awkward and uncomfortable.

We walked across the well-worn flagstones that covered the grounds of the church, shading our eyes from the sun that streamed down from above its tower but gave little warmth. You looked worn out from crying. Lydia too. I couldn't tell what I looked like anymore. It was as if I no longer saw myself, except in you.

'We're having a wake at the church hall,' you told Lydia. 'Will you come?'

She shook her head. 'I'm sorry, I can't face it.'

My breathing became shallow. I had to know if our brother had told Lydia what I'd said to him before he died. 'Why did Cal go to see you that night?' I asked, making my tone as casual as I could.

You looked curious. You wanted to know why he had gone out too.

'He wanted to ask me something,' Lydia answered slowly, as if she was trying to recall the exact details. 'He seemed a bit upset, or angry or ... I don't know ... but before he could say anything ... well, you know what happened.'

Did relief show on my face? Did it seem incongruous? I tried to conceal it, but it must have been visible, because Lydia gave me a questioning look. But all she said was, 'I'll write once the baby arrives. I'll send a photograph.' She turned and walked away, seeming a little unsteady in real snakeskin shoes.

We joined our father and tried to fill the gaps his silences created, even though we had few words ourselves. Our mother also barely spoke; she seemed so hurt and lost as she stood slightly apart from everyone, failing to look at them, failing to connect. People were offering platitudes because platitudes were all they had: *We are so very sorry; let us know if there's anything we can do.*

At the wake in the shabby church hall, our parents remained silent, only nodding slightly as other mourners continued to mutter their condolences. We took round sandwiches and little cheese biscuits on borrowed plates, with shy, forced smiles that shone through tears.

I think our mother was embarrassed by our school tunics (with white shirts and blue-and-green-striped ties), worn that day because we had no other sombre clothing. But she wasn't embarrassed by their West Indian friends who spoke Patois – the melodic sound rang through the hall. Joe's dad gripped our father's hand and wept. Joe stood beside him, the hem of his trousers quivering as his legs shook from all the emotion he was trying to conceal. And then there was David, who had brought the news that Cal was hurt, wearing his threadbare coat. His green eyes always looked incongruous against his dark brown skin and made strangers stare in surprise. He was slumped in a chair asleep, a plate piled high with food untouched on the table in front of him. Each Christmas and Easter holiday, our dad had welcomed him to celebrate with us: 'He has no one,' he used to say. 'No family. He has no real home.' Dad had got chatting to him as he'd travelled on his bus. They'd become friends; they'd played dominoes in the café down the street. 'He's had nothing but bad luck,' Dad often said. 'Life can be so hard for people when they come to this country.' David had wept at Cal's graveside.

Perhaps if we'd been older, we would have been touched to see so many people sharing their grief at the death of our brother, but we were overwhelmed, as if we were obliged to shoulder their sadness as well as our own.

We had abandoned our serving task so people were helping themselves to tinned salmon sandwiches with slices of cucumber, Scotch eggs, crisps and pieces of the cake that Mum had made. It was very plain, as if an embellishment in the form of icing or buttercream would detract from the solemnity of the occasion and sully Cal's memory. We each ate a slice with disappointment. Mum's cakes were usually so delicious, rich and light, but this could have been made by anyone. It was dry and heavy. 'Like Mum's heart,' you whispered to me, with your usual sense of the dramatic, but perhaps it wasn't as silly as it sounded. Dad had insisted that no one would be allowed to go home hungry so he had spent as much as he could to give Cal a good send-off. We tried to celebrate his short life with rum and Coke. We knew our parents wouldn't notice the rum part, not today, but there was no pleasure in it. We listened to other people's conversations, wishing we could leave and be only with each other, chewing gum and reading a book, even though the idea of doing anything so ordinary was almost unimaginable. I think we wanted to see if we could still do day-to-day things or if life had really changed beyond our comprehension. We longed to put aside sadness if only for a few minutes but we could see the impossibility of that.

Once the guests had gone, we cleared the tables silently. You tipped leftovers into bins; I pushed back tables and swept the floor. Dad had stood straight and tall for as long as he could, but now that he could no longer be seen by friends and acquaintances, he allowed himself to stoop, bent by the weight of grief, wiping surfaces he had already wiped. His staccato movements contrasted with our mother's slowness, but each response stemmed from the same bleak place. Father John came in to lock up and we began the walk home.

'I feel so alone,' you said to me, your eyes pleading, filling with tears.

I turned away from you.

Once inside the house, I fled to Cal's room and closed the door. At the funeral I'd wanted to be with you but now I was beside myself with the need to be alone.

I looked at Cal's possessions; there were model airplanes and Dinky cars from childhood, and the records and books he'd collected once he was on the verge of becoming a man. I sat on his bed, recalling the last evening of his life and the things I'd said to him. For the first time I allowed myself the awareness that if I had kept quiet, he would have stayed indoors. He wouldn't have been out on the street, he wouldn't have been punched, he wouldn't have lost his life. Why had I told him about me and Lydia? Perhaps I'd thought that killing his happiness would ease my hurt, with the bonus that it would punish Lydia for choosing him instead of me. I'd been telling myself that I'd wanted to spare him misery further down the line, when, after a few months or years of marriage, he would have to face what Lydia was really like. But Cal had been right. 'You're just jealous,' he'd said before he left.

I still hadn't told you about me and Lydia or what I'd said to Cal. I'd tried, but the words had failed to come. Instead, I was now withdrawing from you; shame and guilt were making it impossible for me to be around the people I loved most. You didn't ask what the matter was – you thought you knew; you thought it was grief, and that my feelings were the same as yours. I wished that was all it was, but I had caused Cal's death, and the hopelessness I felt would never really leave me.

You and I had thought that Cal would always be with us, so we didn't imprint his face or his words on our memories while he was alive in order to return to these at some point in the future when we would struggle to remember how he sounded or the way he looked.

SELINA

Dead. I can't take it in. *Dead.* I say the word over and over to make it real, even though the word stabs me so hard it makes me flinch every time I hear it. I am alone, so very alone. We stand at the graveside. Dead. People offer their condolences. I am wearing a pinafore dress and a red, hand-knitted jumper. Should I have worn black? Is wearing red wrong? A wake. We are at a wake. Am I awake? Is this a dream? It isn't real, it can't be real, yet I know it is. A punch? An unlucky punch? Dead? It was a car – a car – of course it was. Collision course. An accident, they said.

Dead.

I am cold. I am shaking with cold. I will never be warm again.

Twenty-one

Selina

I still miss my brother. I worry that this illness will wipe him from my memory altogether. This thought is more terrifying than all the other frightening things that have been happening to me of late. I've been lost – physically – in a shopping centre and a street, no longer sure how to find my way home again. This doesn't seem as bad as being lost in thought and feeling, unable to remember the people closest to my heart. Zora and I promised each other we would never forget Cal. I try to picture him. Most of the time, I no longer see his face. I get a photograph of him out of the album. He's sitting in the garden with a can of Coke in his hand. He's smiling up at me, his eyes crinkling at the corners. For as long as this is in front of me, I do see Cal. But as soon as I look away again, he is gone. Cal resembled our dad, I do remember that. Cal and Dad were so alike.

Without Cal, our father is lost, ghostly. Zora and I miss our brother, but perhaps we miss our father just as much. He fills his emptiness with things, his way of grieving. At first, the gathering of things makes sense. They are mementos, in a way – things that keep Cal close. It had started with newspapers – he'd collected every word that was written about Cal. And once these had filled our living room, they had been joined by other objects. Bald tennis balls, because Cal had enjoyed watching Wimbledon on television. Empty packets of Potato Puffs, because they were his favourite snack. Old drink bottles and cans, because once we had toasted Cal's eleven plus results with Coca-Cola. Broken Bic biros, the kind Cal had used to do his homework. But now there is a disconnect between object and memory. No sense at all attached to the useless, cracked things Dad brings into the house. He gathers them around himself at random. Dented metal buckets without handles. Conkers. Fragmented flowerpots with clods of earth lodged in the clay. He will mend them, he says, it will give him purpose. They remain broken, the pieces scattered on the floor. No one is allowed to move them. At first, I think collecting is a phase – not butterflies or stamps, but still, lots of people are obsessive about pointless things. But our father doesn't go to work anymore. He needs all his time for scavenging.

I am collecting things that trigger memories, scavenged from jumble sales and markets. There is an alarm clock. It has a hen that bends to peck a chick with every tick. Cal used to have one in his bedroom. It's in my bedroom now, on the bedside cabinet. I've found an old, green, leather purse, like the one Zora used to have. It even has the same purple lining. I've got a second-hand shaving brush. It's just the same as the one Dad kept in the bathroom cabinet. Its bristles are slightly bent in the exact same places. I got an antique ... thing with a pin that is almost identical to the one Mum used to wear on her best brown coat. I've put it on my purple jacket, the one I wear whenever I want to look nice.

Since Cal's death, Mum has given up on her appearance. She doesn't get her hair done anymore. She has ladders in her tights that she doesn't mend. She works even harder than she did when Cal was alive; she has no time for looking nice. Dad needs time away from work to think of Cal. Mum needs to be at work all the time in order not to think of him. When she finishes at the flower shop, she goes to clean an office block. Zora and I know she wants to stay out of the house. It's no longer a comfortable place. Not just because Cal isn't here – the useless things form an obstacle course that has to be negotiated. The furniture is buried beneath rubbish so there is nowhere to sit. Even the television screen is obscured by torn sheets of cardboard. When I ask Mum to tell Dad to stop all the collecting, she is furious. It makes me scared, not of Mum, but of the way everything keeps changing. Sometimes before Cal died, she would get a bit cross about things. Now she is angry almost all the time, like Zora. She screams the words, 'Don't you dare tell me to make Rudy stop! Just let him be. It's his way of coping!'

And your way of coping is to pretend everything is normal, I whisper to myself.

My way of coping with this diagnosis is to distract myself. Going to the photography group helps. We bring old photos of ourselves and our families. Harriet insists on taking me. She keeps saying, 'I know you don't want to be here but I think it will help.' I don't see how it will help at all, but I'm glad that Harriet's beside me. I need her to see the photographs; she will be the keeper of family memories once I am gone.

I open my photo album and say, 'My father came to Britain during the war – or maybe just after? He was in the merchant navy. He married my mother in . . . 1940-something. She was white and her parents objected to the marriage.' I take a picture from the oldest of the albums. It has photos from before Zora and I were born. 'This is Mum on her wedding day.'

A large woman with an orange hat peers at it. She taps it. 'She can't be getting married. She isn't wearing a wedding dress.'

'It was just after the war,' I say to her. 'There was rationing. You couldn't get many clothes then. She didn't have a wedding dress; she wore her prettiest summer frock instead. Her parents didn't come to the wedding. They were angry that she was marrying my father.' I am saying this for Harriet. She needs to know how it was.

I don't ask my mother how it was for her when her parents disowned her until after my A levels. Mum and I are sitting at the kitchen table. Zora is in the bedroom, wanting to be alone, and Dad is scavenging. It's just the two of us.

'I missed my mother,' Viv says, her cigarette poised above a green glass ashtray. 'I missed my father less, if I'm honest. He was a distant man. It's how men were in those days. He expected obedience from me even though I'd left home by the time I met Rudy. My father made me choose. He used some terrible words. He said, "If you continue to go out with that wog, you're no daughter of mine." And there were other words too, even worse words than that. How could he have said them? I still don't understand.' Viv looks away from me, embarrassed to think that such words could have been used by a member of our family – embarrassed to be repeating them. 'So, of course, I chose Rudy. What else could I have done? We were in love.'

Ash falls from the tip of Viv's cigarette, just missing the ashtray, but she doesn't seem to notice, she is too deep in the memory of past hurt. 'They were prepared to lose me, their only child, for the sake of the ridiculous belief that white people were better than black people. I thought, when I had Cal, that my mother would put aside her prejudices and be desperate to see her first grandchild, but she always did whatever my father said, and he forbade it. She was weak like that. Or perhaps that was just how it was for women back then. You did what you were told.'

'You didn't.'

'No, I didn't. I couldn't, even if I'd wanted to. Rudy was too important. Not giving in to their prejudices was too important. Rudy had been part of the war effort. He'd risked his life to help Britain and all he got when he came over here was insults and humiliation.' Viv's eyes flash with indignation. 'We wanted something better for you and Zora and ...' she breaks off. Our mum and dad had wanted something better for Cal too.

*

'It must have been hard for Gran to lose her family,' says Harriet.

'It's how it was back then.'

We were spat on in the street sometimes, Zora, me and Cal. We were only children, but grown men still spat. Their way of telling us we weren't wanted here, that we weren't British. I'd forgotten that. Some things are best forgotten.

'This is a picture of my brother Cal – Harriet's father,' I tell the group, pointing to Harriet in case anyone has forgotten who she is.

'I thought she was your daughter,' somebody says.

'She is,' I reply.

Cal is sitting in the garden in the photograph. He has a transistor radio in his hand.

'Cal liked listening to jazz. He liked reggae too. Whenever I hear that song ... "Israelites"—'

A bald man in a darned jumper and baggy tracksuit bottoms interrupts me. 'Desmond Dekker,' he says. 'I remember that song. It got to number one.'

'Whenever I hear "Israelites", I think of Cal. He died before it even came out. But I remember thinking, the first time I heard it, *Cal would have loved this.* So it became my favourite song. I used to play it all the time. I had a record player. I bought a little one with my grant when I was a student. Cal would have loved that song. Whenever I hear it I think of him. When he was killed, the police assumed Cal must have been dealing drugs, but it wasn't true, he never did anything wrong.'

'The police?' says a woman who is sucking boiled sweets.

'The police brought me back home. They told my husband I was lost.'

The police search our house. They don't care about the mess they make. They think Cal was a criminal. The newspapers also think the worst of him. In their headlines, Cal is treated like a gangster.

Zora and I walk across newspapers, feeling the broken clay crunch beneath our feet. Then empty tin cans join the expanding piles of rubbish. I try to wash these, fearing flies or other even more troublesome pests. But displacing them causes such anguish in Dad that I have to stop. Now a dinging sound is added to the rustle and the crunch as we wander through the house. Zora's eyes meet mine as we cross the room carefully. We vow, silently, to clear up the mess. But not just yet; when our father is stronger, more able to cope.

At first, Zora and I find comfort in one another the way we always have. But by the time Christmas comes, she is as far away from me as she can be. Each night in her sleep, she sees Cal die. She can't bear it. She can no longer bear to be with me, as if, together, we generate too much sadness. And so she distances herself from me, always making sure we sit away from one another, always walking to school alone. So I have to bear the loss of her as well, as she fades out of our doubleness, shrinking into a single, broken person.

One afternoon, she begins moving her things out of our room. She is moving into Cal's room, she says. She can't. The room belongs to Cal. I tell Dad, but he doesn't even register what I am saying. I tell Mum. I thought she would mind that Zora is taking Cal's room, moving his things to the cellar, but she just nods. She doesn't care. Perhaps she thinks it will be easier if all Cal's things are gone and she doesn't have to see them all the time.

Zora is angry with me for trying to stop her moving out of our room. 'We're not conjoined anymore,' she says as she puts clean sheets on Cal's bed. 'I have the right to be on my own. Don't you get it? We're separate people. They separated us in the hospital.'

She takes down Cal's old Airfix models, suspended from the ceiling, and puts them into boxes. She packs away his t-shirts and underwear and puts hers in the chest of drawers instead. Under the bed, she finds bottle tops and empty cereal packets. Dad's been using Cal's room for the storage of useless things. And the living room. And the bedroom our parents share. And the kitchen. He sheds silent tears as Zora puts the bottle tops in the bin.

In spring, the flies come, hovering over dirty milk bottles and old tin cans. At night, while our father sleeps, I add drops of disinfectant to each tin and bottle. I wash them clean, putting them back where I found them. I want to avoid an escalation of our father's anxiety the next morning. I cut paper bags into strips and heat honey, sugar and water in a pan. Then I coat the strips in the syrup and hang them over the stove to dry. Before dawn, I attach string to each, festooning them round the room like celebratory bunting. The flies gradually disappear.

'We should get Dad to a doctor,' Zora and I tell Mum.

She says there is nothing wrong with him. 'He needs to be left alone. He needs time and space to grieve. We all do.'

Her words are echoed by our father: 'There's nothing wrong with me,' he says.

Do they really believe this? They must be able to see how bad things are getting. But our parents can't see anything. They can't cope with the loss of Cal. I'm afraid the landlord will come round and see the state of the place, and then the rent will go up or we'll be turfed out onto the street. Every Friday night, while Mum is still at work, Zora and I keep the rent man at the door. I fetch his money. Zora stands in his line of sight, trying to keep the state of the house from view.

'This is a photo of my dad,' I say to the photography group. I must have taken it before Cal died, before Dad was almost buried under piles of useless things. He looks happy in this picture; he is smiling.

Harriet drives me home. I hold the photo album tight, wanting to keep it safe. There wasn't much money to spare when I was young. I took a lot of pictures but we often couldn't afford to have them developed. I must have been in my thirties before I learnt to develop them myself. I remember taking rolls and rolls of film down to the cellar, where I'd set up a dark room. I felt so proud when the images started to appear.

'We're home,' says Harriet. As I search for my keys, I wonder if I've ever taken pictures of this house. I must have done. I stand by the gate, trying to remember. I look at the garden, and with rising panic, I see it's not my garden after all. But the front door is the same. And the curtains at the windows. I don't understand. 'This isn't my garden,' I say to Harriet.

'What do you mean?' she asks.

'I always keep my garden tidy. And there's a bench. I don't have a bench in the front garden, only in the back. There are blue flowers in the flower beds too. I don't like blue; I wouldn't have put them there.'

'We moved the bench, remember? You wanted to sit in the sun in the mornings. We'll dig up the blue flowers and tidy up the beds together when I come over at the weekend. We'll plant things.'

I like planting things. When is the best time for planting? Is this the right time of year? There are some empty flowerpots by the front door. I got them from a skip. They reminded me of planting things with my dad. They are cracked but they are still usable. I'll plant some bulbs. The pots look very worn but I just can't seem to throw them out.

Dad won't throw anything out and the rubbish continues to grow. Next come bricks. We could use them to defend ourselves, Dad says, if ever there are any attacks. He is remembering the rivers of blood. He is thinking of the National Front. Pieces of piping with the same purpose follow. Glass bottles come after that, multi-purpose items. And the piles of things are reaching a perilous height. Moving back and forth across the room becomes even more precarious.

The street is littered with old beer cans and empty bottles of cider. There are crisp packets and a glove. By my feet there is an old newspaper. It's been raining so it's wet. I pick it all up, even though I don't know what to do with it. They'll put me in a home, or a hospital, like Dad.

Our living room is buried under heavy, leaning piles of newspapers. One day, a rat runs out from underneath the papers and the cans. I can't bear it anymore. I begin to scream but almost as soon as I start, I make myself stop. I am shaking, hardly daring to breathe now in case the sound summons more rats. I call the doctor, even though Zora says I mustn't. They take our father away from us in an ambulance.

Mum is beside herself with anger, and fear. She doesn't know what she will do without Dad. 'You had him put in a hospital? How could you do that?' She launches herself at me. I move to avoid a blow but she pulls back before she can make contact. Her hands cover her face. 'I'm sorry,' she says to me, though she has nothing to be sorry for. I'm the one who should be sorry. What have I done? I didn't mean it to happen; I didn't know what the doctor would do. I thought I was making things better, but now Mum hates me and our father is shut away. In bed at night I am rigid with fear. Late at night, when she thinks I am asleep, I hear Zora crying through the wall.

We visit Dad in hospital, walking slowly to the ward. We are dragging out the minutes before we have to face him. One of the corridors is said to be a whole mile long. Dad sits listlessly in a vinyl-covered chair. I tell him I'm sorry but, drugged to a stupor, he is unable to hear.

'He is depressed,' the psychiatrist says, as if this is news to us. 'Is your mother coming to visit? He keeps asking after her.'

'I expect she will come,' Zora replies. 'She's just extremely busy at work and she can't take time off in visiting hours or she might get the sack. She had to have a lot of time off work when our brother died.' This is only half-true. Zora knows as well as I do that Mum will never visit Dad while he's in here. She couldn't bear to see him confined in a hospital.

'I see,' the psychiatrist says, only he doesn't see. Mum needs help just as much as Dad but she keeps pretending nothing bad is happening, nothing bad at all.

'When can he come home?' we ask in chorus.

'He needs a long rest,' comes the evasive reply.

Zora and I decide we have to clean the house from top to bottom, getting rid of all the useless things. Mum gives us money to pay the dustmen to take the extra rubbish but she can't even look at us. Zora is withdrawing from me even more as well. She wishes that I hadn't called the doctor who sent our dad away.

I wonder what will happen when our dad returns and sees the emptiness of the house. There will be moans of desperation that no amount of medication can hold back.

I feel such emptiness when I am given the diagnosis. I have to fill my time to make it bearable, keep my fears at a distance. One day at a time. I will plant ... pretty flowers in the cracked flowerpots I found in a skip yesterday – or was it the day before? I used to plant things in my garden during the school holidays when I wasn't teaching.

*

Zora is determined that we will both stay at school in spite of everything. We must get good A levels. Go to university. We have to do it so Mum and Dad can celebrate something. Be proud of something. Not just full of loss. We are choking in the thick air of their grief. We sit side by side at the kitchen table, making plans. We are going to Manchester. We will share a room in halls. Or, Zora says (and I think she would prefer this), we will have separate rooms next door to each other. We're going to do English. We haven't decided any- thing else about our future yet. We don't know what we'll do once we've got our degrees. We'd like to work in television, but that isn't realistic. Brown-skinned girls don't work in the media. They aren't on television or in books. But we'll get good degrees and find something we like doing and we'll be outstanding at it, Zora is certain of this.

If Cal had lived, would he have got a law degree the way he'd planned? Or would he and Lydia have slipped into domestic bliss bringing up a baby in a bedsit or a little council house?

A fly buzzes round the living room wall. I thought all the flies had gone. We cleaned everything, made it spotless. We cleaned and cleaned. We got rid of lots of the useless things. But the flies are still here. Perhaps they will never go away.

There is a buzzing insect in my bedroom. I can't sleep for it buzzing about and batting the walls. It darts everywhere. I get up and try to swat it but I'm not quick enough. It keeps evading me. It reminds me of something that I can't quite reach, something bad. I don't know what it is. I try to think, but everything is fuzzy. As if I am seeing the world through a muslin curtain. The buzzing thing with wings buzzes and buzzes, and then, at last, it disappears.

Twenty-two

Zora

Cal's daughter was born on a Sunday: Harriet Cally Russell. We were touched by the middle name Lydia had chosen. How proud Cal would have been. Lydia sent a photograph, taken by the Robinsons, the couple she was lodging with. Harriet was small and sweet with tiny hands and feet. Her cheeks were puffed, as if she was about to whistle a tune. You cried tears of hope. You were full of the belief that Cal would live on in Harriet.

Mum looked at the picture. 'I don't trust that girl,' she said. 'She's flighty. I wouldn't put it past her to disappear somewhere with this baby and then we'd never, ever see our grandchild.'

'Lydia wouldn't do that,' I replied, though I knew Mum was right.

At the hospital we showed the picture to Dad. He turned his face away, as if he too couldn't bear the possibility of an attachment that was likely to be followed by loss.

We posted a black doll for Harriet – we believed that somehow this would give her a sense of us. Lydia sent a thank-you card but there was no invitation to visit. 'We'll go to Brighton to see mother and baby very soon,' you said, but when we phoned to find out when we could go, Lydia told us the Robinsons wouldn't allow it. 'They don't like people coming to the house, they're funny like that. When she's older and the weather's warmer and it's not such a hassle to travel, I'll bring her to London to see you.' You cried again, this time with disappointment.

In May, Lydia wrote a few lines, asking me to visit. *Don't tell Selina* was scribbled at the bottom of the page.

I should have been revising but I left the house to catch a train before you were awake, leaving a note to say I was studying in the reference library, my usual subterfuge.

Lydia was waiting by the ticket barrier at Brighton station. As I saw her, I felt yearning, tinged with sadness. A man stood on one side of her, bearded and tanned, with a blue checked shirt over faded jeans. On the other side, there was a woman with long white hair, similarly dressed. Lydia was failing to conceal boredom behind a fixed smile.

I could see a dark green pram. As I approached, straining to catch sight of the baby, but at the same time trying not to seem too curious, Lydia greeted me so effusively that I was overwhelmed. I returned her hug with a stiff, mistimed embrace that emphasised the awkwardness of the meeting. I pulled away from her and moved towards the pram, which was standing neglected in the corner.

Lydia joined me, moving the blanket that concealed the baby's face. 'Oh yes,' she said casually, 'you haven't met Harriet, have you?'

Harriet had bright, dark eyes and a skin that was almost white. Her nose was small but slightly broad, one of the few signs of her Caribbean heritage. But she was certainly Cal's daughter; her relationship to our brother, her belonging to our family, was etched in the smile upon her face.

I scooped her from the pram and held her close, overwhelmed by a feeling of protectiveness.

The concourse was becoming increasingly noisy, the chatter of disembarking passengers punctuated by tannoy announcements of departures, delays and cancellations. I returned Harriet to the pram and we moved out of the station. There wasn't a car – the Robinsons walked wherever they could, Lydia told me, with irritation. In kitten-heeled shoes, she looked cross as she trundled the pram over uneven paving stones. The Robinsons strode on while Lydia and I lingered behind, trying to talk to one another without being overheard.

'What are the Robinsons like about the baby?' I asked.

'Awful,' said Lydia, 'but I have to keep in with them because they babysit sometimes and I need to get out. They're so po-faced, not a vestige of humour between them.'

'Are they okay with me being here?'

'Why wouldn't they be?'

'Just after she was born, you said they didn't like visitors.'

'Oh that. They're fine with people coming round. I just needed a way of making some space for myself while I adjusted to everything.'

I was angry; I was being caught up in Lydia's games again, treated as if I didn't matter. She caught the look on my face and said, 'I'm sorry. You do understand, don't you? It's not easy, being an unwed mother. The whole thing made me quite ill. I couldn't cope with anything. But I'm so pleased you're here now, I really am.'

I was mollified by these words, as Lydia knew I would be. 'And you're okay again?' I asked.

'Fine now, apart from being bloody bored to death. Pa's given me a decent allowance so at least I'm not poor. And Harriet isn't as much trouble as I expected. She's practically the perfect infant – she even sleeps through most of the night.'

'She's so beautiful.'

Lydia gave the pram a little shake. 'She's gorgeous, aren't you?' Harriet beamed at us.

'Hadn't we better catch them up?' The Robinsons were forging ahead, and the gap between us was widening all the time.

'I suppose so,' said Lydia. 'By the way, I said we'd have lunch with them. I thought it would save me cooking and we'd have more time for a chat. Did I tell you they're vegetarians?'

'Yes, you did.'

'Cranky as anything, this fad, that fad – they're driving me crazy. They adore Harriet. They have this theory that one day we'll all be coffee-coloured and see me as a pioneer in race relations. It hardly matters what colour she is, she's here and that's that, but I could do without being seen as a walking statement on the wrongs of the colour bar.'

The thoughtlessness of Lydia's assertion that Harriet's colour was unimportant set off anger in me again. I remembered all the things that were said about Cal when he died – if a white boy had been killed, it would have been so different. But I said nothing as we moved through a Georgian square flanked by tall, terraced houses.

The Robinsons were letting themselves into the largest of these, on the corner.

We reached the house and eased the pram up the stone steps. 'Shall I lift Harriet out?' I asked as I stood in the hall by a large aspidistra.

'Yes, do. I'll go and check what time Hils is serving lunch.'

I hugged Harriet tight until Lydia returned and said, 'We've got another hour. Come up and see the flat. Don't hold the baby too close – she probably needs changing.'

I followed Lydia upstairs. Her door was fitted with a Yale lock and it was open by the time I reached it. I carried Harriet into a sitting room with doors leading off on either side. It was furnished with a sofa in a purple and green print with matching cushions and curtains. The walls were newly papered in cream; the shade matched the deep-pile fitted carpet. I almost bumped into a glass-topped coffee table; it looked fragile and expensive. It was hard to envisage a baby playing here.

'How have you managed to afford all this?' I asked.

'Like I said, Pa's been generous. It's a bribe, of course. He'll keep being generous as long as I stay out of his way.'

'You called the baby Harriet. Isn't Harry your father's name?'

'I thought it might bring him round.'

'But it hasn't?'

'According to him and Joyce, I'm an absolute Jezebel.' She looked sad for a moment but she shook the mood off, almost physically, with a lifting of her shoulders, and said, 'Come and see Harriet's room.'

It was a proper nursery, full of toys and bright streaks of colour. It had the same orderliness as the rest of the flat, making it seem the way a baby's room looks before the child arrives, rather than one that was actually inhabited.

'It's nice and bright. Where's your bedroom?'

'I sleep in the sitting room – the sofa converts into a bed. There isn't a lot of space and it was either that or sleep with Harriet.' Lydia wrinkled her nose. 'She reeks, doesn't she? You'd better let me take her; I really should get her changed.'

As I passed Harriet to Lydia, I said, 'Selina would have loved to have seen her. Why didn't you ask her? And why didn't you want me to tell Selina I was coming?' I was thinking of the effort it had been to keep my day trip hidden from you. It would be hard not to share all my news of Harriet when I got home again.

'No offence to Selina, but I couldn't face all the tears and sentiment she would have created. You're much easier to deal with in that respect.'

The words, which Lydia knew to be untrue, were deliberately dismissive. By insulting you, she could flatter me – it was another of her strategies for dividing us. Yet even though I knew this, I was pleased; I still wanted to be the chosen one.

As Lydia changed Harriet's nappy, with her usual brisk efficiency, she said, 'You won't tell Selina you've been here, will you? She'll probably come charging down on the train, wanting to know why I didn't ask her as well, and I don't think I can face that yet.'

'I won't say anything,' I replied, though I was intending to keep it from you on my own account, not Lydia's. I knew how disappointed you would be if you found out I'd seen Harriet without you. 'There's something I've been meaning to ask you.'

'Go on,' said Lydia.

'Why haven't you told Selina about the night we spent together?'

'Why would I tell her about that? It was between you and me. Besides, I can just hear her saying I'd led you astray even though it was the other way round. She'd never forgive me.'

'What do you mean, it was the other way round? Is that really how you see it?'

Lydia just laughed, lowering Harriet into a cot, and it was obvious that she wasn't going to elaborate.

I hid my hurt at this version of events behind a weak smile, too proud to allow Lydia to see it. There was silence for a while. Then I said, 'Selina is still in quite a bad way over Cal. Our dad too. He's in hospital.'

'Your dad? Why is he in hospital?'

'He's had a sort of nervous breakdown. He's depressed.'

'Well, he would be, wouldn't he?' said Lydia, holding up her hands in exasperation.

We smiled at one another, then laughed, the tension between us fading. I realised that Dad's depression was being treated as an illness when it was entirely appropriate. If he hadn't been depressed there would have been something wrong with him. Mum had seen this, which was why she had been so opposed to us clearing up the clutter, and Lydia's speedy grasp of the situation was refreshing. There was no tiptoeing round things with her. I remembered why I cared for her so much.

She stood up. 'Come on then, it's time to see what's on the menu at Chez Robinson. We can leave Harriet here. I'll prop the door open; we'll hear her if she cries.'

The meal turned out to be some kind of bean stew. It was too peppery but it was still edible. The Robinsons were irritating, though – they didn't believe in light conversation, only ponderous statements on everything from Indian politics to Russian literature. I was glad when we'd waded through some kind of fruit junket and could escape.

Lydia put on a slightly sturdier pair of shoes and suggested we went out. She normally hated walking and it would be even less inviting with a pram, but she really seemed to want to; she said she liked to get away sometimes and see for herself that there was still a world out there and that life didn't only consist of sterilising bottles and changing nappies. So I said my goodbyes to the Robinsons and we went for a walk along the seafront.

The sun was still out but it was a breezy day; the wind whipped up the waves that crashed upon the beach, tossing pebbles wildly back and forth. Sun worshippers were lined along the seafront in stripy deckchairs turned towards the sea, pale and goose-pimpled in bikinis.

We walked down a ramp, passing stalls selling Kiss Me Quick hats and vivid pink sticks of peppermint rock as the vinegary smell of fish and chips mingled with the salt smell of the sea. I remembered it all from family day trips – you, me and Cal building sandcastles and splashing through the waves – and I was lost in sadness.

'Stop dreaming, Zora, and help me with this.'

Lydia and I eased the pram along the beach. Shells and stones crunched underfoot as we walked towards the shoreline where the mud was full of frothy, swirling pools. I tossed my sandals into the bottom of the pram and tucked the hem of my skirt inside the elastic of my knicker legs. I waded into the sea, feeling the coldness of the water and the tingling slap of the waves that rushed towards me. Exhilarated, I ran, while Lydia looked on amused, her back against a breakwater.

I returned exhausted and cold, my legs and the edges of my skirt dripping wet. Lydia handed me the spare blanket from the pram and I used it to rub myself dry.

'I fancy an ice cream,' said Lydia. 'Do you want one?'

I was still full from the bean stew but I nodded. The ordinariness of licking an ice cream was suddenly desirable. I went to fetch two double ices, strawberry and vanilla, and brought them back to the breakwater. Beside us, Harriet spat squeaky little sounds that made me laugh.

'She's always doing that,' said Lydia. 'She's a strange little thing.'

I swallowed the last mouthful of ice cream and scooped Harriet from the pram, placing her on my lap. It felt good to be hugging her. She was so warm and soft. 'It must be nice, living so close to the sea,' I said as I looked out across the water.

'It's not so bad now, but in winter this place is so deadly

quiet and bleak it's just not true. I hate it then. I doubt if I'll stay.'

'Where will you go?'

'I don't know. I can't think about that now. I need to get the trial over with first. I've been summoned as a witness. Hils and Richard have said they'll have Harriet until it's over. I suppose I'll have to stay with Pa for a while. In some ways it will be nice to be home again, even if it isn't permanent.'

The mood changed once more. The memory of Cal's death fell sharply between us.

'I want to come home for good,' continued Lydia. 'I really need to get away from here.'

I wanted Lydia to come home for good too, not because I missed her – though of course I did – but because of Harriet. Having her around would make such a difference. Our dad might stop hunting for useless things. You might lose the anxiety you now exuded. Mum might reconnect with us. And I might start to be happy again. Did Lydia really mean this? Was she really intending to come back?

'What about your flat? I thought you liked it. Would you really want to leave it? Will you be allowed to come back if your father is so against it?'

Lydia lit a cigarette. 'I'm not going to hang around here for the rest of my life. I'm on my own with her all the time. What do you think that's like?'

'I know it can't be easy—'

'That's the bloody understatement of the year. I get out for one evening a month if I'm lucky. The rest of the time, the only people I see are Richard and Hilda, and I don't need to tell you what they're like. If I stay here, I'm just going to be trapped with Harriet all day and all night. You can't imagine what it's like to be penned in like this. What will I be in five years' time? Or ten? Just her mother, nothing else at all. I don't want that for myself.'

'But you had her, even when everybody said you shouldn't.'

'Don't remind me. Most of the doctors and nurses were vile at the hospital. They treated me as if I was a slut, especially once they realised Harriet's father wasn't white. I hated them, I can't tell you how much. They made me feel dirty.' Lydia's face became brooding and tense. 'It's not as if I ever wanted to get pregnant. I tried to go on the pill but the doctor went on an absolute rant, he wouldn't give it to me. He said it was for married women only and I needed to have more self-control. At the hospital they were as rough as they could be with me. They wouldn't give me anything for the pain. I called out for my mother. Funny really, I don't think of her much, but I wanted her then. One nurse said I didn't deserve any help; I was a disgrace. The only disgrace was her. How dare anyone say that to me? Some social worker wanted me to give her up. She made me feel like I was committing an even worse sin than having sex in the first place by trying to keep my baby. You wouldn't believe the way they pressured me, but I was determined to fight every single one of them. It's my life; no one should be allowed to tell me what to do.' Lydia sounded more cold, more brittle than I'd known her before. I sat tensely, wondering what it must have been like to have been subjected to such indignities. I felt hurt for her, and angry too, and I realised that in spite of everything, deep down I still loved her.

'They all said I couldn't give her a decent life on my own and I should let some nice, upstanding, childless couple have her instead. I wished with all my heart that my mother was still alive. She would have helped; she would never have sent me away. But Richard and Hilda came to the hospital and they kept insisting it was up to me. I don't know what would have happened if they hadn't been there. They can be a complete pain, the pair of them, but at least they made it possible for me to keep her. I would have married Cal, you know. I would have done. We would have been a little family right now. I'm not wishing Harriet away, I'm really not, it's just hard sometimes, that's all. I don't get out like I need to and I feel shut in sometimes. It would have been different if Cal had lived. We'd have done things together. I wouldn't have been lonely.' Lydia came to a halt. She looked shattered.

'Selina and I will always be here for you and Harriet, you know that.'

I was trying to take away her desolation but she just looked at me.

'It was brave of you, keeping her because of Cal,' I added.

'Not just because of Cal.'

'What else, then?'

Lydia lifted the shoulder nearest to me in a shrug, making it clear that she wasn't going to expand on this. She got out another cigarette, lighting it with the smouldering butt of the first.

I still wanted to know if Lydia really meant it about returning. I didn't want to cherish the hope that I might be able to be close to her and Harriet if it wasn't a real possibility, so I said,

'I wish you could come back for good. It would be fantastic. Do you really think you will?'

Lydia didn't answer.

I put Harriet back in the pram. The sun had gone in. It was getting colder now and I was still shivering from being in the water. Lydia got out a woolly hat and tied it tightly round Harriet's head. 'The wind's getting up, it's time we were going,' she said, tucking Harriet into the pram.

I took my sandals out of the tray beneath it and put them on. I felt stiff. As we hobbled over the pebbles, sea birds rose up around us in sudden, anxious flight, dipping and squawking. I lingered behind. I gathered a small pile of flat stones and sent them skimming across the waves.

Twenty-three

Selina

It's like old times, shopping with Lydia, except now I could actually afford to buy something. But we are in a store where everything is over-priced and although I have enough money for the silks and fine woollens, I really don't want them.

Lydia is in her element. She peers at fabrics and pokes suede shoes, slipping her feet inside them. I'm bored. I'd leave if I could but Lydia brought me here by car and I'm not sure which store we are in or how to get home again.

As I look towards the door, I see Cal. My stomach lurches. He is walking across the shop floor with a woman by his side, his back to me. I hurry up to him, desperate to see his face once more. He turns. It isn't him – how could it be? – but the disappointment causes me to lose my balance and I cling to a . . . a thick pole thing in the middle of the floor. An assistant comes over. 'Are you all right, dear?' she says and she helps me to a chair by the changing rooms, where I try to compose myself. I don't want Lydia to see how shaken I am.

Lydia walks towards me, followed by an assistant carrying jumpers and jackets and repeating how well they'll suit 'madam'. I am struck by the difference in the way we are addressed: Lydia is 'madam', whereas I am just 'dear'.

I touch my own face. Sometimes I feel as if I'm wearing a mask, a disguise of some kind, that makes me feel like somebody else. I fear that one day I will look in a . . . reflecting thing and I won't recognise myself.

'Do you remember the trial?' I say to Lydia, once the assistant has gone.

She adjusts the collar of the jacket she is trying on. 'It was all such a long time ago, why would you ask that now? We've never needed to speak of it before.'

We have spoken of it before, I'm sure we have. Perhaps Lydia doesn't want to remember. Then it occurs to me that she might be using my illness to make me think what happened to Cal and the trial were never discussed between us. Why would she do that? There's a word for it . . . I can't think what it is. 'I remember the trial,' I say to Lydia.

Or, at least, I think I remember it.

We know from stories we have heard that the man in the dock is eighteen and has been in care. No family is sitting behind us in the court, praying that somehow he'll get off. If things were different, I might pity him. I can't. Whatever happens, whatever sentence he receives, he will have a future. In twenty or thirty years' time, he will be out. Perhaps even sooner. He will still have time to get a wife, and children too; he will see them grow up. Cal will never see his child. He took Cal's future away from him.

Zora sits very still beside me. She is absorbing every word.

She clenches and unclenches her fists as she stares at the man who murdered Cal.

He is different to how I imagined him. He is overweight with a jagged haircut and he is wearing a suit that is far too small for him. His arms are bursting through the sleeves. He glances round the court repeatedly. He is like a fly, unable to settle, constantly moving about despite being in the dock. Now he is scratching his chin. He rubs his eyes next, and shuffles his feet. He is sullen, angry; frown lines are etched deep above his nose even though he is still young. He came upon Cal in the street. He saw Cal and Lydia: a white woman and a black man. Lydia said he called Cal a traitor to the race. A punch. Cal was on the ground, blood seeping from the wound on the back of his skull – fractured when he fell. The man ran.

We run. We run to Cal. He is lying in an alley. There is no movement. His head is bloody.

The defence barrister sees him as a victim who never had a chance in life. The punch was an unlucky one. If Cal's skull had been thicker, he would have survived. He doesn't say that we, his family, are unlucky too, now that we are having to survive without him.

Our father is lost, ghostly. How will he survive without Cal?

Dad is sitting between me and Zora. The hospital discharged him. They say he is better now. I am just hoping this trial won't make him ill again. He looks scared. Our father never used to be afraid.

I am afraid. We are all afraid. Soon, Enoch Powell says, the River Tiber will be running with blood. Mum turns off the television.

Our mother looks even paler than usual. She is wearing her best two-piece costume as she calls it; a dark green suit, a fitted jacket, cinched in at the waist, and a knee-length pencil skirt with a small slit at the side. Her blouse is cream and her hair has been coloured at The Cut on the high street to take out all the grey. She has dressed up for Cal, but this time she looks sensible, not like the way she looked at the funeral. She wants to do Cal proud. So does Dad. He is also wearing a suit. It's black and it's the only one he has, so it's shiny in places from being worn so much. He has made his face as blank as he can for the trial. He hardly even blinks. I think he is afraid that if he lets his feelings out, he'll never get them back in again. As the details of Cal's injuries are read out, Dad flinches. It's barely noticeable but I can feel it. I shut out the words too because they make me feel sick, so sick inside. Will we remember Cal's death more powerfully than we remember his life? Will we be unable to think of him without also thinking of this man, this coward, who murdered him for some stupid, false idea about who is allowed to go out with who? I feel the waste of it so deep in me, I can't stop crying here in court, in public. I can't stop but I daren't make any sound in case they throw me out. Zora nudges me.

She wants me to control myself, to be like her, steely-still and angry absolutely all the time.

Zora hits out. 'You need to control your daughter,' the police-woman says to Mum.

Lydia is called to be a witness. She looks scared as she walks towards the stand. She hesitates. It's as if she doesn't really know where she is going. I've never seen Lydia hesitant before. When she talks about what happened, she starts to mix up her words. I am worried that the things she's saying won't be enough to make the man in the dock pay for what he's done. The prosecution barrister asks her if the man in the dock is the one who attacked Cal. 'Yes,' she says, though she says it too softly and the barrister makes her say it again a lot louder. She doesn't want to look at the man, even though the barrister tells her to look. The man stares at her very hard – he means to frighten her into staying silent. But she won't be quiet, even though she is trembling as she speaks. I try to catch her eye, wanting to let her know that she is doing okay, that she is being brave. But she doesn't look across at me. I can see how hard it is for her to remember. She doesn't want to think about that night. Like Dad, she flinches when she tells the court what the defendant, the murderer, did to Cal.

Lydia is holding Cal as he takes his last breath.

One of the buttons has popped off the murderer's jacket. It is hanging open now. He is twisting the loose material at the front of his shirt and these buttons are threatening to pop off too. It makes him look demented. Cal would have seen him looking like this as he advanced towards him, the threat of attack in every move he made. He would have tried to protect Lydia. The defence barrister tries to make out that Cal must have started a fight, but we know he couldn't have done. This man knocked him down and then he ran away. Once, I thought capital punishment was wrong, even though the Bible says an eye for an eye is right. But I want the man to pay for what he did to Cal and if I could make him die for it, I would. The defence barrister makes it sound as if she is wrong about the man. He makes her look at him properly, pointing out that she didn't look properly before. She gets some fight back then and says she definitely did look properly. The barrister tries to prove that she is angry, so she isn't giving proper testimony. I hope the jury sees through this. He just wants to get the man let off because that's what a defence barrister does. They don't care who is guilty and who isn't, they just want to win. Lydia cries when she speaks again about what happened to Cal. I am glad about this – I think a jury believes people more when they cry.

We go to the court every single day and we sit through hours and hours of arguments from barristers about who did what. We are so tired, Mum, Dad, Zora and me. When we go home at night, we can't sleep, which makes us even more tired when the next day comes round. Round and round. Statements and counter-statements. I am worried that the jury will get sick of listening and will make the wrong decision and let the man off. I feel tense all the time, like I'm going to break out scream-ing, like I can't bear to hear this anymore, but we have to bear it. The jury needs to see us here, the prosecution barrister says. We remind them that Cal was loved and had a future. If we don't come every day, the man could get away with it.

Cal is going to university. We celebrate with wine and angel cake.

The jury is sent off to deliberate, as the judge calls it. They must be certain the man did it, he says, so they have to deliberate. They deliberate for two whole days.

Two whole days in limbo, not knowing if the man will pay for what he's done or not. Mum sits hunched; she can't shut out what happened to Cal, it's all been resurrected by the trial. Dad is bringing useless things back into the house, even though Zora and I cleared the last lot away. When he isn't busy collecting his hoard, he pretends to read a newspaper. Or he seems absorbed in some stupid TV programme even though he can hardly see the screen for all the boxes and papers and other useless things piled up around it. Anything that means he doesn't have to speak to us and tell us how he feels.

Cal is dead. We feel lost. We feel scared. We feel angry.

Zora and I are sharing a room again. We need to be close to one another. We sit on Zora's bunk, holding hands. We listen to the radio to shut words like blood and murderer out of our heads.

At last we go back to the court; a verdict has been reached.

Guilty, the foreman of the jury says.

I am crying once more, but this time with relief. Mum cries

too. Dad looks blank, as if he hasn't absorbed what's just been said. Zora just looks steely, like she never wants to cry again, not ever. She is sick of having to cry, she said to me this morning. I know what she means. I hold her hand. I look for Lydia but she isn't in the court. When we leave the building, I look for her on the street, but I can't see her anywhere.

A newspaper photographer steps out in front of us. He takes a picture. On the front page of the *Daily Mail* the next day, we all look very small and startled.

Something happened. I was in a changing room while Lydia tried on clothes and now I'm here, in her apartment, having breakfast.

'Did you buy anything?' I'm hoping that whatever Lydia says in reply will help me fill the gap between the changing room and now.

'When?' she says.

'When we were at that shop – the one with the coats that had the fur collars.'

She looks at me in surprise. 'You saw me get a jacket and some trousers – you said how well they suited me.'

Did I? I wish I could recall this but everything is shadowy. I think I spent the night here, in the room with a shiny en suite bathroom, but I can't have slept properly. I'm tired. Bone weary. Before it's even started, I know this will be a difficult day, one where I will have trouble keeping up. I look at the containers of cereal that Lydia has lined up on the island in the kitchen. Except it isn't really a kitchen. There are kitchen things in it but it is just one, great big, enormous room. Lydia offers me muesli or gran . . . something. My teeth aren't up to all the chewing. What was that phrase Mum used to trot out when somebody asked her age? *I'm as old as my tongue and a little older than my teeth.* 'Do you have any . . . flakes?'

She hasn't, of course. I just have toast.

Zora butters her toast and says, 'There's something I need to tell you.'

'Go on,' I reply, steeling myself for whatever she's about to say.

'I went to see Lydia in Brighton. I saw Harriet too. She's a beautiful baby. I'm sorry we didn't go together.'

'Did Zora visit you in Brighton when Harriet was a baby?' I say to Lydia as I open a jar of marmalade.

'I think she did, yes. Why do you ask?'

'But I didn't go with her?'

'No, it was just Zora. You were probably revising for your exams. You were so studious back then. You were so keen, both of you, to get away from home and go to university. I think you wanted to be like Cal.'

Was I really studious? It's not how I remember it.

It's so hard to concentrate now Cal's no longer here. I go to church and light candles for him in the hope that this will stop the wild thoughts that are running round my head, preventing me from studying. I kneel in the pew in the front row and I pray that God will let Cal out of purgatory and into heaven as quickly as possible. He had sex with Lydia and that was a sin, a mortal sin, which means he will be in purgatory practically for ever unless a lot of prayers are said. Do I believe this? I don't think I do. What do I believe? I have to believe something, otherwise Cal is just gone and I'll never see him again; he won't be in heaven when I die because there won't be a heaven – or a hell. There will just be nothing. Nothingness, I decide, is even more scary than a vengeful God.

I return home, but going to church hasn't been the study aide I was hoping for. I read the same words over and over but they still won't go in. Zora is much better at focusing than I am. She can always remember the words on a page whatever is going on for her. Why did she see Harriet without me? She knew how much I wanted to find out if the baby looks like Cal, if she looks at all like us. Why did she go alone?

Lydia pours coffee for us both but she doesn't eat. She hardly ever seems to eat. Perhaps that's how she's stayed so slim. What am I doing here? I should be getting home.

'Did Zora visit you in Brighton just after you gave birth to Harriet?'

'I've told you the answer to that already – more than once, in fact,' Lydia replies impatiently.

I am embarrassed.

Perhaps she notices this because she says, 'Yes, Zora did visit me in Brighton. Sorry, I didn't mean to snap. Would you like some more toast?'

What did I say when I found out that Zora had gone to Brighton without me? Perhaps I was angry. I would have tried to hide it. Or maybe I was more disappointed than anything else, just sad to think I'd been left out. Lydia would have told me in all likelihood. She would have dropped the information casually, as if by accident, via a postcard or during a phone call. She was always trying to divide us.

Date of birth:
Two of us, born on the same day.
Conjoined. I don't think they believe me.
They divided us.

Marital status: ?

'Why didn't you ever get married?' asks Harriet.
'I never found anyone I wanted to spend my whole life with.'
'Lydia's been married twice.'
And almost engaged once. Lydia isn't an advert for marriage; she's a warning against it. Did I say that out loud? I have to be careful what I say to Harriet. I mustn't try to turn her against her birth mother.

Marital status:
Single. Not sad, not lonely – independent.

'We have to be more independent,' Zora says. 'We rely too much on one another.' But she is as unable to separate as I am; we are equally conjoined.

Religion: None. *Atheist*. I've remembered the word.

'Who is the prime minister?'

This is one of the questions they ask when you have to do a test. I checked on a website, so I am prepared. I remember, of course, and I don't even have to cheat, but I wrote the initials on the inside of my wrist just before I came to this appointment, in case of memory failure. Perhaps it's foolish to try to cover up this memory thing, but I don't want to get every single bloody question wrong – it would be too humiliating.

'Where are you?'

I'm in London, at the hospital. I live in London. I've always lived in London – or very close to it.

Lydia wants to live in America when she grows up, she says. 'Britain's dead. America is the place to be.'

Shoe. House. Kitten. Three words I'm supposed to remember. I hold them very tight in my head.

Shoe. 'Hole in my Shoe'. Lydia loves that song. It's letting in water. Who sings that song?

A house is not a home. What does that even mean? Luther Vandross. A house is not a home. My house *is* a home. *Luther.* Martin Luther King. I remember him. I remember hearing on the news that he'd been shot. We cried. We all cried. Why don't they ask me about President Obama or Martin Luther King? I remember them. I want to stay in my house but to do that, I have to get these bloody questions right.

Kitten. Kitten cat. Kitten heel.

I have to keep these three words in my head. Shoe. House. Kitten. I can do this.

'What year is it?'

Zora would remember, or she would pretend to recall it: she'd make up something if she forgot.

'Where do you live?'

Lydia is going to live in America one day. Our friendship will come to an end when that happens, we suppose. 'You'll have to come to visit,' she tells us. 'You'd love it. Everything's bigger and brighter than it is here.'

Yet Lydia wears an 'I'm Backing Britain' badge, with a Union Jack. 'My cousin Adam gave me this,' she says, tapping it with her fingertips. 'He's backing Britain.'

Crowds waving Union Jacks. 'NF' scrawled across the walls. This country's dead, killed by all the immigrants. *If they're black, send them back.*

'My father says this country's dead. He says there isn't any point in buying British – that won't revive it. He's just bought a Porsche. Harold Wilson would prefer it if he bought a Mini or a Morris Minor instead. This country's dead. Once I'm old enough, I'll be living in America.'

A house is not a home.

Martin Luther King is dead.
   'Of course he's dead, why are you bothered about him? Why would you care about the Reformation?'
   Zora and I laugh in spite of the sadness the assassination brings. For once, we know more about something than Lydia does: Martin Luther *King*.

Zora, me and Cal stare at the television screen. It feels like the end of something; a sign of something terrible that's on the prowl for us. We are scared, even though it happened in America. Malcolm X. Our mother was afraid of him; he didn't believe that black and white could get along together. Martin Luther King was more her cup of tea. She is distraught as they announce that he's been shot. Dad likes Martin Luther King but he liked Malcolm X as well. 'Sometimes change must come by force,' he says, when our brother dies and the newspapers tell their lies to sell more copies. Drug dealers, gang wars, that's what they say about Cal.

'What's the date today?'

When is Martin Luther King Day? I think it's a different date each year.

*

'What's the date today?'

The answer is scribbled on my wrist.

A piece of paper.

Draw a clock.

Hands.

Numbers.

Draw a clock. How does it go?

One o'clock, two o'clock, three o'clock rock ...

Fuck o'clock rock. I don't want to play this game anymore. I am not a child.

'What were the three words?'

Traffic. Home ... I forget.

TWENTY-FOUR

ZORA

We celebrated leaving school by fighting our way through the rubbish blocking the kitchen door and lighting a bonfire in the garden beside the overhanging branches of the apple tree by the house where Lydia used to live. We tossed old essays and notebooks into the flames.

We went in to prepare the evening meal, crunching rubbish with our feet. Mum was cleaning offices. Dad was scavenging, most probably. We would eat together when Mum and Dad came home and we would pretend not to notice that Cal wasn't with us. In the kitchen, I started chopping vegetables. You took a neck of lamb from the fridge and put it in a pan of heated oil to sear.

My stomach was churning. My mouth was so dry I couldn't be sure I would be able to speak but I needed to tell you about Lydia and me and what I'd said to Cal the night he died. University would be a fresh start. I didn't want there to be secrets between us once we left home. I had to come clean; I was afraid that during one of the calls you made to Lydia, she would tell you about the night we'd spent together, just to stir things up. I had to tell you before she did.

I watched you put the neck of lamb in the pan and then I said, with tightness in my voice, 'Remember the night Cal told us Lydia was pregnant?' Stupid question. How could any of us forget? 'I told Cal something. It's what made him leave the house. It's something you don't know.'

You were puzzled; you were finding it hard to believe there were anymore secrets between us.

'I told him me and Lydia spent the night together.'

You were relieved. 'Is that all? Mum told us you were stopping over with Lydia. What's the big deal? God, Zora, I thought you were going to tell me something terrible.' As you said the words, relief was replaced by bewilderment. You knew you must be missing something.

There was a long silence. I willed you to catch on so I wouldn't have to spell it out but all you did was rub herbs and seasoning into the lamb.

'When I said we spent the night together, I meant ...' What are the words? Are there any that don't sound sordid or sinful? 'I meant ... I don't really like boys. I like girls best.'

You stared at me, trying to grasp what I was saying. 'But we're twins,' you told me eventually.

'What's that got to do with it?'

'I like boys,' you replied.

'Well, I don't like boys, not in that way. Lydia and I slept together,' I said, tired of euphemisms and wanting to get my confession over with. But sleeping together was a euphemism too – we had sex; sweaty, blissful, sinful intimacy that

Lydia would never allow us to repeat. 'And I told Cal, and I said Lydia didn't love him and she didn't want the baby, she wanted an abortion. So now you know.'

There was another silence.

'Aren't you going to say something?'

'I don't believe you. You're not like that and neither is Lydia.'

Cal had said almost the exact same thing. 'I am "like that", as you put it.' I couldn't vouch for Lydia.

You stood still for a moment, trying to absorb the words. Then you repeated the mantra that you liked boys best, as if that would protect you from being like me. You thought I couldn't be a lesbian because you weren't one. To you, we were the same.

'Father John would say it was a sin.'

I picked up some parsnips and began to peel them. 'Selina, everything's a sin: Cal and Lydia, that was a sin because they weren't married. Thinking about boys. Thinking about girls. Answering our parents back. Not going to church on Sunday. Taking the name of the Lord in vain. Using swear words, even bloody.'

'But sleeping with Lydia went against God,' you stated.

'All sin goes against God. Going against God is the definition of sin, but it's not the God I believe in, if I believe in God at all.'

You were chopping onions – perhaps that explained why your eyes were so red and watery as you absorbed all this. 'Are you saying you don't believe in God anymore?'

'I don't think I do believe,' I replied eventually. 'Do you?'

'I still believe.' The onions spattered fiercely as you tipped them in the pan. You were terrified. If there was no God, we had no purpose. There would be no afterlife. We would never see Cal again.

'So why did God allow Cal to die, then, murdered on the street? What kind of God would do that?' I said, my tone more bitter than I meant it to be.

'We have free will,' you replied, quoting Father John, as if this answered the question.

'I don't believe God, if he exists, would have a problem with me and Lydia – or me and any other girl – being together, I just don't believe that.'

You turned to face me and leaned against the kitchen counter. 'And you told Cal about you and Lydia? That's why he went out that night? How could you have done that? How could you have been so spiteful?'

The onions were starting to brown. I went to the pan, barely aware of what I was doing, and added the vegetables, along with the stock. I stepped aside to let you throw in a few herbs but we were getting in each other's way. Usually when we cooked together, it was seamless; you knew what I was about to do and you moved to accommodate this without even thinking about it, and vice versa. But now we were awkward and our steps were mistimed.

You placed the lamb on top of the vegetables, turned down the heat, and put the lid on the pan.

'Was it true, then, what you said? That Lydia didn't love Cal and she was going to get an abortion?'

I could see that whatever I said, you were going to be full

of righteous anger, so I decided I might as well tell you the whole truth. 'I don't know if Lydia was going to have an abortion or not. I didn't even know she was pregnant until Cal told us. I was angry about everything. I said it because I didn't want Lydia and Cal to get married.'

'You just made it up?'

I said nothing.

'Because you were jealous?'

'No, not jealous, not really. I didn't trust Lydia. After we'd been together, she said it wasn't right. She was playing with me, Selina, and I didn't want her to play with Cal as well. She's weird like that. She likes to manipulate everyone.'

'The most manipulative person is you, or you wouldn't be telling me all this. You want me to forgive you. It's about you wanting absolution and I'm supposed to make you feel better.'

'I'm telling you because I want you to know what happened. I don't want to keep things from you.' I was angry, so angry with you for not understanding.

'Did you and Lydia sleep with each other while she was seeing Cal?'

'Of course not, it happened just once, before Cal and Lydia met. It was a one-off. It didn't mean anything to Lydia.'

And then you got it. You stopped clearing scraps of vegetables from the kitchen counter and rounded on me. 'If you hadn't told Cal about you and Lydia, he wouldn't have gone out that night. He wouldn't have died. It was all your fault!' Your hands were wet but you took my arm and tried to make me look at you. I pushed you away and you banged your hip on the handle of the cupboard by the sink. Then you lunged at me, your fury spilling out. You were shocked, terrified by your own wish to hurt. The blows came fast, your fists and mine working rhythmically to do the most damage. You wanted to kill me. I wanted to kill you. We'd never fought before, not ever, but we kicked each other, aware that we were matched in strength and determination. I don't know how long we were punching each other, biting and scratching, before we fell apart, exhaustion and pain drawing it all to a close. Your lip was bloodied. My cheeks were bruised. There were scratches on our faces. 'I hate you,' you said. I traced the fine red lines with my fingertips and said, 'I hate you too!' and I ran to the room we shared. I dragged the dressing table across the floor and barricaded myself inside. On the other side of the door, I could hear you saying you were sorry and you didn't mean any of it, but I hardened my heart against you and refused to let you in.

Twenty-five

Selina

I open my laptop. I want to send an email to Lydia. It's easier than phoning her or being in her house – there's more distance, and I can cope with that. I'm not sure we're still friends but I can't remember why. Something happened between us, a long time ago perhaps, or maybe yesterday, I just don't know. There are prompts on the screen: Password, it says, but I can't remember it. I wrote it down somewhere but I'm not sure where. What do you do if your password is lost? There must be a way of getting it back. I try to think how to do it but everything is foggy, distant; I can't concentrate. I shut the laptop. I'd throw it across the room except it was expensive and I can't afford to break it. But what use is the bloody thing if I can't get into it? For a moment, I consider praying to God to restore the memory of my password, but then I remember I don't actually believe in God anymore, so there isn't any point.

I need something to do. Perhaps I'll read a book. I find it hard to follow a plot these days, but I've chosen *A Harlot's Progress*, a novel about the slave trade. It doesn't start at the beginning and finish at the end. Instead, it jumps about all over the place. I've read it before; I know this because I've scribbled notes in the margins. But now I'm reading the book with different eyes. I see the poetry in it. I don't have to read it from beginning to end, I can just dip in and see where the words take me. I like the shapes the words make on the page. I like the spaces between them, the things that fall between the lines. I feel excited as I split words from their meaning and hear nothing but the sound. It's a kind of poetry.

I look at the bookshelf in the corner of the room. Zora wrote a book on Caribbean poetry. She was so proud the day it was published. We were all proud; Mum and Dad were as proud of Zora as they would have been of Cal. We celebrated with a meal at an Indian restaurant, all of us together.

I lift the book off the shelf. It's in hardback, shiny, with crisp white pages. I turn to the dedication. *For Selina, with love*, it says.

I'll read Zora's book again and then I'll find some poems. Verses – bite-sized chunks. Just words, often in a strange order, magicking all kinds of feelings in me, even if I'm not sure what they are. More than ever now, I hear the musicality of words, their cadences, even if I can't always join them together.

A bookmark falls to the floor. It's a postcard. It must have been sent years ago – there's a picture of Manchester on it. I pick it up and read it slowly:

Manchester is great. I'm working hard and I'm making friends. I'd say wish you were here, but I really don't.

The words are angry. Why would Zora have sent me something like this?

Since the fight we are barely speaking. Our parents are too preoccupied to notice. We explain our bruises and scratches by telling them we were set upon by some girls from school. It's a cruel lie but we don't realise this until we've said it. Mum and Dad think of Cal, the attack on him. They are scared that no one in the family is safe.

We sit on the stairs in silence, waiting for the post to arrive. It's not a comfortable silence, the way it used to be with us; it's bleak and painful. We are still in matching flannel pyjamas that are too hot in summer weather. Patches of perspiration show beneath our arms. The sun shines into the hall through the glass panel of the door as the postman pushes the letters through the slot. I catch them before they land on the mat. Our A-level results are here. The envelopes flutter slightly as my hands shake. I pass Zora's letter to her and I hold mine so tight that the paper scrunches. I'm too scared to open it; it will be a miracle if I've done well. I watch Zora, who is tearing her letter open with trembling fingers. I can tell by the way her face lights up that she's got the grades we need for Manchester.

She breaks the silence. 'What did you get?' she asks belligerently. These days, she always sounds as if she's spoiling for a fight.

I open my envelope slowly – reluctantly. Even as the writing bounces off the page I can see I haven't passed well enough. 'It will have to be our back-up choice,' I tell Zora with a sick feeling. We won't be spreading our wings the way we thought we would. We will be on the edges of London, going to the teacher-training college we applied to in case we didn't do well enough to get into Manchester University. But I can't imagine being a teacher. I can't imagine being any good at it.

'Teaching will be all right, I expect,' I say to Zora. 'I know it's not what we really wanted, but it's a good career, there are always jobs. We'll have actual jobs at the end of it.'

Zora stares at me for a long time. Then she says, 'You go to teacher-training college if that's what you want. I'm still going to university.' She turns and goes upstairs, leaving me sitting by the phone in the hall. She still hasn't forgiven me for the things that were said the night we fought. I didn't mean to hurt her; I was just so shocked by what she said. Shocked that I didn't even know about her and Lydia as much as anything. Shocked by what she said to Cal. We attacked one another, and that broke something. Perhaps it can't be mended completely, but the fight can't have ended everything for ever, it just can't have done. I don't hate her. I said I did, but of course I don't. How could I hate Zora? But no matter what I say to her, she keeps saying she'll never, ever forgive me.

I hear her moving round her room. After our fight she insisted on separate bedrooms again. Perhaps it was a prelude to the bigger separation she's been planning.

I follow her. 'You're not really going away without me, are you? You don't mean it, do you?'

'Oh, but I do mean it,' Zora replies.

She is gathering up her things and putting them in a suitcase. She can't pack properly yet, there's five or six weeks to go until the start of term. It's a gesture that's meant to show me how angry she still is. As I observe the stiffness of her outline, I know beyond a doubt that she will be leaving me. I am jolted to the other side of the room, even though my body doesn't move. 'Please, Zora,' I say to her, though I know there is nothing I can do to prevent her going. My pleading will probably make her more determined to leave, but I can't stop.

'Shut up,' she says in a cold voice.

I can't shut up, even though I wish I could. 'Please, Zora,' I repeat.

'This is my room. Get out,' she says.

I don't move. I can't.

'Get out!' Zora takes me by the arm and marches me to the door.

I stand outside the room, leaning against the door frame. We've been planning so many things together. There's been months of planning. We were going to explore another city, live away from our parents, learn new things, drink coffee in cafés and dance in nightclubs. But I realise with terrible clarity that all these things are over now. For the first time in my life, I will be alone.

PART FOUR

Twenty-six

Selina

Even though Fran is sitting beside me, I feel alone. We've been on one of our treks. We're about to order lunch in Ye Olde something or other but I might as well be sitting by myself. It's this illness, I think. I can no longer connect with people the way I used to – too many gaps. And there are times when, however hard I listen, I can't seem to hear. Fran takes another sip of wine and says, 'When did you get in touch with Lydia again?'

'A little while ago,' I reply, hoping I don't seem too vague. Time keeps collapsing and it's hard to remember what happened when. I want to ask Fran what I've told her in the past about Lydia Russell – not Russell anymore, what is her surname now? – but I hesitate. I'm not sure I want Fran to know how many holes there are in my memory. It might change our friendship. She might start talking down to me, even though I've known her since my college days.

'I can't wait to start actual teaching,' Fran says, with a lot more confidence than I can manage. She has long fair hair that she plaits around her head and a fringe that tends to get into her light grey eyes. She is slight. She wears clothes that are too big for her, like hand-me-downs from an older sister that she has yet to grow into. Her shoes are white, T-bar sandals, the kind a toddler might wear. They suit her smallness. 'I'm a bit of a chatterbox,' she confesses, as if I haven't noticed. 'It's my worst habit. I hardly let anyone else speak. Everyone tells me off but I can't seem to help it.'

I like this characteristic. It means my silences are less obvious. Being here at college on the edge of London is so scary without Zora. Perhaps we will never see each other again – the thought fills me with such a sense of dread. Maybe I've relied on her too much. It's always been easier to let her take the lead. Now that she isn't here I have no idea how to be.

At night I cry myself to sleep. Zora's absence is so overwhelming, so defeating. But I despise myself for my weakness when I wake up. I'm eighteen now, too old to cry. Fran asks me what's up. I suppose she's noticed my tiredness. She doesn't seem to mind when I say nothing's wrong even though I'm obviously lying. In class, she sits beside me and she shares her lecture notes. She has realised I can't even find the words to write anything down. I'm not as clever as Zora. I'll probably do badly here, just as I did badly in my A levels.

Zora has left me so easily; she doesn't even miss me. Yet I am lost without her. She sends me a postcard saying she is fine, enjoying university in Manchester. She says she's glad that I'm not there. I could never have sent a message like that to her. We're not the same. We call ourselves Selzora, but we are not the same.

*

Fran gets another round of drinks. I need a clear head, or I might start repeating myself, so ask for lemonade. It's too sweet and fizzy, I'm not enjoying it much. I take another sip and say, 'Lydia has invited me to a dinner party, but I don't think I want to go.'

I protest for a while, telling Lydia that dinner parties aren't really me.

'Don't be silly,' she says, 'you need taking out of yourself. It's just a few friends. And if you're worried I'll be doing the cooking you really don't need to be. I've found a wonderful local firm of caterers. They even sort out place cards.'

'Place cards? It's going to be formal, then?'

'No, of course not. I just like to put the right people together. It makes it all go so much more smoothly.'

I don't know what to say to people these days. My memory is full of holes. I'll have to work hard to disguise it, or the gaps may show. I don't want that kind of exposure, not in front of Lydia. So I say, 'It's an awkward journey on the bus from my house to yours, especially at night.' I can't drive anymore. Not so long ago, I went the wrong way down a one-way street and almost caused an accident. It's better if I take the bus.

'I'll send Adrian to pick you up. He'll run you home again.'

'No, really, I don't want to be any bother.'

'No bother at all, trust me, he'll be delighted. Any opportunity to show off his new car – you know what men are like.' Lydia's tone brooks no further argument.

*

'Lydia is always so insistent about everything,' I say to Fran. 'Even now, it's hard to say no to her.'

'Have you told Harriet you're in touch with Lydia again?'

'Yes,' I answer, although I'm not actually sure. Perhaps I've held back, knowing she wouldn't approve. She doesn't want any contact with her mother. She'd think that in seeing Lydia again, I was being disloyal, either failing to remember how much her mother has hurt her or deciding the hurt no longer matters. Perhaps she would be right, but I need to fill in the gaps, and Lydia is the only person who can help me to do it.

'Will you go to this dinner party, then?' asks Fran.

'I don't know. I might,' I say to her.

Lydia's dinner party guests seem well heeled, one or two in their fifties, the rest a bit older. We are served drinks and nibbles in a spacious, open-plan living room. I ask for water and the waitress tries not to look as if it's an imposition. The windows that stretch across a wall slide open and lead into a garden. I sit on a patio on a woollen bench. White lights sparkle in the trees.

'A pleasant enough evening now the wind's dropped,' says a slim man with thin dark hair. He says his name as if it's an announcement: 'Miles Andrews.' He shakes my hand. He introduces the petite woman next to him as The Wife and they talk about nothing much for several minutes. Then Miles says, 'What is it that you do?'

'I was a teacher. I've retired now. What do you do?' I ask, trying to turn the spotlight away from me.

'I'm in finance. I work with Adrian,' he replies.

He and The Wife get bored and wander off. I am left by myself, feeling conspicuous; mine is the only brown face. I wish Zora was here. I wish it so much that, for a moment, I feel her beside me, telling me what to do, telling me what I remember and reminding me of all the things she thinks I've forgotten.

I don't see Lydia approaching until she is almost beside me. She is followed by a tall, slim woman and an even taller man. 'You remember Amy, don't you?' says Lydia, gesturing behind her. 'And this is her husband, Will.'

Amy. The name is familiar. And then I remember: she's Lydia's middle daughter. I haven't seen her since she was young. We exchange pleasantries. Amy tells me she has a nursery in Richmond. I assume she nurtures small children, but it turns out it's plants she cultivates. I must remember to let Harriet know I've seen her half-sister. Have they kept in touch?

'Come inside, everyone,' Lydia says. 'I want Selina to meet Giles.'

We go towards a man who, according to Lydia, bears a striking resemblance to Harrison Ford. More introductions. I'll have to try hard to hold on to names.

'I've put you and Giles next to one another, Selina,' she says as she seats us at a table.

Giles. Wasn't there a Miles as well? How will I manage not to mix them up?

Giles may be good-looking but that is the extent of his charm. He talks at me. Still, if I only have to listen, I won't make any mistakes.

I've always been a slow eater but these days it takes even longer. It's as if I've lost the connection between sight and taste. The two don't coordinate; nothing seems to taste the way it did before this illness. *I* don't coordinate; the pale pastry merges with the white china so it's barely visible. Even my ability to see seems mixed up. Everyone is waiting for me to finish so the next course can be served. I feel self-conscious as I try to swallow the tart with the truffle-and-something filling. It's garnished with too many stringy bits of salad that stick in my throat.

'How do you know Adrian and Lydia?' asks the mock Harrison Ford, finally pausing for breath.

'I was at school with Lydia.' If I have to talk, I'll never get this eaten.

'Ah, the lovely Lydia. I expect she was quite a handful when she was young.' He gives a knowing smile, which makes me think that he and Lydia once had a fling.

There is a conversation going on around us. The voices blend; I have to concentrate hard in order to decipher them. Miles or Giles – the one sitting opposite me – is making his opinions known. 'I have nothing against immigrants. They're not all living off the state; some of them are quite hard-working. Take the Indians – are you allowed to say Indians these days?' He smiles as he says this. I think the last part is his idea of a joke.

'I think you are, darling. They do come from India,' replies The Wife.

The man next to her adds, 'Unless you mean Red Indians. I don't think you can call *them* Indians anymore.'

'Eskimos don't like being called Eskimos,' says the mock Harrison, switching his attention from me to the rest of the table.

'What do they want to be called, then?' asks Miles/Giles.

'Inuits, I think.'

'*Inuits?*' He appears to consider this. Then he dismisses it, with a wave of his hand, as an act of self-aggrandisement on the part of former Eskimos. 'The point I'm making is, the Indians that come here, they adapt, they work hard. Take Rishi Sunak. He's rich as Croesus, pulled himself up by his bootstraps, leads the country now. Yet people still try to claim they're being held back by racism.' He grins at the absurdity of this. 'What do you call yourself?' he asks, looking at me.

'I'm Selina,' I tell him.

He laughs at me indulgently. 'No, I don't mean that. I mean what's your ethnicity? I'm not being discourteous, I'm just wondering what you call yourself. You're not quite black and we don't say coloured anymore. I just want to learn – I don't want to put my foot in it.'

'I think you already have, darling,' says The Wife.

I continue to eat without speaking and the question remains unanswered.

Unfazed, he says, 'At least now we're out of the EU we're not going to be controlled by Brussels anymore, told what we can and can't say.'

At last I swallow the last of the starter. My plate is removed.

'I wish we hadn't left,' says ... Lydia's daughter, who is sitting further down the table.

Miles/Giles groans. 'Don't tell me you're a Remoaner?'

'I voted Leave, as it happens. But everything's gone up so much. I had to buy a dress to wear to my niece's wedding. It was from a website I always use that sells European designs you just can't find anywhere else. It was almost double what it would have cost three or four years ago.'

'Wine is definitely more expensive,' her husband adds.

Lydia says, 'Well I voted Remain. I could see all this coming. We have an apartment in Florence. We're having to consider selling. We used to be able to spend the whole of the winter there but now it's just ninety days, so it's hardly worth maintaining it anymore.'

'It's not as if it actually worked, leaving. The Poles have gone, of course, but all that means is that you can't get a decent builder now,' somebody replies.

I'm starting to lose track. I can't keep hold of the conversation. Too many different voices, too much happening at once. For a while it becomes background noise I can't decipher. But I have to get hold of it again. I strain to understand, and slowly I start to tune back in.

Miles/Giles says, to our end of the table, 'Do you remember that cousin of Lydia's? Adam Russell? He would have been the one to sort out this mess. He had the right idea about things.'

'Keep your voice down, darling. You know Lydia doesn't like to talk about Adam.'

'He wrote books as well. I don't know where he found the time,' Miles/Giles continues, as if The Wife hasn't spoken. 'There was one about Westminster and the goings-on there, I believe – he was rather well placed for writing that, of course. And there were a couple of historical novels. He was unapologetic about the past, and the liberal left couldn't stand him for it, called him a fascist or something. He knew his stuff, though, no doubt about that.'

'Most of his books are out of print now,' Harrison says.

There's something else, something I can't quite decipher. Then a male voice says, 'He got cancelled, didn't he, sometime in the eighties? Before anyone actually used the word "cancelled"? I read an article in *The Telegraph* the other day that said it was time to republish his books because they're just too bloody good to remain unavailable. I always thought he'd make PM but it never came to anything in the end.'

'He drank himself to death, I heard. Couldn't take the loss of his career, ended up with cirrhosis of the liver,' adds someone else.

My hands are trembling so much that I can't hold my glass of water. I put it down on the table. *Adam.* Something happened between us.

Adam Russell stands beside the dispatch box. 'I have always been determined to stamp out racism in all its forms,' he says.

'I would have voted for Russell,' says Miles/Giles. 'The trouble with Johnson was, he lacked statesmanship. Russell had all of Johnson's attributes and a bit of dignity as well. We're too quick to judge people in this country. One wrong word and you're out.'

I want to go home. Nausea threatens to overwhelm me and there is a strange throbbing in my head. A woman places a plate of some kind of fish in front of me. I try to take deep breaths – the smell of the fish is making the nausea worse.

'This looks good,' says Miles/Giles. There are murmurs of agreement. 'At least fish should be a reasonable price now that we've got back the right to fish in our own waters. It's a question of sovereignty – that's what the Remoaners can't seem to grasp.'

'What I don't get is why we're still letting them come in on boats – the illegals I mean,' says somebody at the far end of the table.

'France. It's the French – they aren't controlling the borders,' another voice replies.

I want to speak. I open my mouth to speak but I'm afraid I'll mix up my words or fail to complete a sentence.

'People talk about the rights of immigrants, but what about our rights? Why should our taxes pay for people who weren't even born in this country?'

'I think ... I think what you're saying is wrong.'

Everyone falls silent. They turn to look at me.

Then Miles/Giles says, 'What do you mean, "wrong"?'

I keep my voice steady. 'Everything you're saying is wrong.'

'You see, this is exactly what I'm talking about. You can't say anything these days without somebody taking offence.'

I find my voice. 'I'm taking offence because you don't know what you're talking about. The prime minister ... he didn't need to pull himself up by his bootstraps. He was educated at a private school.' Where was it? I try to think, but the name of it escapes me. It doesn't matter, the important thing is, it cost a lot to go there. 'A year there costs more than most people's annual wage,' I say to them.

Anger is pricking at me. I can't sit still. I think of my father, the hours he had to work. The insults he had to put up with when he came to this country.

'I'm taking offence because so many of the migrants, who worked harder than any of you can possibly imagine, have gone, so things we rely on, like social care, are in a state of collapse. But you're still talking about migrants as if they've contributed nothing.'

I'm not sure how to continue, but I have to say more. I have to make my voice heard. I'm so tired of staying quiet. This illness has made me so quiet. I hate the way I've retreated into silence again. It's like the silence of my childhood. I used to be afraid to speak, afraid to get things wrong, believing that Zora could always do everything better than me. I let her speak for me. And then I grew up and it changed, I became more independent; I spoke for myself. But now I've allowed the silences to come back, in order to conceal my illness. I have to break them. I can't allow this dementia to continue to stifle me. So I say, to a roomful of dinner guests who are bristling with irritation, 'So many people in this country are struggling. Unable to buy food or pay their rent. But that's not because of immigration, it's because successive governments have only cared about the rich. It's not about the cost of dresses or homes in Italy, it's about survival for most people.' I come to a stop. I found all the words I wanted to say, I didn't lose any of them, but still my hands are trembling.

'You can't blame all that on the referendum. It was all those COVID lockdowns and the war in Ukraine.'

I don't want to speak anymore but I know I must, and

my voice sounds stronger as I say, 'Brexit, the Leave vote, it tipped the balance. The rest of Europe has far stronger economic growth ... And people like me are being made to feel unwelcome in the country of our birth by all the racism that's been allowed to push back up to the surface.' I look at Lydia, waiting for her to say something in agreement, but there is nothing. 'I want to go home. I need to go home now,' I tell her.

'At least finish your food,' Lydia replies.

'I'm going home.' I start to get to my feet. Harrison takes hold of my arm as if in restraint. I shake him off angrily.

Lydia signals to ... Michael? ... who bounds towards me.

'It's all right, I'll get a taxi,' I tell him.

'Nonsense, I'm giving you a lift.'

As I follow him from the room, I hear somebody say, 'Is she all right? She seems a bit overwrought.'

'She hasn't been well,' Lydia replies. 'Now come on, you uncultured lot. Hasn't anybody ever told you never to talk politics or religion at a dinner party?'

There is laughter as I leave. Once, I would have minded that. But I found my voice. I said what I wanted to say. I found the words. I wish Zora had heard me. I miss Zora so much. I miss the time when we were Selzora.

Twenty-seven

Zora

It was strange, going to Euston on my own, leaving Mum and Dad behind – and you of course – to catch the train to Manchester. As I sat looking out of the window, I believed I'd finally shaken off Selzora.

The train chugged through smoke-grey towns and endless rows of small, narrow houses, which morphed into terraces of red brick as we arrived in Manchester. The colour gave the place a kind of warmth. It was colder than it was in London and the cliché that it always rained was largely true, but it was a bustling place and I knew I would grow to love it here, even though there were fewer black faces than had surrounded you and me back home. I'd heard Moss Side was the place to be if I didn't want to feel isolated and I decided I'd have to go there.

As I walked towards the university, struggling with the weight of my bag, I was full of excitement mixed with apprehension. I wasn't afraid for me; I was afraid for you, afraid of your disappointment, and where it might take you.

'We'll see each other very soon,' you'd kept repeating.

I hadn't replied. It was easier not to tell you that I would be breaking contact with you. I would write occasionally but I wouldn't be in London again for many months. I knew that if I saw you, you would suck me back, and I wouldn't be able to continue living away from you. I wouldn't be asking you to visit me in Manchester, not because I wouldn't miss you, but because I would.

I lived in a draughty Victorian building that had a touch of the Gothic about it; even with the central heating on full blast, it was never warm, and, steeped in literature as I was, I half expected to meet Bertha Mason on the stairs. You would have greeted Bertha warmly as a friend, a fellow outsider, but I preferred to avoid her.

The large windows rattled in the wind. The hall had leafy grounds full of horse chestnut trees that shed smooth, brown conkers like the ones our father collected, and although early mornings were chilly I would go outside as soon as I woke up and sit on one of the damp, wooden benches in my rain-coat. I'm not sure why it felt good; perhaps it was to do with my need for isolation, which I savoured, even though I was lonely. I would go back indoors reluctantly. My room was a cell that had a desk, a chair, a chest of drawers and a small wardrobe. There was a very narrow single bed, designed to discourage overnight guests. A small bookshelf contained the term's reading for my course.

Each morning, I caught a bus for the twenty-minute ride to the university, and each evening, when I returned to 'Thornfield', I would sit on my bed and absorb every detail of my surroundings as if I still couldn't quite believe I'd escaped and was no longer joined to you. The fact that there was someone else in the world who looked sufficiently like me for us to be interchangeable in most people's eyes wasn't an issue here. Nobody knew I had a twin. They probably wouldn't have cared if they had – we were all so young and self-absorbed.

I was finally free of you, but despite my need for independence, I missed you deeply. If only we hadn't fought. If only you had understood about me and Lydia. If only I could forgive you for believing I had sinned and that you were better than me because I'd slept with a girl. If only you hadn't thought the things I'd said to Cal that night were the reason he had died.

I worked hard, anxious to stay on top of things. I loved being away from London but in truth, I also ached with longing for a home that was no longer there, buried under rubbish as it was. And I kept thinking of you, wondering where you were. I know you thought we had some kind of telepathy and that each of us always knew where the other was, but that was just one of your stories. I was bereft, for a time, without you. We were extensions of one another and without you I barely knew who I was.

I sent you a postcard to let you know I was okay but that was all.

I made a few friends. Of these, Georgia was the one I trusted most. She had the room down the corridor from mine and she was a warm, friendly girl of Jamaican–British heritage. She wore long velvet skirts and attached plastic flowers to her short, curly hair in defiance of the assumption that black women couldn't be hippies. She was tall – taller, even, than you and me – and she made me laugh, which helped lift my mood.

Halfway through the first term, I came to a stop. I withdrew inside myself, needing to hide. I stayed in my room, under the bedclothes, no longer able to move. Georgia brought me cups of tea and thickly buttered Marmite toast, telling me I'd feel better if I ate. She didn't ask questions, she just accepted I was down, and that in my own time I'd come out of it. Eventually, I got out of bed and started attending lectures again, but it wasn't easy to stay focused. I found myself slipping into daydreams, imagining you and me together, doing our degrees at the same university and being happy, once more, in our closeness.

A couple of weeks before Christmas, I sent a card to Lydia. I also sent a stuffed tiger for Harriet – an ugly-looking creature with over-large eyes and a toothy grin. Cal would have loved it. In the New Year, Lydia sent a note of thanks in green ink on a single sheet of Basildon Bond.

That Christmas, I didn't return to London to be with Mum and Dad or you; I stayed with Georgia and her family. Her parents had a farm in the countryside. It hadn't occurred to me that some black people might actually prefer to live away from urban areas, or that a black family would be able to tolerate the isolation and the constant, implicit assertion that they didn't belong in the area. But Georgia and her siblings were third generation; their grandfather, Moses, had been in the British West Indies Regiment, fighting for Britain during World War I. He had settled here after that and he'd sent for Dorothy, his childhood sweetheart, who had arrived in Yorkshire from rural Jamaica. Georgia told this story with pride, asserting her right to call herself British. Her family were determined and defiant and none of them questioned their entitlement to work the land.

I told Georgia that our father had also come to Britain from Jamaica. He had joined the merchant navy and had been on an oil tanker in World War I. When the war had come to an end, he had stayed in London, where he'd met our mother. You and I had never quite understood how our mother had got together with our father. In many ways, she was conventional, unadventurous. Yet she had fallen for the Jamaican she'd met in the café where she worked and their shared love of dancing, big band music and the stories of Edgar Allan Poe had eventually led to marriage. They had been happy – until Cal's death, at least.

'Is your family okay with you not wanting to do farm work?' I asked Georgia one morning.

Georgia pulled on her jumper and said, in a voice that was muffled as the polo neck got stuck around her face, 'They know I'm not cut out for it. I've always liked cities best. As long as I'm happy in whatever I do next, they won't mind.' She got the neck of the jumper in place; I could hear her better now. 'Besides, the house is pretty crowded. They're probably glad of the extra space. There's more than enough of us left to carry on the family tradition.'

Georgia's oldest sister was studying to be a vet in Leeds. A brother was at agricultural college. I didn't ask how they'd come to be a farming family or how they were forging a life for themselves that resisted expectations of black people so completely, but I did marvel at it each morning as I was awoken by the sounds of cockerels crowing and the lively mooing of cows.

I'd posted a book to you for Christmas but I couldn't open your present to me; it was too painful. It was February before I finally unwrapped the soft, orange jumper you'd sent. I knew you would have bought an identical one for yourself. I could sense that you'd been wearing it all through the holiday and into New Year, thinking of me, missing Selzora. As I rubbed its sleeve against my face, I understood that it was cruel of me to leave you on your own at Christmas, a recognition that had come conveniently late; there was nothing I could do to change that now.

Missing you meant it wasn't easy for me to return to university after the holiday – perhaps I should go back to London – to you – I kept thinking, even though I was happy with Georgia and couldn't imagine being without her. I threw myself into my studies to shut you out and felt relief mixed with sadness as I realised how much space there was now between us. I loved roaming round the library, finding things out for myself and applying my new-found knowledge to essays and seminar papers. It was the social side of things that I found hard. Without you, I was self-conscious and nothing came naturally. Georgia said we should join a few societies, so although I was only half persuaded, I signed up for rambling. Georgia went for rambling too and decided the board games society might be fun. She also joined a choir. We'd never been able to sing so the choir wasn't for me, but I did try a couple of dull evenings of Scrabble and Monopoly, and afterwards I wondered if Georgia and I were quite as well suited as I'd thought.

Sometimes, when Georgia was asleep beside me, her breathing low and even, and I was pinned against the wall in the narrow, single bed, I compared her to Lydia. For the most part, Georgia won out; she was honest, kind, truthful and considerate. When she asked how I was feeling, she actually wanted to know, and she never stored up the things I told her to use against me later. She loved me, too, there was no question about that. But Lydia and I had known each other since we were children, and although I told myself that I'd outgrown her, it wasn't really true.

In the New Year, Lydia sent a postcard from Brighton, inviting me to come and see her again. I forced myself not to reply. I was living in Manchester now; a different life. Here, I even had a different name. On the first day in halls, when I met Georgia and she asked what I was called, before I could stop myself, I said that my name was Selzora.

Twenty-eight

Selina

I am alone. There is silence from Zora. I don't know when I last saw Harriet. So when Lydia comes to pick me up in her shiny car with the heated leather seats, I get in. She glides me to her apartment. 'I'm sorry about dinner the other night,' she says, as we stop at a set of traffic lights. 'They were Adrian's friends mostly. I shouldn't have allowed the wine to flow so freely. People are obnoxious when they're drunk.'

A bit of drunken banter, that's all she thinks it was.

I tell Lydia's guests that they are wrong. I use all the right words. Yet when I get home, I feel so sad. Millie-Christine; I can almost see them, here, in the room. There's something vague in my mind, something I can't quite reach. The past still shaping the present – is that it? We used to teach young people, Zora and me. We tried to give them a different version of history through the books we read, the stories we told. The other version, we used to call it, one that began with empire and slavery – the root ... the root of what? What am I trying to get to? The root of the hostility, the othering. The root of not belonging ... Rooms to let – no coloureds ... Rivers of blood ... Leave means leave ... Cal, bleeding in the street. I need to think of Cal, but at the same time, I need to forget him too – thinking of him causes me so much sadness.

'Do you ever think of Cal?' I say to Lydia.

'It was all such a long time ago,' she replies.

I sit on a white sofa in a huge room. There are coloured-glass figures that cast red and green shadows on the tiled floor.

'Would you like some coffee?' Lydia asks.

We drink strong coffee and eat pâté with toast. Lydia is talking about someone called Adrian. I try to keep up. Then she says, 'I do think of Harriet often, you know. I've kept track of her career, read her articles in *The Guardian*. She's quite a crusader, isn't she? I doubt if she's ever met a cause she didn't like.' Lydia's tone conveys hostility, combined with traces of wistfulness.

'She takes after Cal,' I reply.

'How is she these days? Is she happy?'

I nod, nothing more. Harriet doesn't want Lydia in her life. She doesn't want any contact. She doesn't want me to have contact, even after all these years. But there are things I need to know. I just can't seem to piece together the questions I need to ask. So instead, I say, 'Do you have any music?'

'What would you like to listen to?'

'I don't mind.' Music anchors me. It helps me to focus.

Lydia speaks into a round thing in front of her on the

coffee table and Pink Floyd begin to play. I remember this. What's it called? It was Lydia's favourite song.

Lydia and Cal are dancing. Where is Zora? Has she gone home? Adam doesn't want to dance. Dancing is beneath him.

The intercom buzzes. 'Yes?' says Lydia impatiently. She adds something I can't quite make out.

She turns to me and says, 'Don't worry, she won't be staying long.'

Who won't be staying long?

'I don't know why we've kept in touch,' Lydia continues. 'She's so vacuous and we have absolutely nothing in common. Still, I suppose she is a relative of sorts.'

Lydia lets a woman into the room. She is elderly, small and very thin. Her hair is dyed blonde. Lydia doesn't introduce us but the woman seems to know who I am. Is it Lydia's stepmother? What was her name? Jane? No, I think it was Joy.

'What's she doing here?' the woman shouts. 'What the hell is she doing here?' Her voice is posh, clipped. It's a moment before I realise the woman's talking about me – it's me she's angry with. She strides over and hisses, 'I don't know how you've got the gall to show your face after what you did.'

What's she talking about? I should know her. I should know who she is.

She leans over me, her mouth twisted with fury. 'You bitch,' she spits. 'You destroyed us. You ruined everything. We lost everything because of you. His career was over. All our friends deserted us. Everything went! He *died*. He died because of you and your fucking sister!'

She is slight but her fist connects with my face.

An unlucky punch.

I hear myself panting in short gasps, the pain in my eye taking my breath away. For a moment, I am frozen. Then I fight back. I shove her out of the way, but I land on my knees on the floor.

'Oh, for Christ's sake!' says Lydia. She grabs the woman's arm and yanks her to one side. I see my chance. I get up and run – as much as I can run now – stumbling as I make my way into the communal hall. I hear the woman screeching behind me: 'Fucking bitch! Those fucking black bitches destroyed him!' I keep going until the sound fades, opening heavy double doors and gulping in the air outside. At the end of a drive, I lean against an iron gate that I can't seem to open. An unlucky punch. The words keep running round my head. Then I am sick until nothing remains in my stomach.

I should know who the woman is, but I can't think, I just can't think. I don't know who she is. I don't know what she meant.

Not knowing is far more frightening than the punch.

I need Zora. I have to find her. I have to get out of here. I don't know who she is. I don't know what she meant.

Twenty-nine

Zora

I thought I would know myself better once I was without you, but alone, I struggled to know who I was even more. 'My name isn't really Selzora,' I said to Georgia as we lay side by side. 'It's just Zora.'

She stared at me in surprise, assuming, most probably, that this was just an affectation. 'Why *Sel*-Zora, then?' she said after a while.

I told her about you. Then I told her about Cal and Lydia, omitting the part where Lydia and I had slept together.

But Georgia was astute. 'Were you and Lydia in a relationship?'

'What makes you think that?'

'The way you talk about her. The way you say her name.'

'For one night, that's all.'

'But you wanted more.' A statement, not a question.

'Before Cal, perhaps. Not after that.'

'Why not?'

I told Georgia what I'd said to Cal that night.

The two of us were lying on the floor; we'd taken the

mattress off my narrow bed and paired it with the one from Georgia's room, dragging it down the stairs and along the corridor and placing them side by side. Nobody had asked what we were doing. I doubt if anyone would have cared. University wasn't like school and it was the time of free love, as it was called back then – most of the other students believed that it didn't matter who you loved as long as you loved somebody. Now that we had the extra mattress, I no longer had to spend my nights squashed against a wall, though we felt the draught from the gap beneath my door through the winter months.

Georgia turned onto her side and propped herself up on her elbow. 'You couldn't possibly have known what would happen to Cal that night. You would never have said those things if you'd known.'

'But I never got the chance to take them back,' I replied. I needed to change the subject. 'When did you tell your family that you were into women?' I found it hard to use the term lesbian. It was a label, and one that didn't leave much room for manoeuvre.

Georgia stretched out and took a bar of chocolate from her bag. She passed half to me. 'I was sixteen. I knew I was never going to have a heterosexual relationship so I told them one Sunday while we were watching television.'

'How did they take it?'

They were a bit shocked, I think, a bit unsure how to deal with it at first, but in the end, they just wanted me to be happy.'

'Did they know we were sleeping together at Christmas?'

'Yes, of course. I'm lucky, I suppose. Live and let live, Mum always says. Dad too. Do you think your sister would disapprove of us?'

'She'd say it was a sin.'

There was silence for a while as Georgia considered this. Then she said, 'Everything happened at once. Selina couldn't process it all, it was too much for her. Lydia was her only friend and she'd gone off, not only with Cal but with you as well. She probably felt a bit left out.'

Georgia was saying that last part as a joke, but perhaps there was some truth in it. She got up and started to get dressed. It was mid-afternoon and the hall was almost empty; most of the other students were attending seminars or lectures. We should have been in class ourselves but we had spent the day in bed instead, exploring each other's bodies until we had exhausted every possibility of touch and there was nothing left to do but talk instead.

Georgia pulled a t-shirt over her head and said, 'You didn't see her at Christmas.'

'I wanted to spend it with you.'

'You should go to London, try to make it up with her.'

'I can't. You don't understand. It's suffocating, being joined.'

'You don't have to be joined,' Georgia replied mildly.

'We don't know any other way.'

'Go and see her,' Georgia said. 'Then maybe you'll stop being so miserable without her.'

'I'm not miserable and I can't see Selina. She suffocates me.'

'Go and make it up with her, for your sake as much as hers.'

Georgia was taking your side. She was seeing you as the

victim in all of this, the way everybody always did. I could feel anger rising as I said, 'You don't understand at all.'

'I understand that this is hard for you, but it's hard for Selina too. She's the closest family you've got. You need to see her.'

I yanked an unwashed pair of jeans off the top of the pile of dirty clothes I'd been meaning to take to the laundrette in the basement and slipped into the corridor in my knickers and bra, not caring if anybody saw. I was too angry to be in the same room as Georgia. How could she think that visiting you in London, with a grovelling apology, was the right thing to do? I showered and got dressed in one of the old-fashioned bathrooms that had deep old baths with lion-paw feet.

But Georgia kept on pushing, so in the end, I dropped you a note and got on a train.

All through the journey to London I felt dread. I shouldn't have allowed myself to be talked into seeing you again. I stared out of the window. I didn't want to discuss my life in Manchester and I didn't want to hear about your new life either. I wondered what we would find to talk about. We were separate now but I feared that once I saw you, we would be joined once more.

You were waiting impatiently at Euston station. I hardly recognised you. You were pathetically thin and your spherical Afro made your face look small – I felt as if I towered over you. You tried to hug me but I couldn't hug you back. I was full of resentment; I felt as if you'd gone whining to Georgia – even though you didn't know of her existence – and had got her to force me to visit you, to make things right for you again.

We caught a bus to the edges of London. As we walked through the college grounds, pretty and neat, I was relieved I hadn't opted to be there with you. The campus was too enclosed for me, too parochial.

We had lunch in a bar that served everything with baked beans in a thin tomato sauce. I paid for both of us, as if this would make up for all the anger I still stored. I knew I should have been able to put it aside but I couldn't; there was something sustaining about it, something that made me feel stronger. Stronger in myself, or stronger than you? I no longer knew. You barely touched your sausages. You kept chatting about nothing, though you made sure I knew you liked boys – there was a student called Martin you were interested in. Anything to emphasise that in this respect, at least, we weren't the same – you were normal. I could have told you about Georgia but I didn't want to share her, and certainly not while you were wittering on about Martin with such superiority. You might have been nasty about her, accused us of sin. Or, worse still, you might have given us your blessing. What would I have done then? I might have felt obliged to forgive you.

We went to your room. It was bigger than mine, with a huge window. The glass was streaked with grime. The sun was getting in our eyes; you half-closed the blinds. I took off my denim jacket – the room was stifling hot – and sat on your bed.

A female student appeared, dark-haired, dressed in the obligatory jeans and desert boots. You introduced her as Judith. You mentioned somebody else called Fran, just to make sure I knew you had friends, and that I was replaceable.

Early that evening, we returned to Euston station on the bus, talking superficially about your course or mine. Just before my train arrived, you told me how much you'd missed me in the secret words we'd once used with one another. You were staking a claim on me, urging me to stay, standing in front of me, barring my escape. As you leaned in to hug me, I shoved you aside and boarded the train back to Manchester.

SELINA

Zora finally phones, saying she is coming to visit. I'd given up hope of this. I scarcely sleep for days, I'm too excited. At the station, I hug her until she is hardly able to breathe. But there is no reciprocal embrace; her hands remain at her side. We are mostly silent on the bus to college and we sit in the campus café like strangers, struggling to speak. We get salad and slices of cake for lunch, and although the meal is expensive, I treat us both, in the hope that Zora will know this is a kind of peace offering. It's a lot more edible than most of the meals we get in halls but I still struggle to finish it.

We don't look the same anymore. Zora has put on a little weight whereas I have lost a bit. I've let my hair grow into an Afro, Angela Davis style, but Zora has had hers cut. Her tight curls look sleek, making the contours of her face more pronounced. I am wearing purple trousers and a cream, cheesecloth top. She is wearing a deep pink dress that falls mid-thigh, a corduroy, rust-coloured jacket and baseball boots. We are recognisable as sisters, I suppose, but all our joinedness has disappeared.

'It's good that you came,' I say to her. 'Did you get the jumper I sent for Christmas?'

'Yes, thanks,' she answers. I want her to tell me that she liked it, that she knew how much thought went into choosing it for her, but she doesn't say anything more. I sent a card to thank her for the book – Ralph Ellison's *Invisible Man* – but I tell her once more how much it meant to me. I hope she doesn't want to discuss it, though – I haven't actually read it yet. I couldn't face feeling close to her, yet so distant too, as I turned the pages.

I tell her I've made a couple of friends. Fran is in my tutor group. She's very clever, I think. And there's also Judith, who likes the same books I like, though she's doing a different course. She has a boyfriend in the art department. I wouldn't mind a boyfriend too, I say to Zora. There's someone called Martin who seems interested in getting together with me.

Zora doesn't say anything back and she doesn't tell me if there's anyone she feels close to. In a way I'm glad. She might have replaced me with somebody and if that's the case, I don't really want to know about it. We walk through the college grounds and I show her my room, with the posters I got from Athena. I've put them up in the hope that they will help me to feel more at home. There is a Hobbit poster and a map of Middle-earth. I've also put up a poster from the *Easy Rider* film, in case *The Hobbit* seems too childish for a student. Zora wrinkles her nose as she looks at them. I ask what she's put on her own wall, but she doesn't reply. I want her to have put up the pictures of twins she used to collect when we were young. She made a collage and hung it right across our bedroom wall, a kind of homage to our closeness. I used to love looking at it.

'I found something in the college library,' I say to her. I take my suitcase down from the top of the wardrobe and I pass her a book. On the cover there is a photograph of two black women, both the same, in identical ankle-length frocks and boots. They are joined at the hip.

'They were conjoined twins, from America,' I say to Zora. 'This book is all about them. They were called Millie-Christine. They're just like us. I didn't even know they existed.' I can't keep the excitement from my voice. I look at Zora. I thought she would be elated, I thought she would know how important this is, but she barely looks at me or the book and she says nothing.

'Do you remember when we used to go to the library to try to find a book like this?'

She doesn't answer.

'Do you remember *Little Black Sambo*? I buried it in the garden of that old house. You were so scared of him. When I got rid of that book, it was like a weight had been lifted from you.'

'*Little Black Sambo*? What are you talking about?' she says.

It is as if she has blasted a hole in me. I can't speak at first, but after a while, I say, almost in a whisper, 'The book, you hated it, it made you scared, so I buried it. You must remember?'

'No,' she answers, 'I don't remember that at all.'

We walk to the bus stop in silence.

Without Zora is no future.

In bed, when everyone else is asleep, I find the Valium the campus doctor gave me for anxiety and I shove handfuls into my mouth. I miss Cal so much. I miss Zora with all my heart.

Thirty

Selina

'How's your eye?' says Lydia.

I put my hand to my face. It's sore.

'I didn't know Penny was coming round, she just turned up. I wouldn't have let her in if I'd known she was going to react like that. She's been a bit unhinged since Adam . . . well, you know. Anyway, I should have realised it wasn't a good idea to let her in while you were here.'

Penny? Who's Penny? I'm not sure what she means.

We're in Lydia's apartment. I think I recognise it – I think I've been here before but I can't keep up. Lydia has moved so many times – it must be something to do with all the different husbands. She probably moves each time she marries and moves out again once she gets the divorce. We sit in her living room. It's modern. The space is huge and open-plan – barren and cold. A window that turns into sliding doors fills the wall and looks onto a well-kept . . . area with grass . . . a place to sit in. She lives on the ground floor. 'I'm not as mobile as I used to be,' she says, though she seems more agile than I am.

She sits on a large, white sofa and uses a ... control thing to turn on the big television.

'Do you remember when we used to have to get up and use actual knobs to change the channels?' I ask.

'And there were only three channels to choose from. And no internet, of course. My grandchildren can't conceive of a world without "socials". For them everything revolves around showing pictures of whatever you ate for dinner to the entire world.' She laughs and speaks into something. The blinds slowly assume the closed position, shutting out the sunlight. She speaks again and they reopen. 'All mod cons. The estate agent seemed to think this was a selling point. I'm not so sure. If that bloody thing breaks [she points to some kind of speaker] everything falls apart. And God help me if the Wi-Fi goes down,' she adds, pretending to find the possessions she has more of a nuisance than anything else.

I've lost track of the conversation somewhere along the line. Today, I'm having trouble keeping up; so I just nod, as if I'm absorbing everything she says.

There is little colour in Lydia's apartment, apart from large, abstract ornaments made of green, red and purple glass – a bit like statues. They are thrown into sharp relief by the ... emptiness? ... of their surroundings.

The sun shines through the very long windows, causing the glass statues to glisten as they reflect the light. I walk across to the shelves and touch them with my fingertips. They are so smooth and tactile.

'Adrian insisted on those,' Lydia says.

Who is Adrian? I want to ask.

'He said he needed something colourful. They're not my choice. I think they're rather ugly.'

But Lydia has never accommodated anything she didn't secretly like.

'I met Adrian at a New Year's party in New York. It wasn't exactly love at first sight. I found him rather annoying at first.'

She doesn't explain how this perception altered.

'Do you remember that New Year's party we all went to when we were young? It was when I was going out with Cal – one of his friends organised it. What was his name? Anyway, it was absolutely dreadful but I suppose we were all too young to care.'

'No, I don't remember,' I reply, though I do remember it. Joe. That was the name of Cal's friend. The party was at his house. I don't remember it being dreadful though. I remember enjoying it a lot. I felt so grown-up. I don't think I've ever felt quite so grown-up since.

'Would you like the heating on?' says Lydia. 'You look cold.'

Am I shivering? I'm not feeling cold. But I'm not feeling comfortable either, here in Lydia's apartment. It's so spotless and shiny, not lived in. I prefer homes that have a lived-in feel.

I've never felt at home on the college campus. The buildings are stark and modern. Soulless.

It's after midday when I wake up. In the bleakness of my room I realise that the pills haven't had the effect I was expecting. I have a fuzzy head and a strange, bitter taste in my mouth. I'm exhausted too, but that's all. I think of Cal. I think of Mum and Dad. I think of Zora. Last night the hopelessness of everything, the need to find a solution, had seemed so clear. But now, to have acted on it seems cruel and selfish. What if I had died? How would my family have coped with another loss? God has intervened and I have been saved for a higher purpose. But the thought leaves me almost at once. I don't believe in God anymore. I wasn't saved by his hand; I was saved by the fact that I didn't take enough tablets. My knowledge of medicine simply wasn't good enough.

I crawl out of bed, knowing I have to learn to live alone, away from Zora. I have to do it, however hard it is, I have no choice. I still feel numb with hurt but that's all right. It's the pain that's hard; numbness is bearable. I realise this is how I will cope. I will make myself numb whenever I think of Zora and whenever I see her or speak to her. It will be hard, but being hurt all the time is harder. I take a shower. I comb my hair and put on some clean clothes. I have to make this work. I have to find a way of being by myself. I pick up my camera and take pictures of my room. One of my bed, two of the desk and the matching chair. I even take a photograph of the overhead strip light that flickers manically most of the time. I couldn't do it before. I didn't want a record of this. I didn't want to let myself know that living here without Zora was permanent. But it is permanent. The photographs are evidence of that. Photographs capture points in time, making everything permanent, even though they're just reflections of the thing and not the thing itself. They tell a kind of truth. Or maybe because they are simply a snapshot, a part and not the whole, they are as much a distortion as everything else. The thought has me feeling scared again. I put my camera back in its case.

I should eat but I can't face it. I'm a little dizzy and I look like death. Someone will notice if I leave my room now. I could end up being taken to hospital like my father, so I have to be careful. But tomorrow I will go to the dining room and I will eat a full meal. I will make myself read. I will start to write an essay. I will take more photographs. One day soon, I will learn to develop them myself. We are not Selzora anymore, so I must learn to be Selina.

'Selina, hello, how are you?'

A man comes into the room. He is shorter than Lydia and of stocky build. He looks quite affable, rather like the dog we got for Harriet ... what breed was it? Long ears. Short tail.

We asked the breeder not to get the tail ... chopped. It seems too cruel. But he goes ahead anyway and the dog is delivered with a stump where its tail should be. Harriet cries. She keeps asking if it is hurting, as if the dog is going to tell her. I know the training will fall to me and I'm anxious about it. I'll have to do things with it, take it for walks, and I've never liked dogs. I'm just hoping this one is as soppy as it looks.

Maybe it's not his looks that make the man seem more canine than human. Maybe it is to do with the enthusiasm he shows as he bounds into the room, seeming far more youthful than his years. He must be Lydia's husband. He gives her a kiss on the cheek and asks how she is. He sounds concerned, and once again, I wonder if she's ill.

They don't seem well suited. Lydia is so cool by

comparison, so distant, and he is so full of eagerness. I worry, as he bounces round the room, unable to sit down or relax, that he will break one of the large, glass ornaments.

I wait for Lydia to introduce us but she doesn't, and he speaks to me as if we've met before. Perhaps we have. Is it getting worse, this forgetfulness? Lydia's husband does another bounce and perches on the arm of the chair. He says something and she looks at him absently, seeming slightly impatient. Does Lydia's husband know she has a daughter, born while she was still in her teens? Does he know that Harriet's father, our brother, died many years ago when we weren't even adults? Does he wonder about our friendship and how it came to be? Does he know my memory isn't what it was? Has Lydia explained it to him? Is his name Michael or is it something else? Should I be careful not to give the past away or is it not a secret? I keep my mouth closed. It's safer, I expect.

'Michael didn't know about Harriet when we got married,' says Lydia. 'I didn't mean it to be a secret, I just never got round to telling him. He was so angry when he found out. When are men going to stop behaving as if this is the nineteenth century and every woman worth her salt is still a virgin? Jesus Christ, it's not as if men are ever virgins when they get married, is it? Why is there one rule for them and another one for us?'

Lydia seems irritated by her husband. She tells him to go and have a shower. He has been for a run and he is still wearing a tracksuit. He has headphones on; he is bouncing to the beat.

As he leaves the room, Lydia lights a cigarette. She sighs. 'Adrian doesn't stop from the time he gets up until he goes to bed. He goes out like a light until morning and then he's up again at dawn. It's like living with a toddler.'

Lydia isn't good with toddlers. She has a habit of abandoning them.

PART FIVE

THIRTY-ONE

SELINA

Lydia is on my doorstep with a child – *Harriet*. No warning, they are just here. I must have given Lydia my new address, but I don't remember doing it. Did I scribble it on the last postcard I sent, the one that said I'd passed year one of college?

'Can we come in?' asks Lydia.

I can't stop staring at Harriet: two years old, beautiful, with dark hair touching her shoulders. Neat and graceful, like Lydia. And I see, with a mixture of sadness and joy, that she also has the look of Cal.

I am so pleased to see Harriet at last. I take her in my arms, holding her tight. I give her my old teddy bear, the one I've had since I was small. Zora has one just the same. She hugs him to her chest. How like Cal she looks.

I make egg sandwiches for lunch that Lydia doesn't eat. She doesn't look well. Why are they here? The question keeps popping into my head. Why are they here after all this time?

There is a park nearby. We take Harriet to the swings. I've brought my camera. I capture her smile as she comes down the baby slide. We sit on the edge of the sandpit, our sandalled feet resting on its surface. It's hot, the sand is too hot. I lift Harriet out and onto my lap in case it burns her.

'I never thought you and Zora would ever live apart,' says Lydia. 'What happened?'

'I didn't get the grades for Manchester.'

'I know, but—'

I cut in and say, 'I had sex with somebody. I lost my virginity.' I keep my voice low, in case Harriet might somehow understand if she hears. In telling Lydia this, I'm letting her know that I'm as much an adult as she is – as much as Zora is. And I'm saying I can lead a separate life, one without Zora at its centre.

'Male or female?' Lydia asks.

'Why would you think it was a female?'

'Why not?' she replies with a mocking smile.

I just say, 'His name was Martin. We broke up soon after.'

'Welcome to the world of grown-ups,' Lydia answers. There is bitterness in her voice.

We both fall silent. Lydia scoops up handfuls of sand and scatters them distractedly. Her nails look bitten. Then she says, 'The Robinsons have gone away. They've gone to India to find themselves. Of course they have. They're such stereotypes. I'm all on my own. I can't stay in that big house with her, on my own. Will you do me a favour? Will you look after Harriet until this evening? I need to see my father. He and Joyce have split up. Now they're not together, I'm sure I can persuade him to let me come home again, but it will be a lot easier if I don't have to take her with me.'

It's just for a day and I'll get to know Harriet better, so of course I say yes. I can't believe she's here at last.

But I soon find out that I don't have the knack with toddlers. Nappies and safety pins defeat me. I'm not sure what they like to eat. Harriet won't take anything I try to feed her. She wants her mother. She starts to scream. The sound is so piercing, so full of distress, and she won't be quiet. She is turning blue with anger and fright and the pain of missing her mother. Evening turns to night, but Lydia hasn't returned. I fall asleep with Harriet in my arms an hour or two before dawn.

Thirty-two

Zora

Georgia came into the bedroom and said, 'That was your sister on the phone again. She's desperate for you to ring her. Why won't you return her call?'

I rolled onto my stomach so Georgia couldn't see my face. 'I don't want to speak to her,' I said in a low voice.

Georgia slipped back into bed. She tapped my shoulder until I turned to face her again. 'She said it's urgent. I could hear her crying down the phone.'

'She's always crying. She thinks it gets her what she wants.' I didn't believe this, but I wanted Georgia to stop pressuring me to speak to you. I knew you weren't ringing me persistently for no good reason – something was wrong. It couldn't be about Mum or Dad, I'd spoken to them on the phone earlier, so it was some crisis that was only affecting you.

I sat up and started to get out of bed. It was almost eleven, and although I enjoyed late mornings, I always felt lazy and rather restless; eventually it became easier just to get up. 'You don't know what she's like,' I said as I left to go to the bathroom.

I remembered the last time Georgia had persuaded me to resume ties with you and that painful afternoon we'd spent together on your college campus. I'd tried to deal with the hurt of seeing you again and wishing I could stay – yet at the same time being terrified of doing so – by pushing you away more ferociously than ever and I'd been angry with myself for not handling it better. I didn't want to feel like that again; it was easier to resist all contact with you. I had a life in Manchester with Georgia.

Now that we were about to start our second year of studies, we lived together on the top floor of a terraced house not far from the university; it was self-contained so we had our own kitchen and bathroom, a luxury we relished. On hot summer days, we'd put two fold-up chairs in our tiny front garden to sunbathe and people-watch. I did some reading in preparation for next term while Georgia listened to the radio through an earpiece so as not to disturb me, but the music leaked a little as she rocked to her favourite reggae songs. Traffic thundered by, causing me to wonder if Georgia regretted not going home to the farm for the summer holidays where there was only the sound of animals and the occasional rumble of farm machinery to disturb the peace. 'I like it here,' she replied simply, and I knew that it was true. Georgia had a greater capacity for contentment than anyone I'd ever met.

I was starting to realise that I couldn't be truly contented without you – or with you either. Your phone calls were worrying me, just as they were worrying Georgia. I couldn't put off ringing you for ever. I got dressed and went downstairs to make the call.

You were frantic, almost incoherent: something to do with Lydia.

I used the despised words of our childhood, our secret language, to get you calm again. You fell silent for a moment. When you spoke once more, I understood; Lydia had visited you and she had left Harriet behind.

I couldn't take it in at first. She'd abandoned her own child? She'd left her for you to look after, not just for a day or a week, but for ever – or at least until she changed her mind again and returned to reclaim her? I was shouting. Georgia came running downstairs. I explained what had happened, saying I had to return to London. I went to pack a bag.

Georgia followed me into the bedroom. 'I was wrong last time,' she said.

'Wrong about what?'

'I was wrong when I told you visiting your sister was the right thing to do. I know you said you enjoyed seeing her again and that you had a good time, but something wasn't right; you were even more depressed when you got back and it lasted days and days. Do you really have to go to London again?'

'You were the one who made me return Selina's call.'

'I thought there would be some middle ground, something between ignoring her and rushing off to London to be with her,' Georgia replied mildly.

I knew she didn't get it. There was no middle ground with you and me; it was always all or nothing. But I just said, 'Selina won't manage a toddler on her own. There's nothing else I can do. I have to go to sort this out. I won't stay long.'

Georgia didn't reply. She stared at me thoughtfully for a moment and then she found my purse and keys and handed them to me. She also put a couple of books in my case so I could study while I was away.

'I'll phone you every night,' I promised.

As I travelled to the outskirts of London, I struggled to sit still. The closer I got to you, the more agitated I became. Suburbia: dull, tree-lined streets, quiet and respectable, a far cry from Manchester. I was shivering – whether from apprehension or the draught on the bus, I wasn't sure. I was wearing a thin, summer dress but the day was cold. I would end up having to borrow your warm clothes, something I would mind; we would start merging together again.

You held me tight as I stood on your doorstep.

'Where's Harriet?' I asked, releasing myself from your grasp.

'Upstairs.'

Your housemate, Fran, came out of her room to say a brief hello as I approached the staircase. I could tell from her stare that you had told her all about me; she was measuring our likeness to one another the way strangers always did.

Harriet was in a playpen, gripping the bars like a character from *Birdman of Alcatraz*. You hovered anxiously. You didn't know what to say. We hadn't spoken properly for so long that you were tongue-tied. 'I'm sorry,' you muttered eventually.

I nodded but I said nothing. Should I say sorry too? For what? For telling Cal about me and Lydia? For going to Manchester without you? For living with Georgia?

I kept staring at Harriet. She was a striking child. When she stared back at me, she had the look of Cal, but as she turned and gazed round the room, hoping to see Lydia, I realised how much she resembled her mother.

'She's hardly stopped screaming,' you said shakily. 'I don't know what to do with her. How long can you stay?'

'I don't know,' I replied. I pictured us sharing a bedroom, the two of us lying top to toe in your single bed, Harriet in a cot beside us. I would struggle to breathe in such closeness.

You took a letter from the pocket of your jeans. 'It's from Lydia,' you said, your voice still tremulous. 'It came a couple of days after she left Harriet.'

I read it slowly:

Dear Selina,

I've tried to cope with her on my own but I've finally stopped being able to. Cal and I were going to get married. When he died, perhaps I should have had an abortion but it was his child I was carrying, the last link to him, and I couldn't bring myself to go through with it. My father is living in America now. He said I could only be with him without Harriet, so I have to let her go. I am flying out to America in a few hours to join him. I can't cope anymore. I wish I could but it's too hard, I am so lonely, so unhappy these days. You don't know what it's like to be on your own, you've always had Zora. I've always envied you both, having each other the way you do, always somebody there for you. I know you will patch things up, you are too close to be apart for too long. I thought of putting her into care but those places are awful and a mixed race child might not get adopted I'm told. I know you will look after her, for Cal's sake, we all owe it to his memory to make sure Harriet is happy. You will probably be angry with me but I'm afraid something terrible will happen if I try to keep going. The trial made everything impossible, I've struggled so much since then, it brought all the awfulness back and I miss Cal so much. Don't let her forget about me completely. I know she will miss me at first but I'm no good for her. I am enclosing a copy of her birth certificate and a formal letter that names you as her guardian. Pa said you would need those things. There is also a bit of money for nappies etc.

Love, Lydia

'She isn't coming back, is she?' you said, sounding distraught again.

'No,' I replied as I finished reading. 'And she really didn't tell you she was going away and leaving Harriet?'

'Of course not. I never expected her not to come back.'

'Bloody bitch!' My voice was hoarse, full of anger. I couldn't believe Lydia had abandoned her own child.

As she gripped the bars of her playpen, Harriet began to wail. You went rigid. I could see why her cries disturbed you so much. They were high-pitched and full of anguish, as if she knew that both her parents had gone.

You lifted her out of the playpen and said, 'I had a holiday job but I couldn't do my shifts anymore because I couldn't leave her. They sacked me. My money will run out soon. I won't even be able to afford to feed her. And what's going to happen once the other students get here? What are we going to do?'

'I don't know,' I answered, as calmly as I could. I was just as worried as you but I was trying not to show it. If both of us panicked, we wouldn't be able to deal with any of it.

I chose the largest of the empty rooms to sleep in. I knew we would have to sort things out before the other students arrived or I'd end up living there with you and Harriet, impossible for all of us.

'Are you going to stay here with her or try to find somewhere bigger?' I asked as I laid out my spare underwear in an empty chest of drawers.

You sighed and said, 'Term hasn't started yet,' evading the question.

We evaded questions for the rest of the week, not daring to reach the point where decisions had to be made. I took Harriet for as many walks in the nearby park as I could, just to have time away from you. The weather had changed; it was now unseasonably hot, so I let Harriet paddle in a small, concrete pool, watching her kick the water to see it splash over me and laughing uncontrollably when I became soaked. We sat in the sun and I told her stories. I sung bits of nursery rhymes I only partly remembered from childhood. As she turned to watch the ducks on the pond, I swallowed an out-of-date tablet of Valium from the box I'd found in your bedroom. A few yards away, a homeless woman on a bench was injecting heroin into her arm with far more openness but only a little more desperation than I was feeling.

You and I fell into a pattern of semi-separation and I was relieved. I phoned Georgia each evening as promised. I needed to stay connected to the life I had in Manchester.

In the kitchen, eight days after my arrival, we tried to make plans. The other students would be arriving shortly and I needed to get back to university for the start of the new term. 'I'll come down as often as I can,' I said. 'Fran will help too.'

Fran and I had got on. She had come to the rescue early in the crisis, phoning her mother and getting her to drive to the house with a playpen, a highchair and other items that the youngest child in their family had now outgrown. Without these, we would have struggled far more. Fran had cooked for us most evenings – even though she worked in Woolworths throughout vacation time – trying to make things easier. I knew she would continue to be a support for you.

You looked at me, your face contorted with despair. 'What am I going to do? How can I study with Harriet here? I can't take her to college with me.'

'Maybe you could get a childminder?'

'How am I going to afford one of those?'

Harriet started banging the tray on her highchair with a spoon. 'Stop it!' you snapped. Harriet continued, the repetitive beat getting louder. 'Stop it! Harriet, stop it!' you screamed. You tried to wrest the spoon from her grasp but she was gripping it so tightly that you couldn't take it from her. I shoved you aside, afraid that you would hurt her. 'Don't, Selina,' I said.

'It's the noise. It doesn't stop. Just noise all the time no matter what I do. I can't bear it.' You sat down again, covering your face with your hands. 'I just can't bear it,' you repeated. 'But she's Cal's daughter.'

And in that moment I knew I wouldn't be able to leave.

SELINA

I've made macaroni cheese with cauliflower and ham, Cal's favourite meal. Harriet doesn't seem to like it. She plays with it, it's all down her front. Another change of clothes, then. Thank God Fran's mum has given us Jonathan's old outfits.

It will be impossible for me to manage both Harriet and college, that's obvious. I'm exhausted. Zora takes Harriet for walks to be away from me but she does none of the grind, the washing or the cleaning.

Harriet starts banging the front of her highchair with a spoon. I hold in my irritation. She is missing her mother; she is bound to play up. Zora grabs the spoon from Harriet. I start to laugh with a kind of hysterical relief as the noise ceases. Then Zora suddenly says she's staying. I'm so pleased. Or at least, I think I am. I really want her to stay, but I know Zora. She will mind being here and she will take out her resentment on me. I say this to her and she says of course she won't. She tells me I'm being ungrateful and self-centred, as if she is staying for me, not Harriet. As if I should be beholden to her for choosing to be here rather than in Manchester. I tell her to go back to Manchester, then, if that's what she thinks. But she is determined to stay, in spite of Georgia, her secret girlfriend, the one she thinks I don't know about.

It will be easier to manage if there are two of us. I might even get to remain at college. But now that she feels she has to stay, there will be constant tension between Zora and me and it will only get worse as time passes.

I turn my numbness up a notch.

Thirty-three

Selina

In the long living room, shiny glass statues refract red, green and purple light in stripes across my shirt.

'Why did you abandon Harriet?' I say to Lydia, who is sitting on a white sofa, reading a book.

She looks up at me and says, with irritation, 'I didn't abandon her. I left her with you, which was the best thing for her.'

Lydia is very good at convicting herself – and others – that all her decisions were good ones. I am determined not to let her. 'You abandoned Harriet. We brought her up with very little money while you lived it up in America. Have you any idea how much she missed you?'

We are not sure what to be more scared of – that Lydia will return and take Harriet away from us and we'll never see her again, or that Lydia won't come back and we'll be dealing with this forever.

We find a flat to rent where it's just me, Zora and Harriet, but it's small and we are living on top of one another, which Zora hates. 'We are not giving up our studies,' she says, repeatedly and insistently. She transfers to King's College London and begins her second year of English there instead of Manchester. I start term at my teacher-training college later than the other students – sorting out everything to do with Harriet has taken so much time. But at least I haven't had to drop out. No one seems to notice I've come back late. I do worry though, that because of looking after Harriet, I won't be able to keep up.

We use a large portion of our student grant to pay Fran's mother for a bit of childcare. Mum and Dad help out with money when they can. The rest of the time, we take it in turns to mind Harriet. We are both exhausted. Zora is snappy and miserable. I try not to snap back; it will only make her more irritable. What if we can't study and look after Harriet at the same time? What if the money runs out?

I am tired of worrying but I can't seem to stop. Worry is keeping me awake at night. Worry and Harriet. She doesn't sleep. She screams for much of the night. While Zora is dead to the world, I get up; I take Harriet in my arms and try to settle her. It must be hard for her, living in an alien flat with people who are unfamiliar. We are related – she is Cal's child as much as she is Lydia's – but she doesn't know this. To her, we are strangers.

'We were strangers to Harriet,' I say to Lydia. 'I'd never even met her. And yet you left her with me. Why did you leave her with me rather than Zora?'

Lydia doesn't reply but I know the answer: Zora might have suspected something. She might have refused to look after Harriet and then Lydia would have been unable to escape. I was less likely, back then, to see through her.

Is the way she left Harriet the problem between me and Lydia, the source of the unease I feel whenever I'm around her? I don't think it can be. I remember the time when Harriet was young as the happiest of my life.

I make spag bol. Harriet eats it with relish. The spaghetti goes everywhere; it hangs in strands from her mouth and makes its way down to her feet. There are bits of it in her hair and socks. That night as she is in the bath, and Zora and I are trying to remove it, we are giddy with laughter. It's the first time we have really laughed together since she arrived at the house. As the hilarity comes to an end, we look at one another, aware that something has changed for the better. I feel the blankety warmth I used to feel when I was with Zora and I allow the numbness to fade a little. We are here, together again.

There is a smell, Harriet's smell, that sweet smell small children have when they've just been bathed and put in clean pyjamas ready for bed. I read her a story to help her fall asleep, relishing *Paddington* almost as much as she does. During the day, between reading or writing essays, I watch her playing joyfully in a sandpit or a swimming pool and I feel joy too, the first joy I've felt since Cal's death. I sing nursery rhymes to her and she sings them back tunelessly as we hold hands and skip along the pavement towards Fran's mother's house.

*

'You missed Harriet growing up,' I say to Lydia, as we sit on the large, white sofa. 'You abandoned her. You could have ruined her life for all you knew. It's hard to forgive you for that.'

ZORA

You remembered Harriet's childhood as a time of joy, but it was different for me. I loved being with her, of course I did, but more often than not, I was aware of all the things that were no longer open to me: living and studying in Manchester with Georgia. Being separate from you.

Georgia visited whenever she could, spending every other weekend with me. It was the reason I insisted on having my own room; that and needing time to myself, of course – some element of separation. I didn't spell out the nature of our relationship. If you had shown any sign of disapproval, I would have had to leave, taking Harriet away with me to Manchester, and that would have been the end of us. For both our sakes, it was better to stay silent. There were other things I was silent about: I didn't ask Georgia to remain monogamous and I didn't know if there was someone back in Manchester sharing a bed with her in my absence. I'd decided that I couldn't, in fairness, ask her to invest wholly in a relationship that could only be part-time. So much of my energy was wrapped up in you and Harriet. Taking care of you both was taking everything I had; there was so little left for Georgia. And yet, in her impossibly kind and loving way, she didn't ask anything of me. 'There's no one else, just you,' she told me, without being asked. She saw that I had to stay with you and she never opposed it. I was the one who made the demands in our relationship.

For a while, I hoped Dad would be able to pull himself together, if not for you and me, then for Harriet. The solution would have been simple then; he could have returned to work and Mum could have given up her two jobs to look after their grandchild. We explained the situation to them and waited for them to realise how much we needed them to take over. But nothing happened. Dad failed to relinquish his useless things, he didn't go back to work, and you and I both knew we couldn't let Harriet spend time in a house that was a health hazard. She was a curious child. The unsteady piles of rubbish would have become her playground, and however watchful we tried to be, eventually, they would have toppled down and crushed her, as literally as they had crushed you, me and Mum metaphorically.

Even the brief visits we made to our old home with Harriet were perilous, emotionally as much as physically. It became clear to us that Mum and Dad were determined not to connect with her. They feared loving her and then losing her too much. 'Lydia's capricious,' Mum would say. 'She could return to London and take her back just like that.' She would snap her fingers to convey the risk. And it was a risk, we knew, but what was the alternative? Putting Harriet in care?

You and Georgia seemed to like each other, though whether that would have been sustainable if you'd known she was more than just my friend, I'm not sure. You would see her at the table some Sunday mornings and put bacon and eggs in the frying pan for brunch. You would make pancakes because you'd discovered that she loved them. You would try to converse with her, albeit haltingly and with a lot of shyness. You were very welcoming, in your way.

But being in London again when I'd thought I had escaped was even harder than I expected. We were Selzora again, two made into one. With no effort – on my part, at least – we'd come to look almost identical again. My weight matched yours. Your hair gradually took on the same appearance as mine. Sometimes my sense of being trapped with you and Harriet was so great that I didn't know what to do with myself. I would spend days at a time in bed, unable to do anything, shutting the pair of you out. I knew it was unfair of me to leave you to do all the work when paralysis descended, but I really didn't have a choice.

Eventually I would surface. You never talked to me about it but you gave me endless looks of reproach and you dealt with the washing and the ironing pointedly and with a lot of exaggerated gestures. The sticky, sickly wave of unhappiness, when it descended, was so great that I didn't know how to move from the bed, let alone sort out the household chores. Once, you would have understood that and let me be, but now you stomped around the house, muttering about the way everything always fell to you. You obviously enjoyed the role of martyr. Perhaps it allowed you to feel needed, I don't know. I used to know, instinctively, exactly what was going on with you, but those days were gone now.

I'd had my own life in Manchester and now my life was

shared with you again; everything I ever did ended up being shared with you.

After a few weeks of living on very little money, we found a job in a bar so we could afford more of the things that Harriet needed. I did the interview and told the landlord my name was Selzora.

'Selzora?' he said. 'That's an unusual name, or maybe it's not that unusual where you come from?'

Yes, I thought, there are lots of women in London called Selzora.

We led him to believe there was just one of us, but we shared the shifts between us. The other bar staff must have thought Selzora had a split personality; sometimes she was quiet, but willing to do the most boring tasks without complaining, while at other times she was a lot louder and cantankerous, refusing to do anything that didn't match her job description. Sometimes, she spilt things, but no one minded because she was interesting, and she made people laugh. On the other hand, she could be dull but careful, never getting an order wrong or spilling anything.

Both versions of Selzora got into trouble and each was told off by the landlord: the interesting version was often slap-dash. The dull version didn't interact enough with customers.

At home, we laughed about Selzora and the bar, but I was sick of having to think about you all the time; I was even having to *be* you now. Sometimes I acted shy and withdrawn to put our colleagues off the scent because I couldn't see how they could still believe Selzora was just one person. As I took on your persona, I felt like I was welded to you again, with no possibility of a separate existence. But for Harriet's sake, I knew I had to make the best of it. I owed it to Cal to make it work.

Do you remember the first time Harriet called us Mummy? She was three and I was lifting her from the pushchair when the strap became twisted round her. I held her up while you untangled her. 'Mummy,' she said to both of us. Outwardly, I disapproved, and it hurt to think that being mothers to Harriet was only possible if we denied the existence of Cal, and her relationship to him. But inside, I felt triumphant; she loved us more than anyone else in the world – Lydia had been erased.

Harriet was an observant, thoughtful child, but she often lacked self-control – she was prone to tantrums when we first had her and she was very demanding. Lydia would have been just the same at her age I sometimes thought. When I was trying to study, Harriet kept knocking on my door, wanting to be let in. She didn't seem to understand that I needed to work and couldn't give her my undivided attention. She would promise to sit still and not speak but every now and then she would say, 'I'm being very good and quiet, aren't I, Zora?', which defeated the object. In the end, I told her she had to go and be with you. I picked her up and put her outside my door. She looked shocked and came back in again but I put her outside more firmly. I locked the door behind me this time. She began to cry loudly, which made me yell at her. I shouted, 'Shut the fuck up!', something I regretted as soon as it was out of my mouth. But I needed to work and I was losing concentration. The frustration was driving me crazy.

You were furious. 'You can't treat her like that. She adores
you, but you just shout at her. You're behaving like Lydia,
dumping her when it suits you and expecting me to pick up
the slack. Don't you think that I sometimes need a bit of time
to study? Even when she's ill you do nothing at all to help, you
leave everything to me. It isn't fair. It really isn't fair.'

I tried to make you understand. 'Don't you get it? If we
both fail our exams we'll never be able to have our own house
and make a proper home for her. It's just until I graduate.
Then she can bother me as much as she wants.'

You thought I didn't love Harriet as much as you did. You
thought that because you comforted her at night and cleaned
up after her, I had sacrificed nothing. But I was living with
you, in the suburbs.

Of course I loved Harriet, and she loved me fully during
the early years of her life, the way children often love adults
before they see their flaws. And I did spend time with her,
though you chose not to recall this. I would tell her stories
every night before she went to sleep: tales of Anansi, the ones
our dad used to tell us when we were little, about the tricksy
spider man who schemed his way out of trouble. She loved
listening to those stories and I loved telling them.

Our essays were written (mostly in panic) in the small
hours when our eyelids twitched and all we wanted to do
was sleep. We each wrote about the importance of the child
in *Silas Marner*, though we didn't confer – we laughed a lot
when we realised that, unconsciously, we had both done the
exact same thing. For a while after that, whenever we spoke
of Harriet, we referred to her as Eppie. Our essays on *Heart of*

Darkness and *A Passage to India* (also written without collab-
oration) were a little less astute, our tutors thought. We were
perceived as difficult, potential troublemakers. Why did we
feel the need to bring race into all our papers? The works
of these great authors transcended such discussions; their
truths were universal, we were told.

But all the work paid off; I got my degree with a high 2:1. I
would have liked a first – I'd worked hard for one – but in the
circumstances I counted my blessings. Even you passed – you
got through teaching practice, despite all your fears about
being observed and graded. We celebrated raucously with
wine and slices of pink and white angel cake from Marks
and Spencer's – and lemonade for Harriet – trying not to
remember the day we'd got our college offers. We'd assumed
that Mum and Dad would be as overjoyed with our success
as they'd been with Cal's, but there had been little celebration.
Yes, we'd all had cake, but our parents' congratulations had
been muted, as if our achievements were unimportant compared to those of our brother. Perhaps they'd been afraid of
further disappointment, promise unfulfilled – I don't know.
But I do remember how hurt we were, both of us. I dealt with
it by trying even harder. You dealt with it by hardly trying
at all. Now, as we ate our angel cake, I realised we'd been
too young to see that our success could never have made up
for the loss of Cal, not even a little bit. How could it? It was
the same even now. We phoned Mum and Dad to let them
know we'd got our degrees. Perhaps they were pleased but
we couldn't really tell; they'd stopped being excited by things
the night Cal had died.

I'd resisted the idea that we would do the same job but we both ended up as teachers, me in FE and you at a secondary school a few miles up the road. We could give up the bar work now; we could bury Selzora. Our hours would fit in with Harriet's school days. We would be able to buy a house of our own.

We settled into the routine of work and each discovered we were good at our respective jobs, you teaching unruly teenagers with ease – who would have thought it? – and me, working with adults, and writing a book on Caribbean poetry that would probably never be published. But still, it was more than we'd expected to achieve given all that had happened. You continued to nag. 'I'm the one who always has to take care of Harriet. I do all the work round the house, all the cooking and cleaning. When are you going to do your share?'

It wasn't true. I did my share of the housework most of the time, but you just wouldn't let go of it. Once an idea was in your head, you pursued it obsessively.

Harriet came into my study one day and she said, 'Selina is obsessed with being clean and tidy. You don't mind about things like that. You're a lot more fun.' *Obsessed.* I laughed. How did a five-year-old even know the word? She was so sharp for her years.

Georgia had thought that once you and I were each established in jobs that paid well enough to meet Harriet's needs, I would be moving back to Manchester.

We sat in the local café, where there was no danger of you overhearing, and she told me how much she was looking forward to my return. 'There are lots of FE colleges in and around Manchester,' she said. 'And in Liverpool too. That's not too far to drive.'

'I don't know,' I said, tipping a sachet of brown sugar into my coffee, even though I usually drank it without. I didn't like sweet coffee, but the act of stirring sugar round the cup was soothing.

'You don't want to move away from London, do you?' said Georgia, tilting her chair onto its back legs and looking at me in bewilderment.

It was time to tell her. I knew I wasn't going back to Manchester. I'd known for months. I should have told her sooner. You and I were wired into each other again and even though I'd tried to resist, even though I told myself how trapped I was and that my life was being ruined by our closeness, I couldn't seem to sever the join. I was never going to live with Georgia. Perhaps I feared that if I left you, I would cling to her instead and make her as miserable as I was. Or maybe it was an inability to say goodbye to Harriet. Or perhaps, in reality, it was an inability to say goodbye to you. Georgia knew me, but you knew me best. When I thought of 'Us' or 'We', it was you and me, not me and Georgia who came to mind. We'd shared a womb. Claustrophobic though it was, our closeness was comforting, and I couldn't relinquish it.

Georgia looked so hurt. Three years she'd waited, and now I was saying we were never going to live together.

'I suppose I could come down here to live, get another job . . .' she began, but as she looked at me, she realised that I wasn't just saying that I didn't want to move, I was saying we were over.

She cried, there in the coffee shop, and then she apologised, as if she shouldn't have any feelings, as if somehow what I wanted outweighed her needs. And I suppose a big part of me believed that it did. Or maybe I believed there was no selfishness on my part because I was doing it all for you and Harriet.

It was impossible not to miss Georgia. I missed laughing with her about things we'd read or seen on television. I missed sharing a bed and feeling comforted. I missed our occasional nights out at the dance hall, rocking to a reggae beat. I missed early morning walks when fresh dew soaked our shoes and socks as the sun started to appear above the horizon. I missed feeling calm; Georgia had a stillness about her that had rubbed off on me.

I often awoke before dawn wondering why I had abandoned our relationship. Fear, mostly, but fear of what? Why had I thought that living with you and Harriet would necessitate being single? Georgia would have been happy to have continued weekend visits to London. She would have upped sticks to be there, if necessary, and she would never even have asked if she could move in with us. She would have done everything on my terms and asked for very little in return. Perhaps that was why. I felt trapped by your neediness, and I felt just as trapped by Georgia's refusal to make demands. She was sacrificing herself for me and the responsibility of that was impossible to bear. I didn't want to be beholden to her. I didn't want her to turn to me in five or ten years' time and say that she was leaving because she'd given everything to me and I'd given so little to her. You would never leave me, so it was easier to be with you and Harriet, feeling stifled, feeling overwhelmed but able to blame you for my unhappiness. In my relationship with Georgia, I hadn't been able to blame. The unspoken fault had always been mine, and I had minded that.

Thirty-four

Selina

'You missed Harriet's childhood,' I say to Lydia. She is standing by the long window. The glass statues gleam.

'So you said,' Lydia replies with an edge to her voice. 'Can we move on from this now?'

There is still so much I need to know, so I change the subject, telling her I'm thinking of joining a photography group. 'I've always loved taking photographs.' She gives me a look that says I am stating the obvious. 'I have lots of photos of Harriet when she was little.' I can't resist adding this last part even though I know I shouldn't keep wanting to make Lydia aware of how much she lost when she abandoned Harriet.

There is a photograph of Harriet in the green album, the one that only has pictures of her. She is sitting on the sofa looking sleepy.

Zora is evening teaching, so I allow Harriet to stay up past her bedtime. We snuggle up on the sofa watching television. I've put on the gas fire with the living flame and it glows orange-yellow as we eat the chicken soup I've made. I go and fetch my camera and I take a picture; Harriet looks so contented. She blinks in the flash of light and asks if she can have a chocolate biscuit now that we've finished the soup. 'Mummy Z would let me,' she adds.

Harriet is learning to play us off against each other. I think of Lydia. Perhaps I should nip this in the bud but instead I allow her to fetch a biscuit from the tin.

Her cheeks are pink from the warmth of the fire. She is wearing a fuchsia-coloured dressing gown and slippers with the head of a bear on each foot. She has begun to protest that they are childish – 'after all, I am nine now' – and she has asked for a new pair for Christmas.

'Shall we listen to some music?'

Harriet nods and I put on *Kind of Blue*.

'Your dad loved music, especially jazz. He used to play the trumpet. Your granddad got him one, second-hand.'

'Was he good at it?'

'Not very,' I answer truthfully, remembering the flat, squealing noise the trumpet used to make when Cal was practising. We were all glad when he stopped trying.

'Where's the trumpet now? Maybe I could learn to play it?'

'At your grandparents' house somewhere, I expect.'

'Completely buried, probably,' Harriet replies. 'Granddad likes things better than people.'

'Why do you say that?'

'He only pays attention to things.'

Harriet has realised that she is largely ignored when she goes to her grandparents' house. Like her birth mother, she

isn't accustomed to this; it unsettles her. We don't visit often –
it feels too hazardous. We are squeezed into a small space in
the kitchen between the window and the back door. Every
surface groans with piles of useless things. It's not that Mum
and Dad don't love Harriet. It's more that they can't bear to
see her – she looks too much like Cal. And Zora and I aren't
her mothers, we are only her guardians. Harriet could be
snatched away from us at any moment, and how would they
bear another loss?

'What else did Daddy like?'

'He was a really good swimmer; he enjoyed that.'

'I love swimming too,' says Harriet.

There is a photograph in the green album of Harriet in the
sea; she is smiling broadly, splashes of water rising up around
her. When was this taken? I don't remember taking it.

'I wish I could have some ice cream,' says Harriet, hoping to
charm me with a broad smile.

'You've just had a chocolate biscuit.'

'I still wish it though,' she says, snuggling closer.

'Shall we go to Wandsworth on Saturday?'

Harriet nods enthusiastically.

Cal is buried there. We go every now and then to put flowers on his grave. Zora disapproves, she thinks it's morbid, but
I make it into an outing. Harriet and I go and tell Cal all the
things we've been doing and then we eat ice cream sundaes
in a café in his memory.

'What did my birth mother used to like?' asks Harriet.

Zora and I avoid discussing Lydia, even though we are aware that Harriet needs to know about both her parents. 'I don't really remember,' I reply.

'You do!' says Harriet, looking shocked at a lie she knows to be blatant.

I screw up my face as if I am trying hard to recall Lydia. Then I say, 'She liked shopping. She had exquisite taste, your birth mother.' And an exquisite amount of disposable income.

'I don't remember her,' says Harriet. There is sadness in her voice. 'Why did she leave me? Didn't she want me anymore?'

I've had to explain this to Harriet too many times. She keeps asking, wanting confirmation that she wasn't simply abandoned. I repeat the story Zora made up – not made up, exactly; it was more of an embellishment. 'Your birth mother and Cal were deeply in love. They were going to be married. But then Cal died and your birth mother was so shocked and so very unhappy that she couldn't cope with her life anymore. She was afraid that because she was so ill from grief she wouldn't be able to bring you up properly. She didn't want to lose you but she knew she had to do what was best for you. She loved you so much, and that's why she asked us to look after you. Sometimes people give up the things they love most.'

'Why?' asks Harriet. 'That's stupid.'

She has a point, so I pretend not to hear. After a while, I add, 'She wanted you to have the best possible life. We were Cal's sisters and she knew how much we wanted you to live with us, so she brought you to us.'

'Why hasn't she ever phoned me or written me any letters?'

'She misses you too much. It makes her too sad.' I am losing my way in this. I can feel Harriet's desperate need to believe me but I can also feel her doubt. The story is less plausible now she's older. How can I make it believable yet at the same time convince Harriet that she wasn't abandoned, that she was loved? I'm faltering in the fog of my lies – this story will only get harder to tell as the years pass. I can feel her hurt. Damn Lydia. She must have known it would be like this for Harriet when she left her with us.

Harriet is half-asleep. 'Will my birth mother ever be coming back for me?' she asks, with such longing in her voice.

'What will we do if Lydia returns and wants to take Harriet away from us?' Zora and I say to one another, almost every day, and almost every day we put the question to one side because we can't afford to think about it.

Harriet says, 'I love you and Mummy Z. I want to stay with you forever and ever but . . .'
  'But you'd like to know your birth mother too, is that it?'
  She nods.

Could Lydia possibly come back for Harriet? It's been so long that it doesn't seem likely. Zora and I start to ask each other this question a little less often. But just as we are beginning to feel confident that Harriet will always be with us, Lydia returns.

PART SIX

Thirty-five

Selina

I'm struggling with the weight of a tank of terrapins. I wasn't expecting this so I didn't bring the car. Harriet is swinging her satchel beside me as we make our way home at a snail's pace. Terrapins are strange creatures of neither land nor sea, and small as they are, for no logical reason, I am afraid of them. Every time I have to look at them, I feel nauseous. They are being jolted about in their tank and I'm sure their shells are being battered against its sides, even though I'm carrying them with the utmost care.

'Why on earth did you volunteer for this?' I ask Harriet irritably.

She shrugs and, momentarily, I think of Lydia. 'I just like them,' she tells me. 'Their names are Samson and Delilah. We all chose the names. We had a vote. It's what you do when you live in a democracy, Mrs Dyer says.'

'And do you know what a democracy is?'

'It's a place where you have votes,' Harriet answers, in a tone that suggests I'm being very dense.

'How are we supposed to look after these things?'

'Mrs Dyer said you have to feed them every day and sometimes clean out the tank. She wrote it down. It's only for the holidays. You'll hardly have to do anything.' Harriet rummages in her satchel and pulls out a crumpled piece of paper. 'Here it is,' she says, waving it at me.

'I can't look now,' I reply. I can barely see over the top of the tank and its weight is making my shoulders ache. I put it down with a sigh as we reach the house. This is all I need – something else to take care of.

Harriet is leaping from one foot to another. 'Hurry up, Mummy,' she says as I fumble for my keys. 'I'm bursting for the toilet.'

As soon as I get the front door open, she rushes into the house. I hear her stomping up the stairs. I pick up the tank and try to close the door with my foot but it won't shut. As I kick it harder, a woman appears, pushing her way into the hall behind me.

'Hello, Selina,' she says.

I turn round. *Lydia.* I drop the tank. It doesn't break but water streams out. The terrapins lie in a puddle on the floor.

Harriet comes rushing into the hall. 'Oh no!' she cries. 'They're going to die! Everyone at school will hate me for killing the terrapins!'

'No, they're not going to die,' says Lydia briskly. She sets the tank upright, scoops up the terrapins and puts them back into the half-empty tank. 'There. They'll be fine now.'

'Thank you,' says Harriet. She looks at Lydia curiously and I wait for signs of recognition but there are none. She goes into the living room and turns on the television. The *Sister, Sister* theme tune plays.

'What are you doing here?' I say to Lydia.

'Nice to see you too,' she replies with a tight-lipped smile.

'Zora isn't here,' I answer, as if this will send Lydia away again. What if she has come for Harriet? What if she wants to take her away from us? My voice is unsteady as I add, 'You can't come in, we're very busy at the moment.' It's an absurd response, particularly as Lydia is halfway down the hall and beside me at the kitchen door. She smiles again and sits down, uninvited, at the kitchen table. I put the terrapin tank on the counter next to the cooker and go to wipe up the spilt water.

On my return I see that the kitchen isn't as tidy as I would have liked. Harriet's unwashed breakfast bowl is in the sink. There is half a slice of toast, butter-side down, in the centre of the table, surrounded by crumbs. Washing hangs above us on the Sheila Maid; shirt sleeves flap in the breeze from the window I forgot to close. At least we haven't been burgled. If Zora did her share, life would be a lot easier. She could have cleaned up before she left for work. 'What are you doing here?' I repeat.

Lydia gets out her bag and lights a cigarette. 'My father died,' she says. 'I had to come home.'

I can hardly get the words out, but eventually I say, 'Have you come back for Harriet?'

Lydia shakes her head. 'I just wanted to see her, that's all.'

'How did you know where to find us?'

'You're in the phone book,' she says, looking at me as if I'm stupid.

Of course we are: Selzora Bunting. It's easiest.

'You never wrote,' I say to her in a low voice in case Harriet overhears above the sound of the television. 'You never got in touch with her – or us. How could you just leave your own daughter and not look back?'

'I knew you and Zora would take good care of her,' Lydia replies.

We look at one another. She tries to stare me out. Once, she would have managed it, but I am stronger now. She looks away first.

I thought I would be angry if I ever saw Lydia again. I thought I would scream and shout at her for messing up our lives. Sometimes, in my fantasies, I hit her – hard. But most of the anger dissipated a long time ago, because if she had stayed, Zora and I would not have Harriet.

'Is it all right if I get a biscuit?' asks Harriet, appearing behind me.

'This is Lydia,' I tell her hastily, not wanting to give Lydia the chance to introduce herself. 'She's an old friend.' We've always referred to Lydia as 'your birth mother' when we've spoken of her to Harriet, never using her first name. I'm glad about that now.

'Hi,' says Harriet.

'Hello,' Lydia replies. 'You must be ten,' she adds, staring hard at the child she last saw when she was two years old. She is picturing her then and comparing that little Harriet with the one in front of her now, weighing up the changes. Perhaps she regrets the decision she made – perhaps that's why she's here. I am bubbling with fear.

'I was ten last month,' Harriet answers, not questioning how Lydia knows this; she has the solipsistic belief most children have, that adults somehow know all about them without being told.

'Did you have a nice birthday?'

'Yes, thank you. I had a party and I got lots of presents. Mummy S took loads of pictures.'

'I'd like to see them,' says Lydia. Does her voice carry a touch of wistfulness?

Harriet gets up to fetch them.

'Not now,' I tell her hastily. 'I'm not sure where they are.'

'I know where,' Harriet replies, pleased to think she knows something I don't.

'Not now,' I snap.

Harriet looks at me in surprise but she sits back down again. 'My mummies gave me a typewriter for my birthday,' she confides to Lydia. 'I'm writing my own book on it.'

'Are you?' says Lydia, giving her another appraising look.

'I'm going to be a writer when I grow up.' Harriet turns to me. 'Can I have a biscuit, please?' she says again. 'I'm starving.'

'Why don't I take you both out? We can go for a Chinese, or burgers – whatever you fancy,' says Lydia.

Harriet looks thrilled. '*Can we?*' she says to me, her eyes full of hope.

Zora isn't back yet. We can't go without her. 'We need to wait for Zora,' I reply. 'She's doing a PhD. She's working on that today.'

'A doctorate?' says Lydia. Does she actually look impressed?

'Zora's studying part-time as well as teaching. She has a meeting this afternoon with her supervisor.'

'But we can't wait for Mummy Z, she always takes ages to come home. Please, I'm *starving*,' says Harriet.

'Me too,' adds Lydia.

I picture Zora coming home to find Lydia sitting at our kitchen table as if she has just dropped in for a chat and there hasn't been a gap of eight years. I hear her swearing at Lydia. I imagine Harriet listening intently, trying to work out what's going on and why the conversation between the adults is becoming so heated. She will deduce that it has something to do with her. She will be alight with curiosity. Perhaps a meal in a restaurant would be a better option.

'Okay, let's go, then,' I tell them.

Harriet squeals with delight.

In a Chinese restaurant, we order dishes I've never even heard of: duck rolled up in a pancake with a sweet sauce, and chow mein, which turns out to be chicken with cashew nuts and noodles. Harriet says that sweet and sour pork is the best thing she has ever tasted. Lydia picks at the food on her plate, despite saying she was starving. She's ordered some sort of squid.

I get a takeaway for Harriet and me when she comes round. She loves Chinese food. There's something I need to tell her, and I'm hoping her favourite meal will soften the blow.

Harriet cries over her sweet and sour pork as I tell her the diagnosis. I keep trying to reassure her. 'I could never forget you,' I keep saying. But perhaps that isn't true. I believe I'll have some measure of control over this illness, but maybe I won't. Maybe there will be no choice with regard to the things I'm going to forget and the things I'll manage to remember. I fall silent as I consider this. Then I blurt out, 'The truth is, I'm a bit worried that I'm going to forget all the good things and only remember the bad ones once this illness progresses.'

'On the other hand,' she replies, drying her eyes, 'you might forget all the bad things and only remember the good.'

Harriet can always make me laugh. We both laugh, almost to the point of hysterics. It relieves the tension. We have to laugh about this illness, make it seem smaller.

'Do you ever see Lydia?' I ask as the laughter fades. Something in talking about the good and the bad has prompted the question.

'No,' Harriet replies. 'You know I don't see her. I haven't wanted to be anywhere near her since that night she came round.'

'Why haven't you wanted to see her?' If Harriet can tell me, I won't need to keep visiting Lydia to find out the answer.

But Harriet is angry. 'How can you even ask that?' she says, and then, remembering my illness, perhaps, she says she is sorry for snapping.

I take her hand. I understand why she was angry at the question. She believes I know why she and Lydia no longer speak, and that in asking I'm implying she shouldn't have broken contact. I fall silent again. I don't want to admit that I no longer remember. I don't want Harriet to know how far this illness has crept up on me, it will only worry her. I pile another helping of sweet and sour pork onto her plate, hoping that the distraction will cause her to forget I asked.

The food is good but I'm struggling to swallow, knowing that there is a reason for Lydia's appearance after all these years. She wants something. It's more than likely she wants Harriet. I can't imagine being without her. What will we do if she is taken away from us? I try to stifle the fear but the future keeps rushing towards me, a blank future without a daughter in it.

I try to control my anxiety as Harriet eats. The future keeps rushing towards me, a blank future, the kind I dread most. Is that how this illness goes? Will there be fragments of memory, or just blankness once it takes hold?

If I forget Harriet, it will be a future without a daughter in it.

Lydia picks up her chopsticks and puts the seafood into her mouth. She chews daintily. I look at Harriet. She is chewing daintily too, the mirror image of her birth mother. Lydia is bound to try to take Harriet away from us, but I can't ask what she's planning with Harriet sitting beside me and watching us so closely. I should have thought of this. I should have said we'd eat at home. Then it might have been possible to find out why Lydia has come. I pick up a glass of wine and realise my hand is shaking. Has Lydia seen it? Does she know why I'm so afraid? I feel tears starting to form.

*

I start to cry silently as Harriet and I eat sweet and sour pork. What if I forget her? What then? She puts her arms around me and we cry together.

I am crying as I sit in the restaurant. I say I've just bitten into a chilli by mistake. Lydia looks at me with scepticism. I put on a laugh to prove to Harriet that nothing is wrong. She mustn't see how unnerved I am by Lydia's visit. We will be home again soon. Once Harriet has gone to bed, I'll find out why Lydia is here.

The house is in darkness when we return from the restaurant. Lydia wants to see Zora, but she still isn't home. She's probably gone to the pub with some of the other post-grad students. She needs to have a life away from me, she often says. Does she know how hurtful she can be?

Lydia is out to win Harriet over, I can tell. She is regaling us with witty anecdotes. I'm only half listening; I'm straining to hear Zora's key in the lock. There it is at last. Zora is home. I try not to wonder why she would rather be out half the night than here with me and Harriet.

She comes into the kitchen in the middle of a story Lydia is telling about a nosey neighbour back in America. She is making Harriet laugh. I stand up, as if to shield Zora from the shock of seeing Lydia again, but I'm not quick enough; I must have had more to drink than I meant to.

'What the hell are you doing here?' says Zora. The colour has gone from her face. Her fists are clenched and she is trembling.

'Time for bed,' I tell Harriet.

'Oh, *Mummy*,' she groans.

The word Mummy fills me with joy but then I glance at Lydia. She has heard the word several times this evening and it hasn't been applied to her. What's that like for her? I wonder, joy replaced with dread. Has she returned to reclaim the title?

I go upstairs with Harriet, wanting to remove her from the kitchen before an argument erupts between Lydia and Zora. I'm relieved when she asks if she can listen to the radio through her headphones for a while. At least she shouldn't be able to overhear us. I make sure the door to her room is closed before I come downstairs again.

Lydia is drunk now, there's no mistaking it. I'm at the stage our mother used to describe as 'merry' – except that I'm feeling anything but.

'I'm not here to take Harriet away from you,' Lydia keeps insisting.

Zora is thumping the table, shouting about abandonment and Lydia's audacity at landing herself on us again after eight years, without any warning or consideration. I tug Zora's sleeve to urge her to be quiet. Despite the headphones, if there are anymore loud voices, Harriet will be down again, wanting to know what's going on.

Zora subsides. She looks drained. Lydia doesn't seem angry in response. Perhaps was anticipating this.

The three of us sit, still full of tension, though we're all trying to be calm.

'I'm not going to take Harriet away from you,' Lydia repeats. 'In fact, I'm here to ask if you'll adopt her. You've done a brilliant job, she's a lovely child. It would be cruel of me to uproot her now.'

'You didn't come all the way back from America just to say this,' Zora replies, still angry and clearly unconvinced.

Lydia is silent for a while. Then she says, 'My father died. I came back for the funeral.'

'I thought he was in America with you,' says Zora.

'He came home again after a couple of years. He's always been too British.'

'Do I have a grandfather?' asks Harriet. She is wearing slippers with the head of a bear at each toe. One waggles as she rotates her foot. 'I mean, a grandfather apart from Granddad at the junk house?'

'Don't call the house that.' I've asked her not to do this before. There is a sneer in her voice that makes me think of Lydia.

Harriet waits for a while and then she says, 'My proper mummy [her use of the word 'proper' makes me wince], she must have had a daddy, mustn't she?'

'Your birth mother had a father, of course she did,' I answer. 'His name was Harry. I think you were named after him.'

'Did you ever meet him?'

'No, I didn't. I think Zora met him once.'

'Was he white or black?'

'He was white, like your birth mother. Why do you ask?'

'I'm just interested. I'm sort of white and a little bit black, aren't I? People don't really know what I am but they sometimes say bad things about black people as if I'm going to agree with them.'

'What do you say then?'

'I say that my mothers are black, and so was my dad. I hit a girl once.'

'Why?'

'She said black people are stupid.'

Perhaps I should tell Harriet she should never hit people, but I just feel glad of her protectiveness. Lydia may be her birth mother, but Harriet knows that we're her mothers too.

'Your father must have died without ever seeing his grand-daughter,' says Zora.

I don't think she's taken in what Lydia has just said about adoption. I don't think I have either.

Lydia shrugs. 'His choice.'

'Are you serious about wanting us to adopt?' Zora asks. Her fists are still clenched. I can tell by the wobble in her voice that she is trying to contain the anger she feels about Harriet's abandonment. She hardly dares to hope that Lydia might actually be serious about letting us adopt. We've always thought that if she ever returned, she would play her usual games. She would try to use Harriet against us. If an adoption went ahead, she wouldn't be able to retain that power. It's hard to believe this has not occurred to her.

'I'm married now,' Lydia answers, not addressing the question. 'I'm intending to settle in London again.'

'Do you have any other children?' asks Zora pointedly.

Lydia looks uncomfortable. 'A girl and a boy, six and four, Amy and Rupert.'

'So you don't really need Harriet now you have two other children, is that it?'

Lydia pours herself another glass of wine and says angrily, 'You can be such a bitch sometimes, Zora.'

There is a brief silence. Then Zora says, 'What does your husband do?' She has noticed the designer clothes and the Louis Vuitton bag.

'He's in advertising. His company is setting up a branch over here and I wanted to come home again, so with my father's death and all the things that needed sorting out, it seemed like a good time to return.'

I can see that Zora is about to shout at Lydia again, tell her how hard it was for us to look after Harriet – the times, in the early years, when we had to go without so we could feed and clothe her. But if Zora starts another argument, Lydia might respond by slamming out of the house in anger, all hope of adoption departing with her. So I say that it's time we all went to bed and I start to clear the empty glasses from the table. I am relieved when Lydia's taxi comes.

We must have told Harriet that the woman who came to visit and took us to the Chinese restaurant was her birth mother, but however hard I try, I can't remember doing it, or what Harriet's reaction was. Has the memory gone recently or has it been so painful to recall that occasion during the past forty years that I blocked it from my mind almost as soon as it had happened? Harriet must have been upset. She must have blamed us for letting Lydia go that night without acknowledging her as her long-lost daughter. She must have been angry, so angry with us. I can picture us shouting at one another. Was that then? Was it me and Harriet or me and Zora? All of us, perhaps? We got her a dog not long after that. Even Lydia would find it hard to compete with a dog, we decided. I have a photo of him somewhere. I thought I didn't like dogs but I loved that one, he was always so joyful about everything – walks, food, human company – he relished every moment of his life.

I am determined to relish every last moment of my life. I won't let fear of this illness corrode whatever well-time I have left. I won't live in fear, I can't.

Harriet's dog is grey-black with a stumpy tail, which has been docked. Harriet cries about the tail. She calls him Flint. I'm afraid of him at first. I've always been afraid of dogs.

Memories are starting to come and go. It's as if they zap through my head and end up in some other place, buried deeper, harder to retrieve. But I can't allow myself to live in fear.

Lydia's visit creates such fear in us it's almost unbearable. We try not to think about the future but we can't hold back our apprehension. We find our own solicitor to see what would happen if Lydia was to change her mind about adoption and try to take Harriet away from us.

'Lydia Russell clearly abandoned Harriet to your care,' says

Edward Oliphant, as he sits behind his desk. Harriet would love the name. She'd call him Edward Elephant and write a story about him. He is still scanning the letter Lydia wrote. Thank God I kept it. 'But she is Harriet's birth mother of course,' he continues, 'and that is always very important to a judge. Her circumstances are such that she can afford to give her daughter every possible advantage. That will certainly count in her favour.' He doesn't add that she is white, and white faces tend to fare better in court.

I pick up Harriet from school and I do my best not to wonder if soon, the trips back and forth will be over. Perhaps I will no longer see her in her purple blazer, dashing towards me, talking happily about the theatre company that performed a play in the hall that day or the praise she got for getting top marks in her maths test.

I take her swimming. I've been doing this since she was little, every other week. I'm not much good, I can't dive or tread water like she can, but we play. She chases me up and down the pool, always catching me and laughing excitedly. Afterwards, we drink hot chocolate in the greasy spoon on the corner of the street, our hair damp. We plan Zora's Christmas present and what we will have for Christmas dinner, Harriet with eagerness, me with dread. What if she is gone before these things happen? What if our plans are for nothing? I try to prepare myself for losing her, but thinking about the possibility prevents me sleeping at night. Zora and I take out our fear on each other, arguing more frequently about things that don't matter, like who should get the big weekly shop. We are dreading a return visit from Lydia to say she's changed her mind and wants Harriet to live with her again.

I am trying to replay every last important thing. I want to fix my memories into my brain, lock them there so they will never desert me. I fear that one day I may not recognise Harriet; I may not know who she is. I imagine the hurt she will feel, the terrible sting of rejection. I have to keep remembering her. I have to keep remembering everything surrounding her. I take down the photo album, the green one; in this album every picture is of Harriet. She is coming down the slide in a children's playground. She is playing in the sandpit – there's sand in her hair. She is running with Flint, at the end of a lead. She is dancing to the Four Tops with Zora: 'Reach Out, I'll Be There'. She is tiny, in a bath, pushing a boat in the water.

'You missed Harriet's childhood,' I say to Lydia. 'You missed all the memories.'

Here, she is celebrating her eleventh birthday, blowing out the candles on a cake surrounded by a dozen friends from school. In this one, she is sullen and teenage, standing by a tree, arms folded, looking away from the camera. Her first love has just broken it off but we've gone on a long-planned camping trip. She doesn't want to be there. She is angry and humiliated and there is nothing we can say or do to take the hurt away. The sun is shining in the picture, but in my memory, it rained every day.

*

The sun shines into the hall through the glass panel of the door as I take a letter from the mat. It's from Lydia's solicitor; the name of the firm is printed discreetly on the front of the stiff, white envelope. I call Zora down from her bedroom. 'It's here,' I say to her. The envelope flutters slightly as my hand shakes.

I pass the letter to Zora. The adoption is confirmed. We can't believe it. We hold each other tight, weeks of tension leaving us.

Harriet sits at the kitchen table. I watch her face as Zora tells her that we are going to adopt her. She doesn't really seem to understand. She thinks we are officially her parents already. We try to explain the difference between adoption and guardianship. 'Your last name will be Bunting,' we tell her. 'You'll have the same name as us, the same name as your father.' This tangible sign that Harriet is Cal's daughter and belongs with our family is the most important thing, the part we are celebrating most. But Harriet doesn't seem able to grasp the difference.

Then she says, 'If my name isn't Russell anymore, does this mean that Lydia won't be my proper mother ever again?', and the pain we both feel at that moment tells us that Harriet has grasped the difference after all.

'You missed Harriet's childhood,' I say to Lydia. 'You have no real memories of your daughter.' Am I trying to hurt Lydia for all the hurt she caused Zora, me and Harriet?

'You've said this before,' Lydia replies. 'You need to stop repeating yourself.'

*

We take Harriet to visit Mum and Dad, to celebrate the adoption with them. As we approach the front door, we see there are only spring bulbs coming into bloom in the small front garden. No old and broken flowerpots. No decaying, rotten things. In the house, we are able to walk from one room to another. It's not completely clear but now at least there are spaces.

'I've been having a little tidy-up,' says Dad. He hops from one foot to the other and sounds apologetic. It's as if he's suddenly realised the toll his years of collecting has taken on all of us – especially on him. He looks old. 'I've been making some room for Harriet,' he adds, holding out his hand to her.

Harriet really does belong with us now. Mum takes her into her arms and hugs her tight.

Thirty-six

Zora

It was the week before Christmas and Lydia's house was tastefully decorated with sprigs of holly and mistletoe. In the sitting room, lighted candles in ornate holders adorned the mantelpiece. A fire crackled and sparked, and Harriet, Amy and Rupert knelt in front of it, watching their chestnuts blacken. I thought of that Christmas song – chestnuts roasting on an open fire – as you and I perched opposite one another on velvet sofas, me on the green one, you on the maroon. They were built more for decoration than relaxation; the backs were hard and the seat pads unyielding. I struggled to get comfortable. The walls were painted grey and huge, abstract paintings in golds and greens, by an up-and-coming artist I'd never heard of (but should have been impressed by) stretched across them. A Christmas tree, seven or eight feet high, stood in the corner, its lights twinkling softly in the darkening room.

'Be careful, don't burn yourselves,' you said to the children. You were afraid that Rupert was in imminent danger of immolation as he leaned forward to get the fattest chestnut.

'They're fine,' said Lydia dismissively from the other end of the maroon sofa, as Rupert yelped and dropped the fat chestnut onto the grate.

Harriet retrieved it for him. 'Let it cool down for a while,' she said in a motherly voice. She had taken to her half-siblings, but they only viewed her with faint curiosity.

After the adoption had come through, you and I had promised to allow Harriet to see Lydia as often as possible. Our anger with Lydia still simmered, but we did our best not to show it; we didn't want to complicate Harriet's already complicated relationship with her birth mother anymore than necessary. Still, I wished we hadn't agreed to this. Spending time with Lydia always unsettled Harriet for days after; she would be miserable and cross right through the Christmas period now.

She had been bitterly angry when we'd finally told her that Lydia was her birth mother, but more than that, she'd been so sad. I'd sat with her for hours in her bedroom, trying to explain how everything had come about.

'Why didn't my mummy want me?' she said through tears.

I gave Harriet the usual explanation, about Lydia being made ill by grief and giving her up because she loved her so much.

Harriet looked cross, as if she knew I was deceiving her. 'Why did she keep her other children and not me? Why could she make them happy when she couldn't make me happy? She could have tried harder. She could have loved me like she loves Rupert and Amy. I wish I wasn't me. I wish I was Amy instead.'

It was hard not to feel hurt that Harriet wanted Lydia's love so much that she was prepared to obliterate ours.

'Was your dad coloured?' Amy had said to Harriet when they'd first been introduced.

Harriet, usually self-assured, had looked towards me for guidance on answering this question.

'He was our brother,' I'd replied, wanting to head off any views from Amy that might have been hurtful to Harriet.

Amy had nodded but she hadn't said anything more. I wondered what Lydia had told her.

Michael was away for the week, Lydia said. He had returned to New York on a business trip, and to spend a few days with his American mother, who was bemoaning the fact that he and her grandchildren wouldn't be with her for Christmas.

'She's a dreadful woman,' Lydia told us, in the hearing of Amy and Rupert, who looked up with interest. 'I'm so glad to be away from her. All she does is tell me how lucky I am to have a man like Michael as my husband. She never considers him lucky to have me as his wife.' She picked up her cardigan from a tapestry footstool and put it over her shoulders. 'You've had enough chestnuts now,' she said to the children. 'Do you want to go upstairs and play?'

'We want to stay here,' said Harriet quickly. She didn't want to let Lydia out of her sight.

Amy and Rupert were told to fetch books and they sat looking at them quietly. Well-trained children, they had learnt to disrupt their mother's day as little as possible. Harriet listened intently as Lydia spoke.

'Adam's married, of course. Did you know?' she told us as we sipped mulled wine. 'I can't say I've ever taken to her. She's the daughter of some viscount. I think he was hoping her connections would help his career. He intends to be PM one day. There are three children now, two girls and a boy.'

'Who is Adam? And what's a PM?' asked Harriet.

Lydia ignored her. 'Adam is always so determined, I'm sure he'll achieve it. His wife's dull, though. Vacuous.'

Lydia had used similar words to describe her stepmother. 'Was Joyce at your father's funeral?' I asked.

Lydia shook her head. 'Why would she have been? They weren't married anymore. Pa was forced to give her a ridiculous amount of money in the divorce settlement. She'll have spent it on face lifts and a breast enhancement. I never did see anyone more flat-chested. I always meant to ask Pa why on earth he took up with her. I mean, he could have had anyone, but he picked a woman who was both stupid and unattractive.' Lydia turned to you and said, 'Adam's writing books as well, did you know? He won a major prize last year for his most recent novel. He's delighted with himself, of course. Between that and his parliamentary career, there really is no stopping him.'

I got the impression that Lydia was delighted with herself too, basking in the reflected glory of being related to Adam Russell. I had known about his seat in Parliament. He was at the deep blue end of the political spectrum, a vociferous member of the Monday Club. I wondered what he thought of Harriet. No doubt he would see her as being of dubious heritage. Were they second cousins, or first cousins once removed? I'd never really understood how distant family relationships were calculated.

Lydia went to the kitchen. Harriet got up silently and followed her. They returned a few minutes later with a plate of mince pies, baked by Ines, the pale-faced, Swiss, hired help, who remained largely invisible. I remembered encountering Mrs Billington – 'Billy' – in the Russells' kitchen when we were children. The truncating of her name had been indicative of her status – or lack of it. As I recalled her nasty views on savages, and the bad influence we were on Adam and Lydia, I realised she must have resented her menial position in the Russell household and had consoled herself with the idea that we were of even less significance.

'Michael bought me the most gorgeous dress to wear for a big New Year's party we've been invited to,' said Lydia. 'Come up and see it, Zora.'

I had no interest in Lydia's frocks and I would have preferred to have remained in the sitting room, but I wanted the opportunity to speak to Lydia privately about Harriet, so I stood up, noting that, as usual, she was playing favourites – I was specifically invited upstairs to see the dress while you were ignored.

'Can I see it too?' asked Harriet.

'No, you stay here, sweetheart,' I said to her. You picked up your cue and distracted Harriet with chocolates from the box on the coffee table long enough for Lydia and me to disappear upstairs.

'Mike knows so many interesting people,' said Lydia as we climbed to the third floor of the house. 'The party invite was from the actor, Zack Weldon. They've been friends for years and he's in London at the moment. I expect there'll be a lot of showbiz people there. You have to look the part, don't you? I'm hoping the dress will do the trick. Did you see Zack's latest film? It's tipped to win big at the Oscars.'

'No, I haven't seen it yet, but I've been meaning to. I'll try to catch it. Do you remember that time we sneaked in to see *Bonnie and Clyde* at the local cinema? We must have been about fourteen.'

Lydia shook her head. 'I've never seen *Bonnie and Clyde*. You must mean *Blow-Up*, we saw that together. David Hemmings was in it. I used to fancy him like mad.'

'I'm sure it was—'

But Lydia was already in the master bedroom and she wasn't listening anymore. 'Come and see the view from the window. It's why we bought this house. It's listed, you know.'

I looked out and saw the muddy waters of the Thames. A gently bobbing rowing boat was tied to a post just beyond the garden. There were signs of renovation work; the garden was being landscaped – concrete slabs were stacked against a half-finished wall. Lydia told me that the attic was also being stripped; the floors were riddled with woodworm and were being replaced, making the top part of the house unusable. 'It's been months since they started the work,' said Lydia. 'I hate living in a mess. But Mike said he wanted a place with character and this one fitted the bill.'

I needed to talk about Harriet. I moved away from the window and sat on the end of the king-size bed. 'Why did you want the adoption?'

'Harriet had been with you for so long, it seemed like the right thing to do,' Lydia replied as she opened the door to a walk-in wardrobe.

'Come on, Lydia,' I said, needing to convey my scepticism.

Lydia laid out the dress beside me on the bed. It was purple and sleeveless, cut on the bias. Even I could see how well designed it was, and I had little interest in fashion.

'It's very nice,' I said without conviction.

She named some designer or other, expecting me to have heard of him.

'Tell me why you really wanted the adoption,' I repeated.

Lydia sat beside me on the bed and I was reminded of that strange night so many years ago. I edged away from her, thinking of Georgia, even though it had been over between her and me for longer than I cared to remember.

'Don't worry, I don't have any designs on you,' said Lydia, amused by my discomfort.

Did I wish, just for a moment, that she had said something different? Was I affronted that the very idea of attraction seemed faintly absurd to Lydia now? I put these questions aside and asked again about the adoption of Harriet.

'She called you both Mummy,' said Lydia. 'Mummy S and Mummy Z.'

'She stopped calling us that after we told her who you were.' My anger showed; I was disappointed that, since Lydia's return, we no longer merited the title.

'She called you both Mummy and I saw how attached she was.'

'And?' I asked, knowing there must be more to it than this.

Lydia fingered the seam of the purple dress and said, 'Michael is a conventional man despite his showbiz friends. We slept together before we were married, of course, but he assumed he was my first sexual partner.' Lydia smiled at me ruefully. 'Even a few years ago, despite the pill and all the feminists, it was what men expected. Still is, to a greater or lesser extent. It's why they refused me painkillers when I was giving birth to Harriet. It's why I was called a slut by the doctors and nurses at the hospital when I had her. What I mean to say is, I didn't tell Michael about Harriet until after the wedding. He's never really forgiven me. He still minds about her. I think he was afraid that when we returned to Britain, I'd want Harriet to be part of our family. I wouldn't say he was bigoted, not really, but his mother, Barbara, was brought up in Atlanta, during segregation, and Michael has inherited one or two of her views. She knows nothing about Harriet, of course, and Michael wants it to stay that way. So I thought the best way of dispelling any anxieties he might have on that score was to make you and Selina her official, permanent parents.' Lydia got up and returned the dress to the wardrobe.

'And you're okay with that?'

Lydia heard the accusatory note in my voice and looked uncomfortable. 'No, not exactly, but that's the situation, and I'm stuck with it.'

'You don't have to be stuck with it,' I said, fury bubbling up on Harriet's behalf – and Cal's.

'Well, I do now, of course, the decision has been made. Harriet is yours and Selina's, legally speaking, so I am stuck with it. Besides, as I said, she called you both Mummy. It would have been wrong to drag her away from you, even if I'd wanted to.'

We could hear raised voices downstairs. There was some kind of argument going on between Rupert and Amy and you were trying, unsuccessfully, to calm the situation.

'I'd better go down and sort them out,' said Lydia, clearly wanting to end our discussion.

Harriet gazed wistfully at Lydia as she comforted Rupert and told Amy not to hit her brother and I knew that she was imagining being comforted by her birth mother too.

The weather was turning. The skies that had been bright blue that morning were now dark grey and the air was bitterly cold. 'Looks like snow,' Lydia said.

'Will it be a white Christmas?' Amy asked.

'Could be,' you replied.

'We'd better be on our way,' I said. 'We don't want to get caught in a snowstorm.'

You and I stood up to go, but Harriet was reluctant to leave. 'Can't we stay a bit longer?' she asked wistfully.

'I'm quite happy for Harriet to stop over with us,' said Lydia, not checking beforehand if we were okay with this and making it hard for us to say no; Harriet would be full of resentment if we took her away from her birth mother so close to Christmas when she'd been invited to stay. So we left her with Lydia, getting to know Amy and Rupert better, and feeling ... what? Alien in that household? Like a welcome guest? Either was possible but neither position suggested belonging. Harriet had been shy with Lydia at the start of the visit, but that had slowly dissipated, and throughout the day, she had gone wherever Lydia went, following her about the house with a look of quiet desperation, as if she knew that however much time she spent with her birth mother, it would never be enough.

Thirty-seven

Selina

The week before Christmas. I don't think I've sent any carts. No, not carts ... those things you post. I keep meaning to. They're stashed away in a drawer somewhere, ready to be written, but I haven't been able to find them.

I'm with Fran – it must be Sunday. It's cold, threatening ... cold white flakes, though it won't, of course, it never does at Christmas, not in London. Fran drives us to a quiet spot. I've learnt to wrap up warm for our walks over the years. I've got a padded jacket and new walking boots. You used to have to break them in but these have been comfortable from the start. Fran says they're waterproof. She tells me about Artex, this stuff that makes clothes and boots dry. She talks all the time. I think she's lonely. She has grandchildren, she shows me the photos she keeps on her phone, but she doesn't see them much; her daughter is so busy, she says.

'When did Harriet last visit?' asks Fran.

I'm not sure. It's been a while, I think. Did she get me some shopping the other day? Or was that Zora? No, it can't have been Zora, of course it can't. Christ, what's wrong with me?

'Are you all right?' asks Fran.

No, I'm not all right, but I nod because it's easier and I try to get a grip.

'Do you remember Martin?' Fran says as she finishes the red wine she always orders. Her pale face is flushed from our walk and her fair hair is still damp from the sleet. Her wine is organic, I think. She likes organic; she says it's healthier. I suppose it is.

'Martin?'

'You went out with him for a while when we were at college – thin, long blond hair, bald now, of course. I saw him the other day. He ended up getting out of teaching. He said it ground him down. He's working in that big DIY place near the football ground. I didn't recognise him – he recognised me. He must be well over seventy – wasn't he a mature student? I suppose he can't afford to retire. Did you never want to go out with anyone else?'

'Anyone else?'

'Did you ever get into another relationship? I don't remember you ever saying you were with anyone else.'

I shake my head. Zora and Harriet, they were more than enough for me. I came to relish my own company. Being joined was all-consuming, even when we weren't.

Fern and I traipse over hill and dale and I pretend to enjoy it, though in truth, I'm tired. I don't have the energy these days, not like I used to.

'Judith came to stay for a few days last week,' she says, pushing her fair hair out of her eyes as the wind whips it round her face. 'She said, "Remember me to Selina when you see her."'

'Remember me to Selina.' I'm struggling to keep up today, mentally as well as physically. I try to remember who Judith is. I don't want to ask Fern; she obviously expects me to know. Maybe I can work it out. I get myself over a stile with a lot of effort. 'How is Judith?' I ask as I drop to the other side.

'Enjoying her retirement.'

Not much of a clue there. Almost everyone I know is now retired. I try something else. 'How does she fill her time?'

'She does voluntary work at a local community centre and she's got her grandchildren. She has them a couple of days a week. Sarah works mostly from home but she has to go into the office every now and then, show her face.'

Sarah. She must be the daughter. Now I have two names to recall: Sarah and whatever the first one was called. Bugger, this isn't helping. One final question, then – it's like a quiz game. 'Where is she living now?'

'She's still in Rotherham. She's been there since we finished college. It wouldn't suit me, of course, but Jude really likes it.'

College. Judith must have been at college when I trained. I try to picture her but I can't. What with trying to place ... and at the same time pretending I'm not out of breath as I climb all these bloody hills, I'm starting to wish I hadn't agreed to come on this walk. And who the hell was that bloke, the one I'm meant to have gone out with? Fern must be mistaken; I wouldn't have forgotten something like that. She must mean Lydia's cousin, though I never actually went out with him. I kissed him once, I think, at a party. He had to resign from Parliament. There was a scandal. Was it something to do with Harriet? It will come to me in a minute. 'Remember me to Selina.' It's something people keep on doing, remembering themselves to me. Reminding me who they are. Some are subtle about it and I'm grateful for that. Others speak loudly, as if shouting at me will improve my memory, and they say, 'Remember me?' in very loud voices. 'Remember me to Selina.' What was her name again, the one who wanted me to remember her? What did Fern say it was? I still can't place her. Zora remembers herself to me all the time. She constantly requires me to remember her. Remember, remember, the fifth of November. It's not November, is it? I think it's quite near Christmas.

We've almost reached the bottom of the hill. Fern is still skinny. She is the same weight as she was when we were at college, so it's all less effort for her. I'm tired. Yet, as we pass through a wooden gate and plod along a frosty path, I hear the wind echoing round the barren trees and I feel less flat, more like myself. I get out my camera. Fern is looking towards the sky and smiling to herself. I take a picture. I take pictures of the icicles hanging from the trees, their smooth, sharp points refracting light. I capture the frost twinkling on the hardened mud and I start to enjoy this walk, I'm not pretending anymore. She takes me by the arm once the path is wide enough and I tell her about Harriet, the things she's been doing. She's just got a dog, a spaniel, I think. We used to be afraid of dogs, Zora and me, but I'm quite taken with this one. She asks what it's called. I don't know, Harriet didn't tell me. Or perhaps she did, and I've forgotten. I think it's grey. Or black. The colour of coal. Is it called Coal? It can't be, that would be a stupid name for a dog. Long ears. Docked tail. A spaniel.

'Look after yourself,' says ... What is her name? I know what it is. I know her so well; I've known her for years. It's on the tip of my tongue.

She pulls up outside my house to drop me off. People use this expression, 'look after yourself', so often that it's almost empty of meaning. Except that when it's said to me now, it does mean something – it means, don't get any worse. Don't hurt me by failing to remember my name, as if I am no longer important. Don't remind me that I could end up like you. Take control of this illness. Then I can believe that with enough willpower, if the same condition comes for me, I will be able to conquer it too. Don't embarrass me by doing something unlike your usual self, the kind of thing a child might do. Fly into a rage. Cry for your mother to take you home even though she's been dead for thirty years. Just you make sure you look after yourself.

Thirty-eight

Zora

We were almost a family again, Mum, Dad, me, you and
Harriet. Once the adoption had gone through, Dad no longer
collected useless things quite so obsessively. There were still
a few unsteady piles of rubbish dotted about, but it was nothing like it had been before. He even went back to work – not
the buses, too much time had passed and he felt the stigma
of chronic depression too acutely for that – 'I wouldn't fit
in there anymore,' he said. Instead, he worked in one of
the local parks, as a keeper. Ironically, he was in charge of
maintenance, keeping everything clean and tidy, all in order,
nothing out of place. We laughed about that – Dad laughing
loudest – as we sat at the dinner table, eating Sunday lunch,
which had become a tradition again.

Mum had cooked chicken, with roast potatoes, plantain,
rice and peas. She was less tired now that she no longer had
to do two jobs. 'I don't know how on earth I found the time
to do so much,' she said.

There was still a touch of sadness at the table, felt most
sharply, perhaps, when Mum brought the crumble out of the

oven and the grown-ups remembered that last night with Cal. But his daughter was with us now, a part of him.

'That's my father, isn't it?' said Harriet, pointing to the framed photo hanging on the wall to the side of her. It had been put up since our last visit. Cal was looking shy but pleased with himself. He was holding a certificate.

There was silence for a moment, as if no one was quite sure how to remember Cal without pain they didn't want to have to feel. Then you said, 'Yes, that's your dad. I took it when he got his A-level results.'

'I had it enlarged and framed,' added Dad. He looked as if he might cry but instead he forced a smile. Harriet took his arm and stroked it gently. 'What kind of things did my dad like doing?' she asked, refusing to heed the adults' unspoken wish for her to drop the conversation.

'He liked watching wrestling on television,' said Dad after a pause.

Harriet wrinkled her nose. 'I'd rather watch *Starsky and Hutch*. Or *The Fosters*. I like Lenny Henry.'

'Wrestling was fun when we were growing up,' I added. 'The wrestlers took on personas – characters. It was a bit like pantomime.'

'What other things did my dad like?'

'Your dad liked building things,' you said. 'He made a little bookshelf for me once in his woodwork class at school.'

He made it just for you; it wasn't shared. I felt hurt, left out.

'We were only allowed to make one,' Cal told me.

'Then why did you give it to her?' I knew I sounded jealous, but I couldn't help it.

'I didn't do it to upset you,' Cal replied, looking worried. 'Don't get upset about it.'

'We could have shared it.'

'Maybe. It's just that when you're both supposed to share, you end up taking over.'

'That's not true!' I said, feeling even more hurt by this judgement of me.

'It is true,' Cal answered mildly. 'It was fairer to give it to Selina, just for once. I'll make something just for you next time, promise.'

But he never did.

You treasured that bookshelf for years; you even managed to have it sent to halls when you went to college. But it got lost in the move when we bought our house. You were distraught when you realised it had gone.

'Cal believed in fairness,' I said to Harriet. 'He stood up for the things he believed in. He used to go on demos.'

'What did he demonstrate about?'

'He was anti-war. It was the Vietnam war then, in America. He protested about apartheid too. I think he also protested when they banned pirate radio.'

'What's pirate radio?' asked Harriet.

She was disappointed by the explanation. She'd been hoping for galleons or, at the very least, a parrot.

'You look a lot like Cal,' Mum said to her.

'You do,' added Dad.

I looked at them to see if the likeness was causing them distress, but they just seemed pleased.

Mum dished up the crumble.

'That was gorgeous,' said Harriet as she finished the last mouthful.

'It was Cal's favourite too,' said Mum, basking in the compliment.

'Can I have some more?' Not waiting for an answer, Harriet started helping herself.

'Just wait,' I said. 'Other people might want some more of that.'

'No one's going to want it,' Harriet replied. 'Selina and Gran are on a diet. You keep saying you want to eat more healthily and Granddad's left most of his.'

'You could at least have asked. It's rude.'

'I did ask. I said, "Can I have some more?" Everyone heard me ask.'

'It's customary to wait for a reply.'

'I haven't done anything wrong. This isn't fair.'

'Leave her be, Zora,' said Mum quickly. 'She's a growing girl, she's got an appetite. No harm in that.'

'It's rude and it's inconsiderate,' I answered.

My mood had changed. I'd been enjoying the afternoon but suddenly I just wanted it to come to an end. I'd stopped seeing Cal in Harriet and I was now seeing Lydia. There had been so much talk of family likeness round the table, but whereas Cal had been thoughtful, Harriet was often thoughtless. Wilful. Prone to asking why a lot, instead of just doing whatever we asked her to do. It irritated the hell out of me, even though I tried not to let it.

'Does she remind you of anyone?' you asked me a few days later, after a particularly prolonged bout of whys?

from Harriet, followed by an iteration of all the where-fores from me.

'She's so like Lydia sometimes,' I answered.

You laughed. 'No, Zora, she's just like you.'

I didn't see it but it did make me realise something. We all wanted Harriet to resemble us, our side of the family – to be our likeness. We'd been so keen for her to save us, to make us whole again after Cal. You and I had come together once more in order to raise her. Perhaps she had saved our relationship, preserving our joined-ness – you loved her for that. Harriet's presence as our adopted daughter had also been the cata-lyst for our parents' return to some kind of normality. They were living again now, whereas before they had just trudged through life joylessly. We hadn't meant to burden Harriet with our needs, but we were all doing so, one way or another. Sometimes I worried about where this would lead. As an adult, would she spend years in therapy, blaming all of us for our dependence on her, our need for her to be like us, and our fear that she was the only thing that kept us all going? Would she manage to be happy, despite all our demands?

I felt odd moments of happiness, at home and when I was immersed in my work. But I still missed the brief spell of free-dom I'd had in Manchester, even after so many years. I loved you and Harriet, but I wanted to be independent, I wanted that so much. Harriet's adoption had meant everything to me but it had also felt like a prison door had clanged shut. We belonged to one another even more now, you, me and Harriet. Being Harriet's mothers wasn't a voluntary thing anymore, it was our legal duty, and illogically, perhaps, it seemed to carry more responsibility and obligation than a biological parent would ever have to deal with.

Harriet liked school. She never feigned illness to avoid a teacher or a lesson she thought she wouldn't understand. She had friends and was invited to parties at ice rinks and bowling alleys. I remembered how popular Lydia had been.

On parents' evenings, the teachers were full of praise. You and I attended together, ignoring the questioning looks, the raised-eyebrow-invitations to explain our relationship to her; why there were two of us, why there was so little familial resemblance – in their minds we were too dark to be close relatives – and why her birth parents were never present. 'She's a very clever child, but she can be impertinent – flippant, if not downright rude,' they said. 'She needs to curb that tendency.'

On the way home in the car, you blamed me for this. 'She's learnt to be flippant from you, it's how you manage things and you know how she looks up to you. She copies you. Can't you at least rein it in when you're around her?'

'When am I flippant?' I was both angry and surprised.

'All the time, Zora. Just rein it in. When I dropped a dish the other day, you made a joke about how clumsy I was. Now Harriet's repeating what you said as if it's gospel truth, denigrating me, like that's okay. I'm fed up with it.'

You were driving. You pulled up behind a Viva. You were far more patient than I was in every area, except on the road. Now you were tapping the steering wheel impatiently as the driver stalled. 'Idiot,' you muttered. I'm sure that, in the car, even Harriet mistook you for me.

'You don't think Harriet's flippancy is an inherited characteristic we should blame on Lydia?'

'That's exactly the kind of comment I'm talking about. I'm
only asking you to rein it in around Harriet,' you said as you
pulled away from the traffic lights.

We used to share a Mini, but we'd just got a blue Beetle, at
your insistence. You'd done it mainly for Harriet, who found
rusty, old, orange cars an embarrassment.

'I suppose we could be in danger of spoiling her,' I said.
'She plays us off against each other and we let her. Seriously,
we don't want another Lydia on our hands. We need to be
more strict with her, both of us. I don't care if she's flippant
with teachers, they probably deserve it, but if she gets away
with too much at home, she'll end up a spoilt brat.'

We were in agreement now, something that was increasingly rare.

'We're compensating for Cal not being here,' you said.

'Exactly,' I replied.

'We need to be more consistent.' We pulled up outside the
house. You turned the engine off . 'And that means you have
to control your temper, Zora.'

I felt myself tense up. 'What do you mean?'

'You're angry so much of the time. You snap at me and you
snap at her for no good reason. Harriet is really aware of it
and it scares her.'

I turned to face you. 'That's a horrible thing to say. I'm
not angry about anything. And I never, ever snap at Harriet.
I wouldn't, I just wouldn't. It's ridiculous to say that she's
scared of me. If she was scared, she wouldn't answer back all

the time, would she? If anything it's the opposite – she prefers being with me to being with you.' I unbuckled my seat belt but I couldn't quite manage to get out of the car – my foot was entangled in part of it.

'Most of the time, you're not around,' you said, reaching across to release me. 'You've always got some excuse. You're preparing your teaching. You're doing your marking. You're working on your doctorate. You need to spend time with colleagues because departmental decisions are made over beer in the pub. We both walk on eggshells all the time. *Don't upset Zora, she's had a difficult day. Be quiet, Zora's trying to get some work done.* I'm sick of it, to be honest.' You sat on your hands to try to disguise the fact that you were trembling – with anger? In fear of my response?

Free of the seat belt, I got out of the car, my own anger making me speak louder than was necessary. We both stood on the pavement. 'It's very convenient to blame all your anxieties on me. You can't even talk without shaking, but instead of admitting you're not coping, you dump it all on me, make it all my fault.'

'I knew you wouldn't listen. You never listen,' you said, your voice strained.

'That's because you never say anything worth listening to.' I ran to the front door and let myself into the house.

I was halfway up the stairs when you came in behind me and said, 'So now you're going to run away from this conversation instead of listening and trying to put things right.'

Full of fury at your assumptions, I continued up the stairs. I went into my room, but before I could close the door, you were beside me. The house was quiet except for our voices, both of us loud and insistent. We knew we could argue as much as we liked; Harriet was stopping over with a friend for the night. I needed to be away from you so much. At that moment I wanted to be anywhere but in the house. You were standing in the way of that, literally. I shoved you through the door and onto the landing but you sprang back in like a toy that was impossible to stop once it had been wound up.

'I just want to talk to you,' you said.

'Well, I don't want to talk to you.'

'Please, Zora.' The usual pleading. I'd had enough of it.

You stood in the corner of the room, your arms folded. I kicked off my work shoes, the uncomfortable black ones with the pointed toes that I wore in order to feel in charge. A black pencil skirt, a white blouse and a grey, tailored jacket completed the outfit. I pulled these off too and started to get into my pyjamas. If we were going to fight, I wanted to be comfortable, at least. You were also in black and grey, but your clothes were casual, designed for child-wrangling – you were already equipped for combat. And yet, as I looked at you, I knew a fight wasn't on the agenda. Neither of us had the heart for one. We were both tired, and whenever something like parents' evening occurred, we were reminded of our responsibilities to Harriet, and our fear that we wouldn't live up to them.

Was Harriet really scared of me? An image of her, shrinking from me slightly as I complained about the noise from her beatbox while I was trying to get my marking done, barely able to concentrate, sleepy, irritable and agitated from a demanding day at work – trying to do too many things at once – came into my head. Perhaps I wasn't very easy to live with.

I'm not sure what happened next. We probably shouted at one another. You probably accused me of leaving all the work of raising Harriet to you and only taking the good parts, the fun parts of being her parents, as if I was an errant father, a neatly stereotypical view that fitted your perception of lesbians, no doubt. I know I slept badly that night, resenting you, resenting the life I now had – or the life that had been denied to me the day you had allowed Harriet to land on your doorstep.

By morning, I was back in a smart skirt and jacket and ready for work again, as if I hadn't slept on top of the bed and awoken with a splitting headache. As I left for the daily commute, early enough to avoid you, I wondered if some of the things you'd said last night were true. I could be irritable at times. Sometimes, through exhaustion and the demands of work and the sense that the prison door had clanked shut, I would withdraw for days at a time, not even getting out of bed. I knew that you and Harriet tiptoed around me then, quite literally. And Harriet was sometimes scared of me – deep down I knew that too – and I didn't want that for her, I really didn't. I didn't want it for myself either.

So I tried, for a while, to do things differently. I sat on my resentment and I tried my hardest not to let it surface.

Thirty-nine

Zora

We sat at a large wooden table as the dank smell of the Thames was carried on the wind, blocking the scent of the rose bushes that circled the lawn. They made me feel like Alice in Wonderland; soon there would be jam tarts for tea and Lydia would screech, 'Off with their heads!' The table was laden with crab and prawn rolls, an assortment of French cheeses and crisp little lemon biscuits. The adults drank Pimm's, the children lemonade.

'Can I have a Pimm's?' asked Harriet. 'I am thirteen.'

'Ask again in five years' time,' I told her.

Harriet was expecting this response but she still muttered, 'All my friends have tried it.'

'I've just said no,' I replied, unable to hide my irritation.

She looked at you, hoping you might contradict me, but you shook your head. We were continuing to be more united over Harriet.

It had been a close, dull day, though the late-May sun was starting to break through. I took off my cardigan. You did the same. We were still trying to look different from one another, but failing miserably. We were each wearing green shirt dresses, not identical, but similar enough, and chosen independently. Impossible, always, to separate from you entirely.

How old was Lydia that day? Thirty-one, I think. I'd assumed Michael would be there to mark the occasion, but there was no sign of him, and Lydia said nothing about his absence. You took a photo of us all sitting round the table.

A thin woman with an elfin face and well-cut, short blonde hair came into the garden at a half-run, a small boy at her side. 'Surprise!' she said with a circular wave of her arms. Lydia looked as if it was indeed a surprise. 'The au pair let me in. Adam's parking up,' she said. 'He absolutely insisted we had to pop round to be with you on your birthday.'

The woman dragged another chair to the table and sat beside you, holding the boy on her knee. She was so bony that he couldn't get comfortable and was in constant danger of toppling onto the grass. 'We didn't know you had people round,' she said, glancing at you and me suspiciously before turning her head aside.

Lydia didn't seem pleased to see her but she made the usual introductions. The woman's name was Penny and she was married to Adam. The child was Henry.

Adam was striding across the lawn carrying a large box wrapped in purple paper with a silver bow. He was followed by a girl, a year or two younger than Harriet. Another much smaller child, dressed in dungarees, with fair hair that kept falling into her eyes, inhibiting her ability to see where she was going, was trying to keep up. She stumbled and landed on the ground, unnoticed by most of the adults, but she picked herself up and managed not to cry.

Adam caught sight of you and me. He hesitated, clearly wondering if he still wanted to join the party, but then he continued to walk to the table. 'Happy birthday, Lyds,' he said. He set the gift down in front of her. 'We couldn't resist getting this for you.'

There were further introductions: the child in the dungarees was called Charlotte. The older girl was Olivia. More chairs were brought to the table but there wasn't room for everyone. Adam told the children to move: No room, no room, he said. Harriet remained where she was but the rest formed a little circle, squatting on the grass. Penny whispered something to her husband: I caught the words 'embarrassing' and then 'bastard', the term used in its literal sense. You put an arm round Harriet, as if such a gesture could shield her from the vitriol, but she didn't seem to have heard. The casual way the word had been uttered filled me with rage.

'We should be going,' I said, standing up.

'No! Please!' said Harriet hotly. 'Lydia hasn't opened her presents yet and I want to see her open mine.'

I sat down again reluctantly. Harriet had been looking forward to giving Lydia her gift. She'd chosen it and wrapped it herself and I didn't see why she should be denied that pleasure just because the Russell cousins were offended by our presence.

Adam didn't seem pleased that we were remaining. He caught my eye and then looked away with a frown.

Amy and Harriet disappeared and returned with a candle-lit birthday cake. We sang the obligatory song, the adults more than a little off-key – none of us could hold a tune and we'd had at least one glass of Pimm's too many – apart from you, of course; you always drank sensibly, and besides, you were driving us home.

Adam leaned across the table. 'How nice to see you again,' he said to you and me, with the condescending politeness of those who consider themselves superior. 'I hear news of you both from time to time.' He looked at you and said (clearly knowing which of us was which), 'I seem to remember Lydia telling me you were a teacher at a comprehensive.' There was a sneer in his voice.

I cut in quickly. 'Yes,' I said to him, 'Selina won a national award for innovation in teaching last year. What is it that you do?' I knew full well, of course. I'd read one of his books during a holiday in Cornwall two or three years ago, about a political schemer at the heart of Westminster. He narrowed his eyes at my question, and I saw that he was disappointed to think I hadn't followed his illustrious career.

'I'm a Member of Parliament, for my sins. I write a little too,' he said.

'What kind of things?' I asked. My tone implied that I wasn't expecting too much.

'Fiction. I've had some small successes,' he said disingenuously.

'Have you?' I replied.

As he opened his mouth to list his small successes in the hope of impressing me more, I turned to look at Lydia, who was unwrapping Harriet's present. Perhaps we'd be able to leave after this.

Lydia pulled a leather purse from brightly coloured paper covered in bows and balloons. Harriet had saved her pocket money, but it was cheap – or cheap by Lydia's standards. She would pretend to like it but she would never use it and Harriet would be hurt not to see her bring it out.

'It's beautiful, thank you so much, darling,' said Lydia graciously.

Harriet looked delighted. 'There's a card as well.'

Lydia opened it. It was meant to be funny, something about aging disgracefully. You had tried to persuade Harriet not to get it on the basis that Lydia certainly wasn't old, though to a thirteen-year-old, anyone over eighteen was ancient. Lydia frowned slightly, but she faked laughter.

As I looked at everyone – you, Harriet, Lydia, her cousins and the children, I knew I had to get away from London. I'd stayed for so much longer than I'd meant to. You and I had carved out a way of being together that left some spaces for separation, but it wasn't enough. I was floundering so badly in it all, barely coping at work, unable to sleep, numbing myself with tranquillisers and anti-depressants to the point where I was becoming dull, a cypher, an empty box. Most of the time, I felt like an automaton, clanking along, my movements mirroring yours. I didn't know when I would summon the ability to leave but I knew that I had to; my very existence depended on it.

'Our present next,' said the child in dungarees, clapping her hands excitedly.

The purple-wrapped box turned out to be a food mixer.

Lydia looked at it with disappointment and a large measure of disdain.

'I swear by mine,' said Penny. 'It saves no end of time.'

'We thought it would be just the thing for you. Last time we were here, Michael said he hardly ever got a decent meal. He told us how much he missed his mother's cooking,' added Adam.

The gift wasn't designed to give Lydia pleasure; it was meant to draw attention to her failings.

Lydia made no comment but an eyebrow was raised.

'Maybe Michael should learn to cook for himself if he doesn't like what Lydia makes,' said Harriet, in defence of her birth mother. There was a brief, shocked silence round the table and then Lydia laughed loudly, her first genuine laugh of the day. You and I joined in. Lydia stretched her hand across Adam and patted Harriet's shoulder conspiratorially. Harriet turned pink with pleasure.

'Are you going to let her speak to me like that?' Adam said to the two of us.

'I happen to agree with her,' I replied.

Adam looked at me in disbelief and then he said coldly, 'You people need to know your place.'

'And where's that? Behind you and every other white man?'

Adam stood up and leaned over me. 'I was waiting for you or your sister to play the race card. You're all the same, always feeling hard done by, always making out that everything's about race and someone's disrespected you – isn't that the phrase these days? Respect is something you *earn*, but you people are always after something for nothing.'

'Calm down everyone,' said Penny, waving both hands at me in what she hoped was a placatory gesture. 'I'm sure Adam didn't mean that quite the way it sounded, did you, Ads?'

'Don't presume to tell me what I meant,' replied Adam angrily. 'Harriet needs to learn how to speak to her elders.' I expected him to add 'and betters', as this was clearly the basis of his anger.

'Sit down, for God's sake,' Lydia told him wearily.

'Come on,' you said to me and Harriet, 'it's time we were going. We said we'd leave once the presents were opened.'

'Why should we have to go?' asked Harriet, remaining seated. 'We were here first. He's the one being rude, not us. He's a racist. Why don't they all go instead?' She looked at Lydia defiantly, willing her mother to back her up, but Lydia said nothing.

FORTY

SELINA

Lydia's house has changed. I look out of the windows that stretch along the whole of the wall but there is no sign of the river. As I turn back into the room, I see that this too has altered; the red and green velvet sofas have gone and the huge, open-plan room is stark. It's devoid of colour, except for glass sculptures that glitter in the sunlight. My stomach dips to my shoes as I realise something's wrong. I think of it as time folding, it's the only way I can make sense of it. I am so desperate to see things in straight lines again; everything is wavy now. There is a woman in the room who must be Lydia's mother. Her hair is showing signs of grey and there are lines on her face. I touch the skin of my hand; it's cold where it should feel warm and there are creases where there should be none.

'Are you Lydia's mother?' I ask. Except she can't be. Didn't Lydia's mother die when she was small?

The woman looks at me as if I'm stupid. Perhaps I am. Then she says, 'I'm Lydia,' with such irritation that I want to hide. Instead, I look out of the window, but the river isn't there.

'We sat by the river, on Lydia's birthday,' I tell the woman.

The sun shines through the very long windows. The coloured sculptures glisten.

I must have fallen asleep because it's dusk when I wake up again. I'm on a sofa, feeling stiff. There is a grey throw across my knees. I look out of the window. Even in the semi-dark I can see the river isn't there.

Lydia says, 'Can you stay for dinner?'

I nod. Where's the river gone? I should have taken a photograph, then I would remember it. A photograph. Yes, I came to ask about a photograph.

'There was a photograph. You gave it to us. Do you remember?' I ask.

Lydia nods again, almost imperceptibly. She gets up to make cheese omelettes. Is it lunchtime?

I am trying to recall the photo Lydia gave us. I know it was important even though I don't know what it was a photo of. 'Do you want me to peel some vegetables?' I ask as I stand beside her at the sink.

'If you like,' she says, handing me a knife and a bag of red onions.

'Who was in it?'

'In what?'

'Who was in the photograph?'

'What photograph?' she says.

'We were here on your birthday. Someone else was here, someone we used to know.' I look around the open-plan room as if this will give me more clues, but it is feature-less – minimalist. There is almost nothing here, except for coloured-glass sculptures with smooth, round edges. 'Where are all your things?' I ask. There used to be lamps on dark wood tables and big, velvet sofas.

Lydia doesn't answer.

This isn't really Lydia's house. I go to the window and look out again. I picture Penny, walking across the grass – *Penny?* 'Who's Penny?' I ask.

'Do you mean Adam's wife?' Lydia replies, turning from the sink to face me.

Adam sits at the table in the garden. He talks about playing the race card to Zora, me and Harriet. He thinks he has the right to do it.

Penny waves her hands at us. 'Calm down, everyone,' she says.

In the House, at the dispatch box, Adam Russell says he is not and has never been a racist.

'There should be a fire in here,' I say to Lydia. There was a fire at Christmas. One of the children nearly burnt himself, the younger one, who's named after a bear, but I can only think of Paddington and he can't be called that.

Lydia gestures to radiators that stretch from the floor almost to the ceiling and says, 'I can turn on the heating if you're cold.'

'I'm not cold.' It's just that there ought to be a fire in here.

Lydia pours coffee into a red and black cup – some colour at last. She asks me if I'd like some too. I decline. I am declining, but then that's true of all of us. Lydia is also declining. Even Harriet is aging now, though I expect she'll always be a child to me. She keeps protesting, when I tell her off, or ask her why she hasn't done something, that she isn't thirteen anymore.

'Did Adam do something to Harriet?'

Lydia takes her coffee to the long table by the wall and sits on one of the bare white chairs that doesn't look comfortable. She shakes her head, but I know she is lying to me. It's there, on the edges of my memory, I just need to reach out and draw it in.

'Adam did something on your birthday. He said things.'

'Adam was always saying things,' Lydia replies with a short laugh, as if she can fob me off.

'I came to see you. It was a little while after your birthday. You phoned me. I think you were expecting to speak to Zora but it was me.' I join Lydia at a table that is more like a bar or a counter. The hard edge of the chair pokes into my thigh. 'You were drunk, very drunk. You said Michael was leaving you. He was trying to take Rupert and Amy with him to America. You asked me to come over.'

'I don't remember,' Lydia replies.

'You gave us a photograph. Who was in the photograph?'

'It was years ago, Selina, why rake that up now? Adam paid for what he did.' There is a long pause. Then Lydia adds, 'We all pay for everything in the end.'

'Did he hurt Harriet? I'll keep on asking until you tell me.'

Lydia gazes into the distance. 'Not Harriet,' she replies. Then, in a tone that suggests she no longer has the will to evade the questions, she adds, 'I was so drunk that night, I barely remembered the conversation the following morning. How am I supposed to remember it now after so many years?' She picks up a packet of cigarettes and removes one, lighting it with the box of matches she finds by the sink. She returns to the table but sits several seats away from me now, once again trying to distance herself.

Adam stands at the dispatch box. 'I am not and I have never been a member of any far-right organisation.' But there is a photograph. It is published in *The Guardian* and Adam's words are contradicted irrefutably.

'You gave us a photograph of Adam in a uniform.'

'That photograph,' says Lydia, narrowing her eyes as if trying to shut out the memory. 'You wanted me to help you, so I helped. That picture was one my father kept. I found it when he died. I should have thrown it out there and then, but I didn't. I gave it to you instead. And even though I did all that to help you, you wouldn't forgive me, you and Zora. Harriet hated me too. I haven't seen my daughter for years and years. She won't see me. I've asked her to visit repeatedly, but she won't.'

Harriet is stubborn. When she decides something, there is no moving her. I tried to get her to stay in touch with Lydia, if only to ensure that she still saw her half-siblings. I thought she might regret it one day if she didn't. But she has always refused.

Lydia stands up as if she is going to leave the room, but then she sits down again. 'You don't know what growing up was like for me, living with my father and Joyce. You and Zora have always had each other – every minute of every day there was someone you could share things with, somebody to love, somebody who loved you. I didn't have that.'

There is silence. No sound at all. 'Why does Harriet hate you?' I ask, hardly daring to breathe.

'She hates me for keeping quiet – do you really not remember?' Lydia speaks with bitterness. 'You all hated me for knowing what Adam did to Cal, but keeping quiet about it.'

PART SEVEN

FORTY-ONE

SELINA

I wake up, and for a moment I think I only dreamed it. I try to catch my breath. The dream possesses such intensity it's hard to separate the nightmare from reality.

Some of the forgotten things the dream has etched, marking in the details but askew. Streets are flat and two-dimensional, leading impossibly into one another. Overlapping. Winding like the pathways of a labyrinth. I'm encased in concrete and stone until I cry out for space, running towards the open air.

The truth was lost long ago in Lydia's testimony. But I remember hurting, shouting, running, burying the nightmare deep inside ourselves.

I need to know, says Harriet.

Once, someone told me that if you remember all the details of a recurring dream, it goes away and doesn't come back again. Memory neutralises its power. Shielding my eyes with my arm, I try to focus on it. Slowly the dream unfolds, truth and lies merging as I capture it, only half-asleep.

*

The sound of the radio, pitched like a siren,
is screaming through my head.
War ina Babylon. Is it a song?
You were there, I say to Adam.
You killed Cal.
He doesn't hear. He doesn't see.
I am invisible to him.
Enoch Powell was right, he says.

What was my daddy like?
Dream about him now, I need to know.

The street is full. Sirens, shouting.
There's a scream.

Wake up!

You have to dream it for me now.
Is my daddy still alive?
You have to wake him up.

There's a woman with a pram. There is a baby in it. Her
face is stiff with fear. She doesn't look at anyone, she just
walks on, one arm stretched across the pram to shield the
baby's head. The woman's face is mine; the woman's face
is Zora's.

Am I the baby in the pram?
You're not born yet, Harriet.

I want to hold Cal's hand.
I try to grip his fingers in the dark.

What was that?

Breaking glass.
Adam's smashed the headlights of a car.
Blood is seeping through
the soles of our bare feet.

What did Adam do?
Lydia's voice is shrill; I don't remember now.
Yet there is blood on Adam's fist.

Where is Christopher Walker?

Christopher Walker has no family.
Christopher Walker has no friends.
Christopher Walker won't be elected.
Christopher Walker won't write books.
Christopher Walker is black as a bug.
Christopher Walker dies in jail.

we're being swamped by immigrants
we must arm ourselves and fight
our country's being taken over
we don't know who we are

I don't know who I am, our mother cries

I don't know who I am, our father says, buried under useless things

I don't know who we are, says Zora, running from the house

We don't know who we are, we scream

Forty-two

Selina

I re-member the man in the dock.

We know from stories we have heard that Christopher Walker has been in care. No family is sitting behind us in the court, praying that somehow he'll get off. He looks so lonely, so different to how I imagined him. He is big, but he has a gentle face, though he seems older than his eighteen years. He is wearing a suit. He doesn't look comfortable in it and the sleeves are too short. He glances round the court, looking scared, as if he can't understand why he is there. The policeman says he punched Cal for no reason. Whenever anyone speaks against him, he flinches and looks down. He pulls the hem of his shirt out of the waistband of his trousers in his agitation. He wrings the front of it. He doesn't know how to deal with this. He doesn't know what's going on. The prosecution barrister tells the court he was uncontrollable in his rage, animal in his ferocity. The defence barrister says he's never had a chance in life. I look at him and see that he has nothing, he has nobody. Having nobody makes you guilty of something.

Lydia is called to be a witness. She is calm, but her testimony doesn't add up. The defence barrister points out inconsistencies half-heartedly. He has another trial next week, one that isn't legal aid. If this one doesn't finish soon, he'll miss a big fat fee. Lydia is asked if the man in the dock is the man who struck Cal. Yes, she says, refusing to look at Christopher. She can't face him. He stares at her in disbelief, silently begging her to tell the truth. He is afraid that he will be going to prison for something that he didn't do. Fear makes him sweat. This will tell against him. It makes him look nervy, guilty. No one will see that he is just afraid; they will be afraid of him instead. He opens his jacket because he is so hot and scared. He's been told by his barrister before the trial that he must stay calm but he can't, he is desperate now, he thinks he's going to be convicted of something that he didn't do. When Lydia sheds tears, he knows that he is done for.

The judge's summing-up is biased. It is grounds for appeal, but no one has the will to see Christopher Walker free. The jury deliberates, but his fate was sealed before they even retired. For two days, he hopes against hope that they won't convict him.

GUILTY, the foreman of the jury says.

Nobody sheds any tears.

On the front page of the *Daily Express* there is a photograph of Christopher Walker, staring into a camera – hair wild, eyes bulging – monstrous, like the Incredible Hulk.

FORTY-THREE

ZORA

I didn't believe you at first. We were standing in the kitchen. I shoved you – hard – when you told me about Adam, pushing you into the sink, wanting to believe you'd made it all up to hurt me, to make me hate Lydia again, even though she had long since stopped being important to me.

Your hip hit the handle of the drawer. You were in pain, bent double. Then you recovered and you lunged at me, your fury spilling out – our fury spilling out. We couldn't hurt Lydia, so we tried to hurt each other instead, the blows coming fast, your fists and mine working rhythmically to do the most damage.

'We'll wake Harriet!' you hissed.

Our fight ended almost as quickly as it had begun. 'What are we doing?' we said to one another, ashamed of our displaced anger.

We sat side by side at the kitchen table in the dark, my hand clutching yours. We cried. We cried for Cal, for Harriet. For Mum and Dad. We cried for each other. We cried for Christopher Walker.

A sound: loud and insistent.

You started and pulled away from me as the battering of the front door seemed to make it shake. We stood side by side in the hall, each holding our breath, not daring to move.

Your boy is hurt. He's in the alley. You have to come now.

I shoved my bare feet into my shoes so they wouldn't get cut to ribbons as I ran along the street.

It was a moment before I realised this couldn't be the knock that would send us running to the alley where Cal lay covered in blood; it couldn't be the knock that would mean he was dead.

'Leave it, don't open the door,' you said, holding me back by the sleeve of my dress. 'I don't want to see anyone, not now.'

But the knocking was persistent and Lydia's voice called out, 'I just want to talk to you. I need to explain. I know you're in there.'

You gave me a fearful look but then you nodded and I let her in.

Lydia pushed past us before the door was fully open. We followed her into the kitchen. 'I have the right to explain,' she said.

'You have no rights,' I replied, moving towards her, anger threatening to overwhelm me. You held my arm and I came close to hitting you in retaliation, failing once more to find the right target.

We didn't offer Lydia a drink. We didn't offer her a seat at our table, but she sat down anyway. Tension sparked between us.

'I have to tell you what happened the night Cal died. I'd

change it if I could, you must believe me. But what's done is done.' Lydia sat back in her seat and looked at each of us. I couldn't read her expression. Defiance? Regret? A mixture of the two?

We didn't speak. Our silence caused her to take a strand of her hair and twirl it between her fingers. 'It really wasn't my fault. I couldn't have foreseen any of it.' She sighed deeply and looked away from us again. 'Adam was full of indignation about my pregnancy. He was staying with us for the last couple of weeks of summer. Cal phoned and said he needed to see me, so I slipped out of the house. Adam followed me.' Lydia stopped. She took a cigarette out of her bag and held a lighter to it. Then she inhaled as if her life depended on it.

'I didn't know Adam was there, I swear I didn't,' she continued, blowing smoke across the table.

You sat in total stillness, your face turned away from Lydia. We didn't want to hear what she had to say but we knew we had to hear it. We needed to know what really happened the night that Cal was killed.

'Adam came up behind us and grabbed hold of Cal. He pulled him into an alley, said he needed to be taught a lesson. It was like they said in court – one punch and he was down. There was nothing I could do. I just didn't see it coming. Adam ran off. I think he was in shock when he saw Cal wasn't moving. It was accidental; he didn't mean to harm Cal the way he did. It was inconceivable that he could actually have killed somebody.' Lydia stubbed out her cigarette and looked at each of us, trying to tell if we believed her.

'And yet he did kill somebody,' I said. 'And then he let

Christopher Walker take the blame. He died in prison, did you know that?'

Lydia looked at me. 'I'm sorry about that, I really am, but the police told me I had to say it was Christopher Walker. They said he was dangerous, out of control. He had to be taken off the streets. If anyone's to blame for his conviction, it's the police.'

She lowered her voice as if the words she was saying shouldn't really be heard. 'They called me a nigger lover because of Cal. They were disgusting. They shouted at me as if I'd committed a crime. I was there for hours; they kept insulting me, wearing me down until I gave in. I didn't want to hide what Adam had done but I had to, you must see that?' She looked scared as she added, 'Are you going to tell Harriet? Are you going to tell Harriet that it was Adam who killed her father?'

'I don't—' you began.

But before you could finish the sentence, Harriet was there, in the room, her face grey. 'I heard you. I heard what you just said. You and Adam killed my father and you pretended it was somebody else. How could you have done that? You killed my father, you killed him!'

'I didn't kill Cal. Adam killed him,' said Lydia, her voice hard.

'You were an accessory to murder,' Harriet replied, drawing on her knowledge of TV drama.

'Go back to bed, Harriet,' you told her.

'No! I'm not going anywhere,' she answered, looking small and vulnerable in pyjamas printed with dachshunds. You tried to remove her, physically, from the room, but she pulled away from you. 'I have to stay here. I want to stay! He was my father!'

'Let her stay,' I said, my own fury dissolving, as if it was now being channelled in and through Harriet. 'She needs to hear this.'

'No, she doesn't,' you answered. 'Not like this.'

'Harriet needs to be here,' I said.

'No, she doesn't,' you repeated, and, taking Harriet's arm, you tried once more to remove her.

'I'm staying here,' Harriet answered angrily. 'Zora says I can stay.' Harriet shook you off and took her seat at the table.

There was a heavy silence. Harriet was staring at Lydia as if she was trying to work out who she really was.

I turned to Lydia and said, 'Okay, what are we going to do about all this? You keep saying you're sorry, you regret it. Prove it. You have to go to the police. Tell them you lied in court.'

'That's perjury,' Harriet whispered, running her fingers along the edges of the table.

'You let an innocent man rot in prison,' I continued. 'You lied, Lydia, and Cal didn't get justice. Because of you, Adam, who is a murderer, got off scot-free. What do you think that's like for us? What do you think this will do to our parents – Harriet's grandparents? They were coming to terms with Cal's death. What will happen to them once they know there was no justice for Cal after all?' I said it as baldly as I could, wanting to underscore it for Harriet. If she heard the unvarnished version, Harriet would probably sever ties with her birth mother permanently, the only punishment Lydia was ever likely to receive.

But you put your arm around Harriet, as if you could shield her from this knowledge.

'There's no point in me going to the police,' Lydia replied. 'Don't you understand? They were the ones who made me lie. They're hardly going to admit that, are they? And no one's going to want to arrest Adam. He knows too many powerful people. Everyone is going to close ranks. Don't you think I'd have put this right if I could? They'll say I'm a liar. They'll say that either I lied in court or I'm lying now. There isn't any actual proof of anything.'

In the long silence that followed, I saw that Lydia was right.

I stood up. 'Okay, you can go now. Just get out. We never want to see you again.'

Lydia got up shakily. Then she seemed to change her mind and she sat down again. She reached into her bag and pulled out an envelope. 'I've brought you something. It won't prove Adam did it, or send him to prison, but it will put an end to his political career.' She took out a photograph. She turned to Harriet. 'I found this when my father died. I've brought it to show all of you how much I regret what happened.'

She placed the photo on the table. We stared at it. Adam was standing in a brightly lit room. He was wearing some kind of uniform. There was a swastika on his arm; the initials RBG were embroidered beneath it.

'What does it mean, RBG?' asked Harriet.

'When he was a student, Adam and his friends set up a group – The Rivers of Blood Group. They believed Enoch Powell was right,' Lydia answered.

'Who's Enoch Powell?'

'A politician,' you said. 'He gave a racist speech before you were born. The papers called it the Rivers of Blood speech.'

'The RBG decided there would have to be a violent solution to "the immigrant problem" as they called it,' Lydia continued. 'The group only lasted a couple of years. It never really went anywhere; it just petered out.'

We continued to stare at the image. We pictured Cal lying in a pool of blood, his head broken. We thought of the last time we'd seen Adam Russell, at Lydia's house. 'I wondered how long it would take you to play the race card,' he'd said.

It was evidence. Adam Russell had lied in the House when he'd said he'd never been part of a far-right organisation. He would be forced to resign. He would never lead his party; he would never lead his country. His books would be taken off the shelves. He would fade into obscurity – or, more probably, faint notoriety. It wouldn't get justice for Cal and it wouldn't clear Christopher Walker's name. But it was something. And it was all we had.

Harriet looked at Lydia. She whimpered softly and I saw that anger had turned to pain. 'You left me when I was a baby. You didn't care about me. You protected Adam because he was your cousin. Your cousin mattered to you more than me. You let my father be killed and you let somebody else take the blame. I am never, ever going to forgive you,' she said, blinking back her tears.

There was a photograph. We sent it to the papers, you and me. On every front page there was an image of Adam Russell, standing to attention in a uniform.

Forty-four

Zora

I was finally free of Lydia. The last vestige of longing to be with her had gone. I felt less troubled, despite all the things she'd told us. I even thought about getting in touch with Georgia, though it was probably too late – she would be settled with somebody else by now. But I saw possibilities that hadn't really been there before and I knew that one day I would find someone to be with.

You and I were painting the kitchen. Cal was too much in our thoughts; decorating provided a distraction, easing our renewed sense of loss.

I put my roller down. 'There's something we need to talk about.'

You carried on painting.

'Stop for a minute, will you?'

You didn't want to stop. It would soon be dark and then it would be harder to see what we were doing. 'Daylight is best,' you insisted.

I waited for a moment, but you continued to slap paint

across the wall by the window, so I said, 'Just stop, Selina, I'm trying to tell you something. I've got a new job.'

'I know you have. I always know what's happening with you.'

I was surprised that you still stuck to this belief in spite of all the evidence against it. 'It's in Leeds, so I'll have to move away.'

We had to be apart again. We were still hurting after Lydia's betrayal, and although I felt freer and more able to think of the future, my sense of injustice was sharpened to knife point. You dealt with your unhappiness by being kinder; I dealt with mine by lashing out in retaliation. I didn't want to be like that, I didn't want to shout and rage at you when you were hurting too. And I was so stifled in your presence that my ability to control my anger was slipping away. I couldn't compound the pain we each felt any longer – I loved you too much.

'What's the job?' you asked.

'It's at the poly. I was invited to apply when I submitted my thesis. It's a step up from what I'm doing now. I'll be running a foundation course for people who want to do a degree but didn't get the right opportunities and left school early. There will be some undergraduate teaching too. If I'm doing that, I might even be able to get my Caribbean poetry book published.'

Your face was alight with pleasure at my success. You threw your arms around me, squeezing me tight. It took me by surprise; I'd been expecting you to mind desperately that I was leaving you behind. I began to wonder if you'd fully understood.

'A fresh start,' you said. 'It's the right thing. Me and Harriet will miss you, of course we will, but you have to do it, it's such a fantastic opportunity.'

I was right. You hadn't understood. I would have to spell it out for you. I eased you away from me. 'Selina?'

'What? What's the matter?'

I didn't want to say it, but I knew I had to. I felt in my pocket, hoping – and failing – to find a cigarette. The words came out so quickly that they were barely coherent. 'I'm sorry, but Harriet needs to be with me.'

'With you?' you replied in bewilderment.

'I've found a really nice house with a huge garden. Harriet will love it, she really will, and you can come over whenever you want, every holiday if you like.'

You stood in total stillness. Hurt radiated from you. I knew I had to ignore it; I couldn't let you hold me back anymore. I had to sever the join. I spoke more slowly, measuring each word. 'I know this will be really hard for you, but it's for the best. You couldn't cope on your own with Harriet before, so I had to come back to live with you. You won't be able to manage Harriet by yourself so I have to take her with me.'

You sat on the little stool by the door as if your legs could no longer hold you. Bent over on it, you seemed so much smaller. You dragged your arm across your eyes as if to stop tears falling. 'That was years ago,' you said flatly. 'You wouldn't have coped either if things had been reversed and Harriet had suddenly been left with you instead of me. I hadn't ever had to deal with a small child before. I didn't know what to do. How could I possibly have managed on my own? But it's different now. I've taught kids for years. Of course I'll manage.'

'She's coming with me, Selina.' I said it as firmly as I could, leaving no room for dispute. Fleetingly, I wondered if it was cruel of me to be taking Harriet away from you, but I believed that in the end, you'd see it was the right thing for all of us.

'Don't do this,' you said, your voice containing a howl that you only just managed to suppress.

I turned away from you so I didn't have to see the anguish on your face. 'It's for the best,' I repeated.

You stood up and tried to position yourself so you were in my line of sight but I continued to turn aside. 'You haven't thought this through,' you said. 'What about school? This would be the worst time to move her, she'll lose all her friends. She's only just lost Lydia, and now she's about to lose you too. That can't be helped, but the last thing she needs is another loss on top of that.'

I adopted my most reasonable tone, calm and measured. 'There's a really good school in Headingley and I've managed to get a place for her there. It's just as good as the school here, if not better. They get fantastic exam results. She'll make lots of new friends – you know how easily people take to her. And she'll be able to put the whole Lydia thing behind her a lot more quickly if she leaves London. She'll be fine, I'll make sure she is, I promise.'

'What about what Harriet wants?' You were determined to make eye contact; I was determined not to let you. With every step you took towards me, I took a step back.

My heart was beating too fast. Your heart was beating

too fast too, I could feel it; your heart and mine fluttering in sync. I had to break it. I had to break your heart. 'Okay then, why don't we ask Harriet which of us she'd rather be with?' I said.

Finally, you looked down. You stared at the floor. 'She'll say you, won't she? She's always preferred you. You're special to her. I'm the one she can take for granted. Please don't take her away, Zora.'

'I have to,' I replied coldly.

'Why do you have to?'

'I just do,' I answered.

Without Harriet, I would be alone. One of us had to be. I didn't want it to be me.

SELINA

I'd thought the worst times were over but now I'm going to be alone again. I rehearse loneliness so that I'm prepared, running scenarios through my head, visualising Harriet's empty room – and Zora's. I practise trying to fall asleep at night when there is no sound at all, no breaths taken by anyone apart from me, no other heartbeats, no warmth, no closeness, no sense of being loved. I try to think of ways my life will improve without them: without Zora, there won't be anymore arguments. She will be happier. Without Harriet, I will be able to focus on my work. I will get my preparation and marking done more quickly. I'll have the bathroom all to myself; no waiting when I'm in a hurry in the mornings. I stare at photographs of Harriet, committing them to memory, as if to make sure she'll be with me even when she leaves.

I stare at photographs of Harriet, committing them to memory, trying to make sure that as this illness takes hold, I will still know who she is.

'What about my friends?' says Harriet, as Zora tells her about the move. She kicks the leg of the kitchen chair. 'What about Selina? I don't understand. Why can't we all stay together?'

I can hear the misery in Harriet's voice so I'm trying to look as if the move is what I want too. If she doesn't have to deal with my feelings she will be more able to deal with her own. The effort is causing such tension in my face that my jaw is starting to ache.

'You'll be with Selina some weekends and through the school holidays. And your friends can always visit,' says Zora.

'I'm not going to Leeds!' Harriet runs from the kitchen, knocking over a glass of orange juice in her rush to escape.

'I haven't finished yet. Come back here right now!' shouts Zora, her anger causing Harriet to run even faster.

I follow Harriet to her room, leaving Zora in the kitchen, and I sit on the bed beside her. 'I think you'll like Leeds. It's just that you need time to get used to the idea.'

'Is that what you're saying to yourself? That you just need some time to get used to it?'

Harriet has always been perceptive. I draw her closer to me. 'At least hear what Zora has to say. She's found a really good school for you. And the new house has an attic bedroom with a sloping roof. There's a little cupboard in the wall where you can put all your most important things. She told me about it. That room is one of the reasons she wanted the house. She's planned it for you.'

'I'm not a little kid, I don't need hidey-holes anymore. This isn't fair, it's just not fair and I'm not going, I don't care what Zora says.'

She leans against me. She is so warm. When she was little, we cuddled all the time. I've missed that now she's older. I'll miss it even more when she's gone.

'I'm not going,' she repeats dully.

'I think you'll like it.'

'When I've had time to get used to it,' she replies, mimicking my voice. 'I don't understand why you can't come too.'

'I have my job here.'

'You could get a new job.'

'I have to stay here.'

'This is like when Lydia dumped me on you and Zora, isn't it? You've had enough of me as well.'

Her tone is harsh, truculent, and in it, I see the troubled adult she could become unless she understands how loved she is. I try to put my arm around her but she pushes me away. I take her hand instead; it remains limp. 'Don't ever think that, Harriet, not ever. It's just that living with Zora . . .' I'm about to say that living with Zora will be better for her, but then I realise, with frightening clarity, that this isn't really true. I look towards the window, avoiding her gaze.

*

When is Harriet coming? Why hasn't she been to see me?

Harriet's fingers wrap around mine. 'I do love Zora,' she says.

'I know you do, sweetheart.'

'But I can't go and live with her. She isn't like you. You're calm about things. You hardly ever shout and I always know what's happening with you. It's different with Zora. We argue. She thinks I should just do whatever she says straight away. I'm hardly allowed to speak and it's getting worse all the time.' She strokes my palm. 'Why do you always give in to Zora and do the things she wants?' Her tone is wistful, but there is an undercurrent of anger.

Is Harriet angry with me? Is that why she hasn't come?

I start to tell her that I don't always do what Zora wants, but I know that Harriet is right – mostly I do give in to her. It's partly habit – something I've been accustomed to since childhood – and partly that I am better equipped to deal with disappointment than Zora is. I'm more able to cope.

'I'm not going. Nobody can make me. I want to be by myself now,' says Harriet, letting go of my hand again, tacitly conveying that I've failed her.

I've tried not to worry Harriet. I've tried to cover up the holes in my memory, but maybe they've shown. Perhaps I haven't been strong enough. Have I failed her?

*

Downstairs in the kitchen, Zora is making tea. She fills two cups and we sit opposite one another, drinking slowly, her movements mimicking mine and vice versa. There is silence. Then Zora lights a cigarette; she always smokes indoors even though I keep asking her not to. I'm gearing up to confront her about Harriet, but the words remain locked inside. Then, as she stubs out her cigarette on the saucer in front of her, I force myself to say, 'I can't let you take Harriet away with you.'

She looks startled. 'I don't think it's up to you,' she replies after a few moments.

'Who else is it up to? You?'

'She wants to be with me.'

'She wants to be with both of us, but that isn't possible anymore. I know you have to go, I know you're not happy, it's right for you to leave, but Harriet has to stay. This is her home. You'd do your best for her in Leeds, I know that, but you need more space than I do, you need room to breathe. Harriet will be a constant disruption and you'll end up arguing even more than you do now. She's a teenager. She isn't a small child who will do everything you tell her without question anymore.'

'Harriet has never done anything without question,' answers Zora drily.

'She's like you, she needs space, she doesn't want someone on her back telling her what to do – when you can be bothered to be around, that is.'

Zora looks as if she is about to end the conversation and walk out of the room.

*

There is silence from Zora. Is Zora angry with me too?

'I'm sorry, I put that badly,' I say quickly. 'I just meant that Harriet is angry and resentful and it's only going to get worse. She's grieving for the mother she lost for the second time when she found out about Adam. She'll need a lot of support to get through that. You love your work. When you're working, you give it everything. There won't be any room for Harriet. And, Zora, you don't put her first. It was so wrong to let her sit there and listen to everything Lydia said the night she came round. You should never have done that and I should never have let you. Harriet has to stay here. She needs stability. You can't give her that. I can.'

'Harriet had already heard most of what Lydia had to say if you remember. She needed to hear the rest of it,' Zora answers angrily.

'She didn't need to hear it, not like that. She needed to be told quietly and calmly by us – just the two of us. What you did was cruel. You did it to spite Lydia, and you didn't think about Harriet's feelings – can't you see that?'

'She's coming with me,' answers Zora defiantly, but I can tell how scared she is.

'No,' I say, as gently as I can, but I know I must also hold on to my determination. 'It's not happening. You're not taking her. You can't; it wouldn't work. You don't want to take Harriet because it would be better for her, you want to take her because it would be better for you – you believe that if you have her, you won't feel lonely or abandoned, or hurt. It can't be like that – for Harriet's sake, it can't.'

Zora sits without moving. She is angry. She is disappointed. I'm afraid for both of us, but I have to say these things, I have to say them. We need some air. It's hard to breathe in here. Zora is taking heavy, gulping breaths. I open a window wide and then I sit down again beside her. 'You haven't really been all right since Cal died. Remember when you told me what you said to him and how it made him go off to find Lydia? I blamed you, I know I did, but only in the moment.'

Zora is standing by the stove. The lamb we've prepared together is simmering in the pot. 'If you hadn't told Cal about you and Lydia, he wouldn't have gone out that night. He wouldn't have died. It was all your fault! I hate you!' I scream at her.

'I only blamed you in that moment. But you think I've continued to blame you, because you blame yourself so much. It wasn't your fault, Zora, if Adam hadn't hit Cal that night it would have happened the night after, or the night after that. You have to let it go, and Harriet can't be with you while you're sorting yourself out. You need time by yourself – time to *be* yourself.' I take Zora's hand and I hold it tight; she knows I am saying I love you, the way I always have.

It's starting to get dark. I draw the curtains and switch on the lamp. We are sitting on the sofa in the light of the gas fire we bought together – it warms us and its flickering flames seem almost real. I turn to Zora and I say, 'Do you remember when Mum overheard us arguing? Do you remember what she said? It was when you decided to move into Cal's room instead of us sharing anymore. I didn't want you to go, remember?'

Zora is packing up her things, shoving them into carrier bags she will take down the hall and into Cal's bedroom. Her movements are quick and angry.

'I can move into Cal's room if I want. We're not conjoined anymore,' she says.

'You and Selina were never conjoined,' Mum announces from the doorway.

I am shocked into total stillness. Zora remembers it. She remembers everything about it. She used to tell me what happened every night before we fell asleep.

Zora says, 'Of course we were joined. I remember.'

But Mum tells her she must have dreamed it. 'I have my faults, but not remembering giving birth to conjoined twins isn't one of them.' For the first time since Cal's death, she smiles.

'But what about our scars?' asks Zora, pulling up her skirt and showing her the deep wound on her left hip and upper thigh. I have one too, almost the same, on my right.

Mum sighs. 'You were small, four or five. You probably don't remember it. The man who used to live downstairs was a night watchman. He had a guard dog, a Dobermann, that he took with him to the warehouse where he worked each night. It got loose one day while I was cooking your tea. When you were little, we shared this house, each family taking it in turns to cook – there was a gas stove on the landing. I left you on your own in the living room. There was no space on that landing, you couldn't be with me. Perhaps I didn't quite shut the door. Or maybe Cal or the dog itself somehow managed to open it. I heard your screams and ran upstairs; the dog was attacking you both. I hit it over the head with a poker but you were taken to hospital.

It explains our fear of dogs.

But our mother must be wrong, Zora decides. 'I know we were conjoined,' she says. 'I know what really happened.'

She is angry with Mum, so angry, but she doesn't show it because Mum is still in pieces about Cal. She waits until Mum leaves for work, and then she lets the anger out, stomping all over the house and shouting at me as if I am to blame. I try to calm her down again but that just makes her rage even more. 'Of course we were conjoined. We must have been. I remember it. It is true,' says Zora. She is so certain of it.

I take Zora's hand again. 'I don't think we ever were conjoined, Zora. And even if we were, I know you'll be all right without me and I'll be all right without you.'

Zora's face is pale. I expect her to argue or even fight with me the way she did once when we were young, but she just sits there, staring at me, saying nothing.

ZORA

I looked at you; it was like looking at myself, the version I used to be – if only in my own imagination – the one who was strong and calm and capable. When had this reversal occurred? I wanted separation, I needed it, but as I looked into your face – the face that was so like mine – I saw that separation had already happened; it had happened years ago. And it wasn't you who needed to let go of me; I had to let go of you.

SELINA

Zora is leaving. She pushes a package into my hands. I open it slowly: *The History of the Carolina Twins: As Told by Millie and Christine McCoy.* A thin book, but so very precious – rare, Zora tells me – she had to get it sent over from America.

We laugh so much we can't seem to stop. Zora is giving me a book about being joined to mark our separation.

FORTY-FIVE

SELINA

Opposite me at a table outside a café on the south bank of the River Thames, Lydia sips a glass of red wine. 'Do you remember when we were at school and we were asked to write an essay on the year 2000 and what the world would be like in the twenty-first century? I remember working out that I would be nearly fifty by then. I couldn't imagine ever being that old.' She laughs, making the wrinkles round her eyes and at the corners of her mouth look deeper.

She puts down her glass and gives me a look of appraisal. Then she says, 'You're still angry with me, aren't you?' She sounds irritated. No, exasperated is closer to it. She thinks I should be able to put the past aside. She thinks that because we're in our seventies, the things that happened when we were young should no longer be coming between us.

'Let's order lunch,' she says.

I look at the menu. The café was Lydia's choice and everything is stupidly expensive.

'Don't look at the prices; I'm paying. Have whatever you like,' she tells me.

She is still trying to patronise me. And then, as I look at her, thinking that as much as things have changed, they have still remained the same, it returns. A fragment from the conversation we had so many years ago. The one that sealed our differences and separated Zora, me and Harriet from Lydia for the next forty years.

'It was Adam, my cousin Adam, who killed Cal. I had to cover it up, I didn't have a choice.'

The waitress arrives at our table. 'I'll have the chargrilled chicken paillard with steamed red quinoa,' says Lydia. 'And a side salad – no dressing on the salad.'

I order a fancy version of fish and chips. I wait until the waitress has gone before I speak again. I am not struggling to keep up; this is one of my good days. 'Why did you testify at the trial that it was Christopher Walker if it wasn't? Why didn't you tell the truth?'

Lydia lights a cigarette. 'The police made me lie. Don't you remember?' There is a pause and then she adds, 'And I knew I couldn't ruin Adam's life for one unlucky punch. How could I have done? I'd have had no one then, not once Cal had gone. Christopher Walker would never have made anything of himself. He would never have turned his life around; what use was he to anyone? Adam was at Cambridge; he wasn't a criminal but they would have sent him to prison. Look what he achieved. He got a double first. He became a Cabinet minister. He was a writer, he won awards, everyone said how gifted he was. His life really meant something – until that photograph was in all the papers.'

'That woman who hit me – Penny? She was Adam's husband?'

'You mean Adam's wife. I'm sorry she attacked you like that. Adam wanted to know how the papers had got hold of the photograph so I said you and Zora must have dug it up without my knowledge. I couldn't tell him the truth; I would have lost him.' Lydia is quiet for a moment and then she says softly, 'Only I did lose him, of course. I lost him to drink in the end. You have to understand, I didn't mean for Walker to go to prison, of course I didn't. I thought if my testimony was weak enough, he'd get off.'

'He fitted all the stereotypes. His guilt was assumed by everyone from the time of his arrest.'

'Perhaps. And I'm sorry about that, but what else could I have done?'

Lydia looks at a boat that's slowly making its way up the river. Tourists will take photographs of one another from the upper deck. We will be captured in the background, barely discernible, right on the margins of the picture. There will be two little dots, not quite recognisable as people. I finger the strap of my camera case but I don't take a picture. I no longer want to remember Lydia.

There is a long silence. Then Lydia says, 'Adam was so angry with me for getting pregnant. It was none of his business of course, but men thought they had the right to interfere back then.' She drains her glass of wine and adds, in a low voice, 'Still do, a lot of the time.'

*

Cal is bleeding. His head is covered in blood. An unlucky punch, the barrister says. Zora is trembling beside me.

Lydia slept with Cal. Lydia slept with Zora.

The waitress brings our food to the table. I eat mine slowly; I'm not really hungry. There is a question I want to ask but it keeps eluding me. Light is in my eyes. I shield them with my arm and look towards a duck that's bobbing on the sunlit surface of the water. Then I know what I wanted to say: 'Why did you sleep with Zora?'

Instead of answering, Lydia puts out a hand to bring the waitress to a halt as she hurries away from a nearby table. 'Could we have another bottle of Shiraz?' She turns to face me again and I think she's going to speak but she takes her phone out of her bag and checks it for messages.

'Lydia!' I say to her.

The fierceness of my voice seems to startle her. She puts the phone down on the table; the lit screen turns dark. Then she says, 'Why do you want to bring that up after all these years? What does it matter now?'

'I have to know, Lydia.' I think I've asked this question before but I can't recall the answer.

There's a photograph of Harriet. It should be in my wallet. I am relieved to find it there – these days there's always the chance that something has been misplaced. Harriet is coming down a slide, clutching my old teddy bear. I place it on the table, in front of Lydia. It's the very first photograph of Harriet I ever took. She is missing her mother. There are tears on her face.

Harriet screams and screams. She won't be quiet. I have to phone Zora. Once Zora is here with me again, everything will be all right.

Lydia puts down her knife and fork.

'Why did you sleep with Zora?' I ask.

Lydia is quiet for so long that I don't think she's going to reply. She glances at the photograph of Harriet, sighs and says, 'I'm not like you and Zora. You were always so incredibly close, you felt everything with such intensity, bleeding from every pore – Cal too. I don't really feel very much, most of the time. It takes a lot to make me feel something. I just wanted to feel, even vicariously. Amy said something to me once: she said, "You have no feelings, Mother," in such an accusatory way. Perhaps she was right. I always envied you and Zora your relationship with one another, with all its highs and lows. My life has been flat.' She pushes the photograph away from her.

I push the photo back again but Lydia won't look at it anymore. She picks up her knife and fork and prods at the quinoa, pushing it to the edges of the plate. 'When I was young with Joyce, it was all just flat. It wasn't that different with my father; we barely spoke to one another. I knew next to nothing about him as a person. I couldn't have told you what was important to him – apart from his rather dubious business deals, of course. Did you know that he and his brother – Adam's father – were in business together? They were so alike. I suppose the apple didn't fall far from the tree in many respects. When Adam hit Cal, it wasn't out of rage. It was cold. You couldn't even describe it as moral outrage about my pregnancy, though he convinced himself it was. He wanted to teach Cal a lesson, he said, and he'd been fired up by that speech of Enoch Powell's. He gave me all the usual spiel about immigrants taking over, but I doubt if he really cared about that. It was more that, in taking action, as he saw it, he was able to see himself as significant, and not the rather hollow person he actually was. That was how we functioned as a family.'

The waitress brings the wine to the table. Lydia pauses to take a few sips. Then she says, 'Being pregnant changed things for a little while. Everyone was so critical, so harsh in their judgement of me, and I think I felt that, and it was good, in a funny sort of way. And then after Harriet was born, and after the trial finished, it was back to flatness again, feeling nothing. When I left Harriet with you, it wasn't because I was afraid I would hurt her, not in the way you must have thought I meant it in that letter I sent. I actually thought she would die of neglect, born out of my indifference. Indifference – that's been the strongest emotion I've experienced for most of my life, if you can call indifference a feeling. Perhaps I've been lonely, Selina. Perhaps that's why I agreed to meet you that day in the café. Perhaps that's why we're here now.'

Lydia is still speaking. I think I've missed something she said, but I'm not having any trouble keeping up – this is one of my good days.

'But I'm not sure,' she continues, 'because I don't really know what loneliness feels like. If you don't know how an emotion feels, how can you know if you've felt it? Does an emotion actually exist in someone if it's not felt?'

Sometimes, when I've lost the words, all I have is feelings. They envelop me. They offer comfort, of a sort. When I feel, even when I feel afraid, I know I'm still connected to the world outside myself.

I put the photograph of Harriet back in my wallet.

Lydia looks at me. She's wanting absolution again. 'When I slept with Zora I think I was trying to make sure she would always want me, always need me in her life. And I knew it would stir things up, especially when I got with Cal. As long as you and Zora were at odds with one another, one of you at least would always have to turn to me. In part, that's why I decided against an abortion. You and Zora would be the baby's aunts, so you would always be in my life, one way or another. Loneliness is dull. Flatness is dull. It sucks the life out of you slowly, like the cancer that's destroying my lungs.'

Lydia gets out her purse. She wants to pay the bill. 'I gave you that photograph, remember? The one my father kept? The one of Adam in that ridiculous uniform? I did it out of my friendship with you and Zora, and for Harriet. And in the end, I lost Adam because of it. I lost the only person who knew what it was like for me when we were growing up. He and I had the same memories – family birthdays, family Christmases. He even remembered my mother. He died young – far too young – because of everything he lost when that photograph was published. I wanted to help you all, and I lost Adam because of it. I lost you and Zora too, and my eldest daughter. You're the oldest friend I have. We won't lose touch again, will we, Selina? We will always be friends, won't we?'

We were friends once, Lydia, Zora and me. I put my share of the bill on the silver tray and walk towards Waterloo station.

EPILOGUE

SELINA

I am waiting for Zora. She said she'd come. I can't remember when I last saw her. I've cleaned the house. I have made up the spare bed. Glass gleams.

There's polish, I can smell it, that lovely honey and lavender smell. Mum buys the polish from the hardware shop at the end of our street. She is dusting the living room. She is humming to herself.

What time is she coming? I wrote it down somewhere. I can't wait for her to come.

I've tidied up. I've rearranged the boxes. Rolls of undeveloped film. When I was young, I couldn't afford to get all the pictures I took developed, so I stored them in boxes. Eventually, I learned to develop my own photographs. One day, I'll get the rest of them done. Then I'll have more photographs to look at – more memories to savour.

*

It's getting dark. Perhaps I've got the wrong day. Could it be I've got mixed up again and she's coming here tomorrow?

The doctor said sudoku is good for the memory. I scribble numbers, erasing them and then rewriting them but I can't find the order in it. I would rather be out, taking photographs. What time is it now?

Time goes by so fast. I don't feel how I thought I'd feel when I got old. My body aches a lot of the time. I don't bend so well anymore and sleep sometimes fails to come or comes when I need to be awake. But I seem to spend as much time in my younger years as I do in my old age. Is it like this for everyone? Or is it that I have trouble keeping up? Every now and then, the past is so … vivid, so … compelling, that's the word I'm looking for … it draws me back. And I remember something as if it happened this morning. When is Zora coming? She should be here by now. Have I got the day wrong? Perhaps she came yesterday, but I'd remember that. It's more likely it's tomorrow.

I awaken with a start. A woman is standing beside me. 'Mum?' she says. There is a question in her voice, as if she doesn't know if it's me or not.

'Of course it's me, silly,' I reply.

'How have you been?' she says. 'I've brought some shopping.'

I reach for her hand. 'You came, Zora,' I say to her.

'Mum, it's Harriet.'

Why does everyone keep trying to confuse me?

*

'Mummy?' Her hand is in mine. It's so soft. We can't let her call us Mummy; if she calls us that, Cal will no longer be her father. We are her aunts. We are not her mothers. But she won't stop calling us Mummy. She likes the word. *I* like the word. She wants to be close, as close as she can be. She snuggles up to me. I am not her mother, yet I am her mother too. Zora and I have joint mothership. Zora is laughing at the word. We are the mothership, she says.

'The house is gleam,' I say to Zora. 'I gleamed all day yesterday.'

She smiles and says, 'It's Harriet.'

She squeezes my hand. Her hand is soft.

Harriet doesn't come to see me. Harriet has gone away.

'I was here the day before yesterday, remember?'

Remember, remember the fifth of November. We burn the guy. A . . . burning of the past. A ritual burning of the past.

We put all our old essays on the bonfire. It's good to see them going up in smoke. We laugh.

Harriet is making circles with the sparkler she is holding. She laughs as embers fall around her. I take a photograph.

'Let me find the picture. I want to show it to you. It's a photograph of Harriet.'

'*I'm* Harriet,' she says.

I start to laugh. She can't be Harriet. She's a grown-up. And yet, there is something about her that I like. I'm not afraid of her. And even though I know she isn't telling me the truth, I know that she is kind.

'When is Zora coming?'
'Zora isn't coming, Mum. Zora died, remember?'

I am cold. I am shaking with cold. It envelops my whole body. I will never be warm again. Zora's car, hit by a stolen vehicle. An unlucky punch? I watch them put the coffin in the ground. Do I look all right? Should I be wearing black? I've put my best red jumper on. I want to look my best for Zora. No Selzora, never again, just Selina now. Was Harriet with Zora? Has Harriet gone too?

'I'm still here,' she says.

Of course she is still here. Zora will never leave me. Zora is always at my side whether I want her to be or not, telling me who I am, who I was, what happened today, what happened yesterday – what happened when.

There is this story Zora tells, about how we were born joined. We never were; her memory is full of holes. And now she's treating this problem I have with keeping up as some kind of tragedy. Not even my tragedy – her tragedy, of course.

There's music. The box thing has come on. I know this song. I know what it's called, it will come to me in a minute. We used to dance to this, Zora, me and Harriet. The Four Tops, that's it. 'Reach Out' . . . 'Reach Out and Touch (Somebody's Hand)'.

Harriet is squeezing my hand. Her hand is soft.

The Four Tops. I played this to Harriet when she was little. 'Reach Out and Touch (Somebody's Hand)'. A blast from the past.

Zora thinks I'm wrong about the past. But memories don't stay put, they . . . change . . . They change like the seasons. Sometimes the changes are small. But sometimes they shift into something? . . . something not quite real. My memories aren't the same as Zora's. Which of us is right? . . . How can we know? . . . If past and present sometimes fold, isn't it that way for all of us?

I am scared about the future. I know where this illness will lead. But, Zora, I still have a life. It is pieced together differently, perhaps, but I am more . . . more than just the sum of our misremembered parts . . .

warm despite the cold. Each day I breathe . . .

hold on to every moment that I can . . .

I am still here, Zora, *I am still here* . . .

ACKNOWLEDGEMENTS

I would like to thank the Alzheimer's Society for their very useful information. Dementia Talking Point (https://www.alzheimers.org.uk/get-support/dementia-talking-point-our-online-community); Dementia Voices (https://dementiavoices-id.org.uk) and Dementia Diaries (https://dementiadiaries.org) have been such important sites. Thank you, forum members and contributors; your posts give so much towards an understanding of the condition. Wendy Mitchell's brilliant books, *Somebody I Used to Know* and *What I Wish People Knew About Dementia*, have been indispensable and have clarified so many things. The novel that Selina is reading in chapter twenty-five is *A Harlot's Progress* by David Dabydeen (Vintage 2000).

Judith Bryan, Pauline Edwards, Theres Fickl, Kate McGowan, Gerri Moriarty and Jane Taylor have listened patiently as I've tried to get to grips with the writing of this book, and I'm very grateful.

A dear friend said of the last book, 'Well, I thought it was good when I read it and I know you've tarted it up a lot since then.' I would like to thank editors Clare Hey and Mina Asaam at Simon & Schuster for their very helpful, thoughtful and supportive suggestions for this book's tarting-up process.

Finally, there is my wonderful agent, Milly Reilly, who always offers invaluable advice with intelligence, kindness, patience, tact, and a remarkable eye for detail. I can't thank her enough for her support.